THE GREAT MAN THEORY

BY THE SAME AUTHOR

Apartment

Loner

The Love Song of Jonny Valentine

Kapitoil

THE GREAT MAN THEORY

A Novel

TEDDY WAYNE

BLOOMSBURY PUBLISHING
NEW YORK • LONDON • OXFORD • NEW DELHI • SYDNEY

BLOOMSBURY PUBLISHING
Bloomsbury Publishing Inc.
1385 Broadway, New York, NY 10018, USA

BLOOMSBURY, BLOOMSBURY PUBLISHING, and the Diana logo are trademarks of Bloomsbury Publishing Plc

First published in the United States 2022

This is a work of fiction. Names and characters are the product of the author's imagination and any resemblance to actual persons, living or dead, is entirely coincidental.

ISBN: HB: 978-1-63557-872-0; EBOOK: 978-1-63557-873-7

LIBRARY OF CONGRESS CATALOGING-IN-PUBLICATION DATA IS AVAILABLE

2 4 6 8 10 9 7 5 3 1

Typeset by Westchester Publishing Services
Printed and bound in the U.S.A.

To Phoebe,
my brightness

Idiot wind, blowing like a circle around my skull
From the Grand Coulee Dam to the Capitol

—Bob Dylan, "Idiot Wind"

I

"I am a Luddite," Paul typed.

> My ailing laptop, a prerequisite for this manifesto and my profession, is by now capable of word processing, email, and little else. Eleven years ago I acquired a cell phone whose functions are limited to calling and texting, and have not upgraded it since. My home is without a television or a tablet. I do not post, comment, or "like," as I have no social media accounts and thus no online "brand" (nor, it would appear, that conspicuous an offline one). I have never—and this may come as a shock—taken a selfie.
>
> And yet, as much of a curmudgeonly crank as this abstemious lifestyle might make me sound, I'm also an idealist at heart.

After this opening inventory of renunciations (and its redemptive punctuation), he delivered the précis of his argument: our subsuming addiction to screens has, more than any other economic or cultural factor, fostered today's perilous political climate. Technological immersion has fomented the rise of right-wing extremism, giving platforms to abhorrent values once disqualified from decent society; neutered the left with a hashtagged resistance that substitutes apoplexy for action; and, perhaps most perniciously, anesthetized us all with spectacle and distraction, blinding citizens to our imminent jeopardy while smothering our desire for progress with an endemic cynicism.

"The stakes, bluntly put," he concluded, "are a matter of life and—"

Paul stopped before the last word. Beyond being a cliché, that final sentence employed the very hyperbole he was diagnosing as a malady of the digital age. Subtlety in language was paramount, and asserting the existential risk of our screened lives through a stand-alone sentence at the end of the prologue was the handiwork of a turgid hack, a blaring news chyron. The caps-locked president.

The Luddite Manifesto: How the Age of Screens Is a Fatal Distraction would have more integrity than that. After twenty-odd years of publishing little-read essays on niche subjects in obscure literary magazines, he had a chance, with his first book, to reach a wider audience. The topic generally interested people, nearly all of whom recognized their addiction to their digital devices, occasionally with concern, more often in shrugging acquiescence. If he didn't pander, if he wrote the book he knew he had in him, he might actually get them to pay attention.

The eyestrain-deterrent-cum-motivational-phrase he'd set up for his computer flashed on its twenty-minute cycle: THE SCREEN IS A FATAL DISTRACTION—LOOK UP! He'd been writing for two hours straight, heedless of its instruction. He blinked away the dryness, unclamped his chunky noise-canceling headphones, and took in the room. The heads of the other patrons genuflected before their own silvery computers and black phones. A few screens he could spy on displayed work applications, but most were social media feeds, the reflections waterfalling down the lenses of their users' trendy eyewear. He was the oldest person present, an increasingly frequent phenomenon of late. Already aging out of the quinoa-and-chickpea-salad coffee shop demographic at forty-six.

His seniority was usurped by a man with springy coils of white hair who wandered in with a rolled-up copy of the *Times*, his shirt reading SUPER CALLOUS FRAGILE RACIST SEXIST LYING POTUS. He ordered a coffee with milk, couldn't hear over the music when the barista asked him what kind of milk, seemed bewildered by the plant-based varietals she then rattled off, and clarified that he'd just like a little whole milk.

Paul had a soft spot for this species on the verge of extinction, the throwback Brooklyn liberal, and it always made him happy to spot one puttering about in its native habitat of Park Slope, the last neighborhood in which they throve. As he left to collect his daughter from her day camp, he passed the man's table. On the front page of his newspaper was a headline about fracking and earthquakes, the literal coming apart of the planet from greed and overconsumption.

The despairing thought that typically resulted from an encounter with these old-timers: all that utopianism and organizing and protesting—for this blighted world, now led by the very worst member of their generation. You could blame venal politicians, avaricious bankers and CEOs, the yuppie defectors from their ranks, the vast swath of America that had remained indifferent or mulishly resistant. But maybe these people, the only ones who'd cared in their heyday, still hadn't sacrificed enough for the cause. And now all that remained in their arsenal were acerbic made-in-China T-shirts.

His phone shivered with a call he'd been expecting for weeks. He doubled back to a corner of the room.

"How are you, Paul?" his department chair asked after they said hello, and from the measured timbre and salesmanlike deployment of his name, he could tell he was about to receive bad news.

2

Near the end of the spring semester, he'd lodged a request for a 6 percent raise with his next senior lecturer's contract, and his chair, Nathaniel Zielinski, had promised to do his best once he squared away the upcoming budget. The English department at their third-rate private college in Manhattan appreciated Paul's professionalism—he hadn't called in sick in eight years, his student evaluations typically marked him as tough but fair, he kept his mouth shut at faculty meetings—if not his publishing profile, and he anticipated they would meet him in the middle, a satisfactory outcome. Next year, with the publication of *The Luddite Manifesto* forthcoming, he'd have a stronger negotiating hand as a viable candidate for a tenure track professorship, either as an internal promotion at the college or somewhere else within a Metro-North ride to maintain weekend visits from Mabel.

But now he was listening to Nathaniel's my-hands-are-tied litany about general austerity, line items withdrawn, once-slack belts refashioned into Victorian corsets. A completely predictable apologia; the administration would seize any excuse not to fairly compensate untenured faculty. Winning a 2 percent raise last time had required an undignified month of lobbying.

"I take that as a no on six percent," Paul said. "Can you do three?"

"I'm afraid to say the financial situation's substantially worse than that," Nathaniel told him. "All the departments are being forced to make payroll cuts, which means—I'm very sorry about this, Paul—we can only retain you on an adjunct instructor basis."

A firing would have been almost more humane than a demotion. Senior lecturers had benefits and modest job security, with biennial as opposed to semester-long contracts. Then there was the matter of salary.

Nathaniel stammered when Paul asked what adjuncting paid.

"I'm sorry," he repeated after sharing the puny figure. "That's all we're allotted. But we can give you four classes a semester."

"More work for less money?" Paul asked. "Sign me up!"

"And I hate to tell you this now, too, but we're overhauling the writing curriculum," Nathaniel continued. "Student interest in traditional creative nonfiction has waned quite a bit in recent years, as you've probably noticed from the enrollment numbers. We're asking you to teach a newly designed intro to nonfiction writing class for first-years."

"Glorified freshman comp, you mean." He hadn't taught such a low-level class since the beginning of his teaching career. "It would've helped if you'd told me this a few months ago so I could have looked around for other work this semester. It's almost August."

"I understand. I've been fighting this budget the whole summer, hoping it wouldn't happen, and I just got the final word. I know it's not ideal, but does this sound amenable?"

Paul would have preferred the less fancy but more honest *tolerable*, or the humbler *doable*. Being *amenable* to Nathaniel meant being "agreeable," not "willingness to be submissive." But that's what it was: the powerful demanding that the powerless submit to their rules in their game, skirting the unseemly, Anglo-Saxon truth with a Latinate euphemism.

"Paul?" Nathaniel asked. "Did you hear me? Is that amenable?"

3

His future direct deposits more than halved, Paul stepped out of the air-conditioned coffee shop and into the afternoon's wool blanket. This June had been the hottest in history, and July was on pace to set records, too. Even in climatically conscientious Brooklyn, people acted as though extreme temperatures were a new norm to marvel at, like fitter and more skilled Olympians pushing the right wall of human performance.

He'd pick up a class or two at another college in the city to cover the shortfall. There would be less bandwidth, as the cyborgian phrase went, for *The Luddite Manifesto*, but he'd truncate the margins of his days, brew more coffee. He'd chosen this profession, if not its instability. Most of the world had it much harder. He'd survive.

Still: fucking Nathaniel. He could've reminded the administration that Paul was the department's longest-serving lecturer, a title that with each passing year had become more of an embarrassment, the oldest minor leaguer never to crack the majors. But every favor Nathaniel asked on Paul's behalf of his higher-ups now was one less he could demand for himself in the future. He was a few years younger than Paul and had never visibly demonstrated any meaningful interest in teaching or scholarly work. He simply wanted to be in charge of others, and his Machiavellian means to that end was inciting neither fear nor love, but presenting himself as a preternaturally nonthreatening bureaucrat, a marina manager whose solitary concern was that no boats ever rock in his vicinity.

Paul spotted Mabel's cohort on a grassy hillock in Prospect Park, a cluster of preteens supervised by two counselors. Half the campers were soldered to their phones, and both adults, too. Jane hadn't seen the harm in giving Mabel one. She'd used Paul's overheated bias against him, as she had done more and more near the end of their marriage, semi-playfully calling him Professor Webb, after a "curmudgeonly crank" (he'd lifted the Homeric epithet for the prologue of *The Luddite Manifesto*) of an English professor she'd had in college who disparaged seemingly all new technology and culture: answering machines, "rap music," even VHS tapes. As a result of the students' antipathy for him, they automatically despised the old novels and poetry he taught to which, with a more inspiring guide, they might have been receptive. If he kept this up, she warned him, Paul would only instigate Mabel's rebellion.

But this was one co-parenting fight he'd won, after wearing her down with reams of data and arguments against mixing children and smartphones: decimated attention spans, self-esteem issues, the creep of materialism, time spent not reading, cyberbullying, potential exposure to monstrous men, scarier developments to come in the dystopian future. They still needed a line of communication with their daughter, given the logistics of shared custody, and had compromised, for now, on a bulky phone that, like his, had restricted functionality. Mabel pulled it out in public with great, status-anxious reluctance.

She was on the edge of the group, in her camp-branded teal shirt, ponytailed and summer-bronzed, toeing a patch of dirt. His irritation with Nathaniel lifted for the moment. When Mabel was a baby, and he and Jane weren't yet defeated by the fatigue of parenthood and the iterative quarrels and détentes of a faltering marriage and the is-this-all-there-is nihilism of early middle age, he sometimes wondered when the paroxysm of joy that gripped him upon seeing her would peter out, as it inevitably had to. But the raw magic of her existence hadn't yet faded; he was a fool for her, still instantly smiled upon seeing her face. He believed that it was in fact his curmudgeonly, cranky stance toward most everything else that induced this response. It opened up a Mabel-sized space in his heart, an unexpected warm spot in an ice-cold lake.

To think, as he often did, of what nearly happened almost a dozen years ago.

4

Paul hadn't felt much when Jane had become pregnant. Nor when her bump swelled and he could see the extraterrestrial fetus on the sonogram and hear the squishy underwater thumping of its heart, or even feel it kicking. He'd chalked it up to his lukewarm interest in procreating; whereas Jane had wanted a baby, especially a daughter, more than anything else, his reaction to the project had been tepid cooperation. When he'd readily consented to giving their child Jane's surname of Bailey, he had claimed to others it was in feminist solidarity, but the real reason was that he didn't care much about his name's living on in this unborn human. Close male friends he'd confided in about his numbness had assured him that men seldom developed an attachment during the pregnancy, but that he'd be flooded with profound paternal emotions once he met his daughter in the flesh.

Jane's labor likewise failed to excite anything in him other than helpless anxiety as it dragged on overnight. When Mabel was delivered and eventually thrust into his unpracticed arms, he supposed he felt something, though it was more an acknowledgment of the moment's historical import rather than overwhelming love for this wizened homunculus of a stranger who was about to upend his heretofore streamlined life. She looked like every other newborn he'd ever seen; nothing marked her as distinctively his. His concerns mounted with each passionless minute he held her. He was different from his friends, defective. Not cut out to be a father. Assessing himself as the head of their household, he conjured up horrific hypothetical scenarios. If he, Jane, and Mabel were all in a sinking boat and he could save only one of them, it would be Jane. And if rescuing Mabel meant surrendering his own life, a trade-off Jane would instinctually make, he wasn't sure he'd have that same measure of courageous devotion.

A couple of hours later, a salt-and-pepper-haired doctor who looked like a soap opera physician came into the recovery room. He wanted to run an echocardiogram on their baby. The doctor's responses to their questions were vague.

"Purely precautionary," he said. "We just want to rule some things out. Don't worry about it."

A nurse rolled Mabel away in her bassinet to the neonatal intensive care unit on another floor. Paul and Jane were told the test would take forty minutes, and since Mabel was sleeping so soundly, she needn't be sedated. Paul stayed with Jane in the recovery room, feeding her unconvincing reassurances.

After ninety minutes with no updates and intensifying fears, they were told they could see Mabel and the doctor. Paul pushed Jane in her post-delivery wheelchair down to the NICU, a dark hallway resembling an air traffic control unit, with computer stations that displayed health statistics he didn't understand. Soft beeps issued, at once calming in their regularity and ominous in what a sonic deviation might portend. He steered Jane through the cramped space until they reached Mabel, sleeping in her bassinet near another baby. A nursery of newborns slumbered in an adjacent glass-walled chamber. It was sundown now, the only window showing a dusky gray sky rimmed with orange.

"We don't think it's anything, but we're bringing in a pediatric cardiologist just to be on the safe side," said the soap opera doctor.

"Why does she need to be up here?" Paul asked. "Can't the cardiologist just look at whatever test you gave her before?"

"We'd like to keep her here for now," the doctor responded in a tone that made clear the ostensible preference was a mandate. They were welcome to stay with their baby while they waited, he told them.

"Don't worry," he said again before he left. Then, glancing into the bassinet, he remarked, "Looks like a little dumpling," presumably on account of Mabel's hefty birth weight of nine pounds five ounces.

Paul hated this suave doctor, his blithe placations and flippant farewell. This was a blip on the radar of his day before he went home to dinner with his own healthy kids, just another case he would refer back to with anonymous identification markers for the patient.

"You want to stay?" Paul asked Jane.

She looked stricken, exhausted, bloodless.

"I think I should try to get some sleep," she said.

If Jane didn't want to remain with her newborn, her recent labor and delivery notwithstanding, her internal state had to be harrowing. Paul agreed, volunteered to stay, and weakly told her for the sixtieth time that everything would be fine.

After a nurse wheeled Jane back to the recovery room, Paul pulled a chair up to the bassinet. A hospital staffer soon came by, asked how he was doing, then what religion he was.

"My religion? Why does that matter?"

"If you'd like to speak to one of our chaplains," she said.

"None," he said. "Atheist."

"We have a secular humanist on our staff as well."

"No thank you."

"And your wife?"

"Also none. Please don't bother her now."

"And the baby's religion?" When Paul gave her a look, she said, "I'm sorry, but the hospital requires me to—"

"Buddhism," he snapped. "She got into it in utero."

"I have to write down what you say," she told him apologetically.

"None," he said. "Sorry. You're just doing your job."

The conversation left Paul more unsettled than before. Why were they preparing him for the possibility that he might require spiritual guidance? Was her condition direr than the doctor was letting on? And the *baby's* religion . . .

Was he allowed to touch Mabel, or might that disrupt whatever they were monitoring? No one had prohibited him, and she was, as of a few hours ago, his. His baby. Strange that after thirty-five years of independent selfhood, with relatives reaching only backward in fixed history, he was now permanently linked with a human hurtling toward an undefined future.

With a hesitant index finger he prodded the center of her pudgy little fist, where the pinky curled into a right-angled C. Like a clam opening and closing, the baby's wrinkly purple digits reflexively released before clutching him above the top joint in her hot, moist grip.

He watched his daughter through the clear plastic panel of the bassinet, remaining motionless for fear of disturbing her.

At some point an Orthodox Jewish man sat by the baby next to them. Paul nodded, and he nodded back before gravely observing the bassinet and texting. Paul envied him the certainty of his faith when answering the hospital staffer's question. In the glass-walled room, a Black man stood sentinel over a bassinet and intermittently paced. There weren't any mothers on the floor. Though they traded no words, Paul felt a kinship with these two fathers that he'd never before felt with strangers, a rare moment of recognizing the truth in the cliché that all people were fundamentally the same.

Mabel's face was turned away, her cheek bulging like the surface of its own small moon. Her bare chest looked so perfect, smooth and unmarked; he couldn't believe anything was wrong with the organ beneath its innocent surface. Was she still supposed to be sleeping? Other than her hand, she hadn't moved the entire time; was she too weak?

The sky blackened. They kept the lights low in his area, the lambent computer screens an eerie, bluish supplement. The Orthodox man departed, then the Black man. Paul's imagination rioted with medically ignorant speculation and premonitions: surgeries, chronic conditions, constant vigilance. Having never been tested by a real tragedy, he didn't think he had the fortitude to withstand one. Other new parents, other fathers, would rise to a challenge like this. "Why *not* me?" he'd heard people with hardier constitutions than his say when dealt misfortunes.

He'd felt foolish speaking to Mabel in the delivery room around others, even Jane, and had said little to her beyond welcoming her to the world. Now, alone, he talked without embarrassment.

"Mabel," he said softly. "I know this isn't how you wanted to spend the first day of your life, but you're going to be okay. I'm going to wait here with you as long as I have to."

He listened, as if expecting a verbal response, but heard only the quiet beeps in the unit.

Though he had been irritated by the chaplaincy offer, there are no atheists in a NICU, and Paul found himself appealing to God. He wouldn't pledge faith and piety—both of them would know that was a lie—but he offered a zero-sum bargain, one that would tempt the retributive deity of the Old Testament more than the lenient one of the New: if Mabel was healthy and safe, now and in the future, he would consent to an undetermined number of years being shaved off his own life.

After he signed this mental contract, the doctor's glib parting words intruded upon his thoughts.

"Little dumpling," Paul said in snorting imitation.

Mabel squirmed momentarily, the first real sign of life other than her belly's barely perceptible tide of respiration. He had grown so accustomed to her fingers' wrapping his that he'd nearly forgotten it was still there. As she stirred, he thought her hand would finally unclench, but it was just the opposite: her grip tightened.

Paul, who had believed he was soothing his daughter, realized that she wasn't, of course, the least bit distressed. His baby was the one unwittingly calming him, her tiny fist a life preserver.

"Little dumpling," Paul repeated, superstitiously.

"My little dumpling," he said once more, this time with warmth.

The pediatric cardiologist, a grandmotherly woman, finally arrived with a comforting smile and folksy appellations. False alarm, Dad; baby girl's heart is perfectly fine; she can head back to Mama.

An undamming of tension, a deluge of relief. A nurse rolled the bassinet to the patient elevator and the recovery room. Jane tearfully collapsed into his chest at the good news.

"I was so fucking scared," she said. "I don't know how you were so strong and steady."

These weren't adjectives Paul was used to associating with himself, especially not during the past few troubled hours. He held her and looked down at Mabel, still dozing. His speech to her had birthed a new identity. He was this baby girl's father, her dad. He would have to protect her, to be a strong and steady man for her—or keep up appearances—even when he doubted his capacity for it.

And his plea to God hadn't been cobbled together out of fleeting desperation, destined to be forgotten. It was a compact whose consequences he would honor thereafter, regardless of whether its notary were divine or mortal. If he ever had to, he knew now, he would give up his life for his daughter.

5

"My little dumpling," Paul said to Mabel in Prospect Park.

She looked up from the shallow trough she'd dug with her sneaker. "Oh. Hi, Dad," she said.

"*Oh. Hi, Dad*," he parroted.

They walked south through the park, the grass still damp from a sun shower that afternoon.

"We could use a worm refill," Paul said.

Five years ago, as Mabel's curiosity about the animal kingdom had blossomed, he'd bought her a fifteen-gallon aquarium and converted it into an insect terrarium as a blandishment for his book-and-periodical-dominated apartment. Together they'd garnished it with pebbles and plants and periodically hunted in Prospect Park for pill bugs, beetles, and worms. Mabel would give names to some of the more distinguishable critters, and they would at times spend half an hour watching them explore their enclosure, with Paul narrating in a British voice to emulate a David Attenborough nature documentary.

They stooped over, surveilling the ground like circling hawks, and caught two worms, which they stored in an empty Altoids tin he kept in his backpack for this purpose. Twenty minutes later, in his one-bedroom fourth-floor walk-up, Mabel dropped them in.

"Welcome to South Slope," Paul said brightly, their longstanding christening.

"Welcome to South Slope," Mabel echoed in a singsong voice.

He was proud, as ever, that he'd raised a girl who not only was unafraid of touching worms, but also was full of love for the natural world, even its lowest species. He had no special affinity for the environment, nor did Jane; his distress about global warming was less for the fate of the earth and its creatures than for the survival of humans. Before her birth he'd worried about Mabel's not sharing the (few) traits he liked about himself. He hadn't considered the numerous ways she might improve upon his personality.

"The worms adapt to their new soil like a duck to water," Paul said in his Attenborough voice. "If cut in half, these remarkable creatures can survive and become two separate worms."

"I've told you a million times that's a myth," Mabel said. "The head can grow a new tail, but the tail doesn't grow a new head."

"The young human female," he said, still doing his impression, "does not like it when her father plays dumb." She was focused on the worms, and he couldn't get a read on whether she was annoyed by him. He dropped the voice.

They claimed their favorite red vinyl booth at the diner on the corner with time to spare for the early bird special, their Friday ritual. Over the sound system, Auto-Tuned lyrics interrupted syncopated bloops; the song might as well have been sung and played by a band of robots. It was even louder than the coffee shop. Either public spaces were getting more cacophonous or he was simply growing more intolerant.

"You know that a ten-decibel increase in noise, which is the difference between a conversation and a vacuum cleaner, is linked to a five percent decrease in cognitive functioning—meaning your ability to think?" he asked Mabel. It was a nugget he'd picked up from his book research.

"You told me that a month ago," she said. "Maybe there's a problem with *your* cognitive functioning."

The diner served breakfast all day, and he always let her order pancakes for dinner.

"And is it possible to turn the music down a little?" he asked the waitress.

"Sorry, the owner wants it like this now," she said. "Encourages customers to come in."

Paul suppressed the urge to question the wisdom of alienating the customers they already had.

"When's your book going to come out?" Mabel asked when the waitress left.

He was touched by her interest. She'd barely acknowledged it when he'd sold it.

"Well, I wrote the prologue today, so at that pace—"

"What's the prologue?"

"The first chapter, essentially, which lays out the major—"

"The *first* chapter? You just started? I thought you already sold it."

"I sold it by describing what I was going to write, but I hadn't written it yet. I've been researching and outlining for a long time. Planning a project is half the work."

Mabel pinched a strand of her brown hair, a shade lighter from the summer, and examined it. "Hannah's dad writes for the *New York Times*. And she said he just interviewed the president."

Paul nodded neutrally. If the interviewer were a complete stranger, he'd say something snarky about reporters who traded their reputation for access to this clownish travesty of a leader.

"And she said he wrote *six* books. Is that a true fact?"

"I'm sure your friend isn't lying to you."

"But he's younger than you. How come you haven't written *any* books?"

"I'm working on one now, as we've established. And I've written a lot of essays over the years. Put together, they'd equal a few books."

In fact, he had tried to package nearly all of his published work as an essay collection a few years before and had no takers. He'd masochistically forced his agent to share all the rejections from book editors. The most cutting response: "The idea of an omnibus from a writer no one's heard of is so disastrous from a sales and publicity perspective that I'm nearly tempted."

"You give them to me when they come out, and I've only seen, like, seven of them. Her dad writes almost that many every week. She showed me on her phone."

Mabel had approximated correctly; his literary output had slowed lately. In the last few years his completed essays and pitches to editors, even ones he'd worked with in the past, had been going unreturned more and more, requiring pestering, timidly worded nudges from him just checking in to make sure his email from two months ago hadn't gotten lost in the inbox vortex. When they did get back to him, it was invariably a polite pass with the half-hearted apology that this wasn't quite the right fit for their audience. Paul had never been a wildly in-demand luminary, but he was respected among the circle of low-circulation literary journal gatekeepers who knew his generalist work, and he was certain he would have found a willing publication for these submissions twenty, fifteen, even five years ago. Things had changed—gradually, then suddenly. Now no one wanted an exhumation of newspaper advertisements for musical instruments in the 1930s and what they could tell us about the Depression (an essay he'd worked on for four months that had been rejected twenty-three times so far). They all craved fast-food clickbait, reactive responses to what was "trending"—even the prestigious places, albeit through the highbrow prism of appraising the tastes of hoi polloi from their castle turrets. The quality of the work had become a secondary concern, as had any notion that the writer might aspire to invisibility, deferring to his subject. No, these days the scribe had to take center stage, an ego machine of first-person perspective, and that character had to hold provocative opinions that brooked no uncertainty—the more dogmatic the better—and to restate those beliefs in prose a middle schooler could understand, over and over, until she or he became a reliable "brand," generating baked-in attention from the internet-captured masses for whom there was no middle ground between the denunciative and the obsequious. The slangy monarchical reverence for their favorites as "king" and "queen" was a depressingly symbolic fad, commoners happily groveling at the feet of their literary rulers.

The spoils had gone to the loudest, most shameless and combative, and often least qualified voices in the room—in Paul's field and, with more tragic repercussions, to America's ersatz king.

"I wrote a lot I haven't shown you, before you were old enough to understand what they were and before you were born," he said. "And Hannah's dad writes news articles. Those are completely different from essays."

"Why?"

"The essays I write are very long and require months of research. Articles are usually just short summaries of what happened yesterday, plus a bunch of quotes from experts to substitute for original thinking.

The etymology—the original meaning—of the word 'essay' is 'to try,' and that's what my essays do: they try to grapple with complicated—"

"What's 'grapple'?"

"Wrestle, or struggle. They grapple with complicated issues, and in my opinion, the only subjects worth writing about are those that demand sustained grappling, and may not have a definitive answer. In fact, I try to end essays on a note of ambiguity—that means more than one interpretation—so the reader can keep grappling with—"

"Hannah never even heard of the places your articles were in."

"Again, essays, not articles. And, to quote Schopenhauer, 'the person who writes for fools is always sure of a large public.'"

Mabel looked confused.

"What's Hannah's last name, by the way?"

She told him, then asked, "Why? You want to look up her dad?"

"No. I should just know your friends' names."

An amusical beeping drew their attention. At the neighboring table, a dad squinting at his phone sat with two kids around Mabel's age, both absorbed in their iPads, one of which was producing the sound effect. The man wasn't wearing a wedding ring and was what Jane affectionately referred to as a "crazy-hair dad," a father whose unkempt locks signaled no requirement to look sharp for work and who clearly stretched intervals between haircuts out of thrift or laziness. (Paul trimmed his hair sporadically in front of the bathroom mirror and indulged in a cheap haircut a couple of times a year to tame the back of his head.) The area was a natural landing spot for their slovenly tribe, the crazy-haired dads whose divorces had forced them to downgrade from tony Park Slope proper and accept the long, uphill walks to the F train over snaggletoothed sidewalks for proximity to their children. His half-joking motto for the neighborhood, whose sleepy, ramshackle ambiance he'd come to love: *South Slope—when life throws you a curve.*

Paul didn't verbally convey his judgment over the tech devices to Mabel—she'd heard this lecture enough times—but allowed himself a subtle head shake.

The waitress reappeared with the paper cup of tater tots the diner served as a kid-friendly hors d'oeuvre. Mabel had never liked them, so they were all his.

"Remember when I used to do this?" he asked, skewering two tots with their forks and doing a Charlie Chaplin dance with them.

"You're getting my fork all oily," she said.

"Sorry." He decapitated and degreased her fork before prodding her with questions, mostly about the new public middle school she'd be starting in the fall, until their food arrived and she asked if they could both read. He never declined this request from her, and reading while eating was one of his favorite pastimes. Mabel had a young adult novel in her backpack, and he leafed through a community newspaper from a stack by the entrance. These publications, no matter how amateurishly produced, always entertained him, the stories of petty crime and local eccentrics and furors over real estate developments. This one was particularly amusing, with its house-style fondness for yellow-journalism tabloid headlines. He would have loved to be a turn-of-the-century New York reporter, filing dispatches from the rough quarters of the city with a verbal panache that the public wholly appreciated—no cries of "fake news" back then, even though much of it actually was.

He was about to share a choice phrase from the paper with Mabel for a laugh—RUFFIANS DEFACE BANKING ESTABLISHMENT ON 7TH AVENUE—but her snippy reaction to the Chaplin routine made him keep it to himself.

"Dad? Dad!" Mabel said with an exasperation that suggested she'd called for him several times already. Their check was on the table.

"Whoops," he said. "You left half your pancakes. Were they not good?"

"They were okay," she said. "We had a big afternoon snack."

He paid, leaving a tip made much more generous by jettisoning his spare change. The diner was cheap, especially with the early bird discount, but he needed more teaching work, and soon.

6

On the way to his building they passed through a tunnel of scaffolding. Even in shabby South Slope, developers had amenity-stocked housing to erect and longtime residents to evict. Soon the entire city would be nothing more than an agglomeration of slickly anodyne glass-and-steel structures, all its gritty character and history overwritten.

"Need any clothes?" Paul asked as they walked by a stoop where someone had set out piles of used children's clothing. He never bought Mabel anything new—that was certainly Jane's department—but he'd created a sizable wardrobe for her at his place from sidewalk scavenging and flea markets.

"No," she said without looking at the items.

Suddenly Paul grabbed a diagonal bar from the scaffolding above and hauled himself up to stand on the lower horizontal beam.

"What're you *doing*?" Mabel asked.

It wasn't like him to do this—he'd never climbed scaffolding in his life—but he wanted to jolt her out of the half coma she'd been in all afternoon.

"Why am I doing what?"

There was one more beam above him before the roof. It was trickier to pull himself up without solid ground below, but he snatched it and swung his legs skyward, clinging to the beam with crossed arms and feet, hammock-style.

"You're not supposed to do that," she said. "It's against the law."

"You're right. I could go to climbing jail. You can't climb scaffolding for overpriced, cookie-cutter condos that pockmark the neighborhood."

Passersby looked up at him.

"You ever hear the phrase 'civil disobedience'?" he asked her. "It means—"

"*Dad*, people are staring."

Knowing better than to embarrass her by association, he lowered his legs to the first beam, planning to disembark from there. But his foot slipped and he landed awkwardly on the sidewalk, falling on his behind.

"Shit," he muttered.

Mabel laughed, her first laugh since they'd been together.

He'd wrenched something in his lumbar region from the impact. But it was worth it to hear that tinkling, helpless giggle of hers, its joyful musical purity. When she was a toddler, he'd tickle her more for his pleasure than hers. Raising her up to touch the ceiling, peeking at her through the neckhole of his T-shirt, setting her on the back of a couch and letting her slide down—it was so easy to unleash her honking cackle, to delight her and in turn delight himself; she was happiness on tap.

"Hilarious," he said as her laughter built on itself. Shards of pain radiated up from his tailbone. "Next time I almost get myself killed, I'll get it on tape for you."

"'Get it on tape'?"

"Seriously? You don't know that expression?"

She shook her head.

"Get it on video," he said. "Sorry—*live-stream*, as your friends might call it."

"No one says 'live-stream,'" she told him. "Just say 'streaming.'"

7

Paul was shocked to learn that Mabel had never seen *The Wizard of Oz*, so they lay on his bed, his laptop dividing their lower bodies, and watched it. His ancient machine couldn't handle streaming video, live or otherwise, making his only alternative his extensive DVD library, which he'd been able to build easily from abandoned discs on stoops. They'd been on a roll with old musicals; that summer she'd loved *Singin' in the Rain* and *West Side Story*.

"Are you *crying*?" she asked half an hour in.

"No," he answered truthfully. "My eyes get dry when I look too long at screens. Everyone's do, because you don't blink as much, but it gets worse as you get older. That's one reason why you should look up from the screen every—"

"Okay, o*kay*." When the credits rolled, he asked Mabel how she'd liked the movie.

"S'all right."

"It's *all right*? Are you kidding? It's one of the most—"

Jane had often had to remind him that his taste wasn't incontrovertible fact, that you couldn't browbeat someone else into sharing your preferences, that being an intransigent advocate could be just as off-putting as a closed-minded, Professor Webb–style critic.

"It's about defeating an evil ruler and fighting for a better world," he finished. "That idea is just as important today as it was in 1939, when Adolf Hitler was in power."

She yawned. Paul told her to brush her teeth.

"Dad, is it okay if I sleep on the couch?" she asked when she was ready for bed.

"Why would you want to do that?"

"I just think I should."

This day had to come, of course; he'd just kept assuming it would be in the future. He had been concerned at times that she was too old to share his queen bed and that he was warping her in some intricate psychological manner that would reveal itself only a decade or two later with other men, but they had grown used to the arrangement. His lumpy secondhand couch sagged, too.

He said he'd take the couch and retrieved the tube of hydrocortisone from his medicine cabinet. Mabel had suffered from eczema ever since she was an infant, livid splotches of red skin that riddled her body (sparing her face, fortunately), erupting most often when she was in bed, and caused insatiable itching. When she was a baby, he and Jane had to put her hands in mittens or else she would scratch herself bloody by the morning. They'd tried bleach baths, ultraviolet therapy, a panoply of homeopathic remedies off the internet and from farmers' markets. Nothing worked except potent topical steroids. They didn't trust the judgment of a child not to overdo the dose, so they continued to apply the ointment themselves.

The most inflamed patches were on her back and abdomen. She lay on her stomach and lifted her shirt. Paul coaxed out pearls of the hydrocortisone onto his fingertip and rubbed them into the red marks, hoping the scaly deserts would turn into oases overnight.

"Other side," he said.

She flipped over, and he targeted a constellation on her belly. He not only didn't mind this procedure (aside from sympathizing with Mabel's dermatological discomfort and wishing she hadn't been afflicted with it), he sort of looked forward to it, to tending to his daughter, providing a literal salve for her pain. Before she was born, he'd thought the physical caretaking of a child would be solely a burden, tedious and unpleasant phases of diaper changing and food prep to muck through until she was finally and blessedly independent. Much of the time, of course, it was. But as Mabel shucked off his help over the years, it was mostly proving the opposite: he missed having her rely on him for everything.

He read to her, a nightly activity since she'd been a year old, when, among the division of parental labor somewhat arbitrarily meted out, Paul was assigned bedtime. Though he otherwise disliked reading aloud—in class he nearly always pawned it off on a student—this turned out to be one of the main attractions of having a kid. After grinding through the horrendous rhyme-schemed cardboard volumes for young children, he loved sharing with his daughter the books and authors he'd discovered in the local library as a kid: Roald Dahl, E. B. White, Frog and Toad, an illustrated British series called The Church Mice that no one he knew had heard of. Mabel had always been a very willing audience. They'd snuggle in bed—"co-co-nay-nay," a bastardization of *cozy*, was her term for it as a toddler—her warm little head nestled against his armpit. He'd get into the characters' voices, hamming it up with an animation he never exercised elsewhere. Often she fell asleep as he read, and that moment she succumbed, curled up on him like a shrimp, had always made him feel most like a parent.

For weeks they'd been absorbed in *Where the Red Fern Grows*, a book he'd read multiple times when he was around Mabel's age, and they were close to the end.

Paul had forgotten the power the novel still had over him, surfacing feelings that few externalities besides his daughter could provoke. He'd cried often as a child and teenager when reading but couldn't remember the last time it had happened as an adult from an adult book—maybe two or three times in the past twenty years. Once in a while, however, reading to Mabel brought it on through some combination of the direct emotional simplicity of the text itself and who his audience was.

She, too, was deeply moved by the climax, when the two hunting dogs rescue the boy who owns them from a mountain lion, but at the price of the male's life. The female, bereft from the loss of her partner and lacking the will to live, dies a few days later.

"I know, it's sad, Mabes," he said as she smeared her face into his shirt. "But they died because they loved Billy and each other so much. Try to think of it that way, as a happy ending."

Under his own tears he was ecstatic she'd responded this way, especially after her cool reception to *The Wizard of Oz*.

He suggested they stop for the night, and as he waited for them both to return to equilibrium, he sniffed her head, basking in its wonderful aroma: her shampoo's lavender notes and a baby-powder-like scent she'd always had.

"Good night, my little dumpling," he said, kissing her forehead once she was under the covers. "I love you. If you miss me, just get me."

"Good night," she said. "I love you."

To economize he normally slept with the window unit air conditioner at seventy-five degrees on hot nights, but he set it to sixty-eight for her, feeling guilt with each falling number over his incremental contribution to global warming, anger at the bigger villains behind it, despair over what the world might look like someday for Mabel. He should have been born thirty years earlier for a host of reasons, but she should have, too.

In the living room, he googled Hannah's father.

8

Hannah's father covered national politics for the *Times*—Paul recognized his byline—and he really did have six books out at age forty-three. Even more galling, he appeared to spend all his waking hours on Twitter, participating in every half-witted meme du jour, yukking it up with blue-checkmarked colleagues, even indulging in the occasional selfie (so long as there was a modicum of justification beyond preening). Paul could see him as the kind of guy who furtively monitored his phone under the dinner table to see if he was going viral. His articles were well written, but the tweets' sloppiness and fatuous idioms ("I'm here for it," "We have no choice but to stan," "*chef's kiss*," the abuse of "literally") astonished Paul, as it always did when he encountered professionals debasing themselves on the medium. Weren't these people embarrassed to put their names on typo-stained, punctuation-free sentences composed from ready-made language that bred ready-made thoughts, no matter how insignificant their publication? Or did none of this matter when everyone else was pissing in the pool, not least the semiliterate president, whom they all allowed to set the narrative every hour?

More poking around revealed that Hannah's father had gone to Columbia for journalism school, Princeton for undergrad, an elite boarding school before that. He was, judging by his blue-chip résumé and unflappable appearances in cable news clips, what Jane called "good at life": he understood how the world operated, had the wherewithal and executive functioning to maximize his advantages, and projected the rarefied air of being the sort of person for whom things always worked out. It didn't hurt to have his pedigree, either—according to a *Times* vows announcement (Hannah's mother was a deputy mayor and fellow Princeton alum), his parents were both Yale professors.

Paul's father, dead almost two years, had had an aptitude for numbers and logic but was limited by his high school education and had been able to go only so far professionally. He'd bounced around sales jobs over the decades in dreary industries (plumbing supplies, pet food, a nearly allegorical stint at a coffin manufacturer shortly before it, too, went under), earning a steady income but dissuaded by a scarcity mentality, born of his Depression-era childhood, from investing in the stock market during its extended bull run. He'd declined a couple of opportunities to go into business with more enterprising friends; one had failed, but the other had stayed in the black until the man's well-heeled retirement. Paul's mother had been a receptionist at the same life insurance company in New Jersey for nearly fifty years. She'd met and married her husband at thirty-nine and had Paul at forty.

The shelves of their home growing up had been cluttered with more tchotchkes than books. The unimaginative dinner conversation revolved around their days and people they knew, seldom current events, rarely history, never abstractions. It wasn't surprising, then, what his parents' reaction was when Paul announced, the summer after his freshman year at Wesleyan, his intentions of becoming a writer.

He had taken a creative nonfiction seminar that spring, mostly because he thought it would be a gut class to balance out his rigorous psychology courses, his planned major that had met his parents' approval. The professor was a young man who'd recently published his first book of critically lauded essays. All the girls had inevitable crushes on Julian Wolf, a horn-rimmed, effortlessly clever East Village–based writer who commuted twice a week from Port Authority to Middletown on the Peter Pan bus, and the boys admired him as an older-brother figure who led an exotic life, mingling with Manhattan's literati, publishing occasional journalism in the manly *Esquire* (a first-person account of the running of the bulls) and the cerebral *Harper's* (a report on a fringe cult in California) and, once, in the hallowed *New Yorker* (what initially appeared to be an original essay on the Depression that, two pages later, turned out to be a review of a dry critical study of Dos Passos—why didn't they just make that clear up front?—but still, the *New Yorker*). Paul enjoyed the syllabus much more than his psych textbooks, especially Gay Talese's "Frank Sinatra Has a Cold"; his father was a Sinatra fan, and Paul had grown up to his crooning over their record player on weekends. For the first assignment he wrote a personal essay in response to it, about being the only child of ascetic Silent Generation parents when all his peers had been raised by Boomers who'd smoked pot and had casual sex to British Invasion albums.

Julian had loved Paul's essay and helped him publish it, thrillingly, in the school's lit mag. Soon they were meeting up weekly, first for coffee on campus, later in the semester for beers at a grungy bar in town. Given his mentor's worldliness, he'd assumed Julian hailed from an elite coastal background. But his North Carolina family was less well off than Paul's, and he'd given his bootstraps a vigorous pull every step of the way, sequestering himself in libraries, scrounging academic scholarships, writing ten-thousand-word articles on spec.

"You can't merely be talented. It's just as important to be a hustler if you want to compete against the rich kids," he told Paul one afternoon during happy hour, pointing his Marlboro at a booth crowded with Wesleyanites who were raggedly dressed the way only the securely affluent can get away with. "Their signal advantage is being well fed. Yours is hunger."

He served off-syllabus recommendations to Paul, who devoured them: Didion, Orwell, McPhee, Baldwin, each new text massaging open his cramped worldview from eighteen years in middle-class New Jersey. Paul's happiest academic memories were of working on his papers that spring, staying up all night before they were due, torquing the sentences, making the verbal joints as satisfyingly snug as could be. They were probably his happiest writing memories, too. It had been more innocent then; the only approbation he'd desired had been from Julian. Otherwise the class had sparked the intellectual awakening college brochures always promised but rarely delivered, the pleasure of deep engagement with a subject, the steady elevation of one's craft through apprenticeship. He could distinctly recall one Saturday night, drafting an essay in longhand in his room as an opium party blazed down the hall, when he'd realized he preferred to be exactly where he was, sober and lucid with a pot of midnight coffee. He joined Wesleyan's newspaper, the *Argus*, that semester. The banner headline stories—school scandals, town-and-gown disputes—held little interest for him, but he found his niche: the off the beaten paths of campus life and Middletown, a portrait of an oddball liquor store owner, recounting the strange history behind the construction of one of the Foss Hill dorms.

During his first dinner home that summer, after he'd told his parents he planned to be a writer of "creative nonfiction," his father asked what that meant.

"Journalism," Paul said. "But not newspaper journalism where you cover a beat. 'New journalism,' it's called. It's more of an art form."

Using the word *art* had been a mistake.

"And you can make a living from that?" asked his father.

"You can get staffed on a magazine or teach. Or freelance." It was still a time when these jobs were in abundance.

Freelance did not appear to dispel his father's concerns.

"Psychology is a more stable field."

"Well, it's not what I love. And my professor thinks I'm good."

"A lot of jobs you can get by if you're good," his father said. "To make a living as a writer—a real living, where you can provide for a family—you can't just be good. Psychology's more stable."

He didn't respond, but the implication hung in the air: his father may have believed that Paul was good, but not *good enough*.

He was likely drawing his assessment from the small body of quantifiable data at his disposal. Paul's grades in school had always been strong, though he never threatened to vie for valedictorian. Same for standardized tests. An A-minus, ninetieth-percentile caliber of student.

But excelling at conventional scholastic metrics didn't make for a successful writer. The canon had fewer members who'd been high-achieving test takers from the cradle than it did late-blossoming screw-ups.

Paul had detected another intimation, with his father's repetition of psychology as "more stable." Two years earlier, his parents had found him on the floor of their bathroom, vomiting up a bottle of aspirin. They'd rushed him to the hospital, where he recovered swiftly. There had been no obvious catalyst, no romantic heartbreak or school-related failure, which made the episode more mystifying to them, stolid people already not predisposed to empathetic psychological interpretations. That was the only attempt he ever ended up making, and no one spoke of the incident again. Paul had never even told Jane about it; in the little time he spent thinking about his motivations, he'd attributed it to impulsive teenage confusion and a capital-*R* Romantic desire to dive into the most intense of human experiences.

Regarding his paternal advice, Paul later factored in his father's projections stemming from his own hugging-the-shore ambitions, his plodding, Willy Lomanesque career of little ventured and less gained. But he also remembered it every single time he placed a piece in a journal, a small, private fuck-you to his dad, even if the payments were not, indeed, nearly enough to support a family. It also entered his mind—more forcefully—with each rejection. If he'd been better than merely good, he would have published that essay, won that grant, landed that job.

His father's cautionary words had later exerted an earthbound tilt on his career trajectory. After Paul graduated from Wesleyan, he applied to dozens of journalism positions and received one offer, from a newspaper in New Jersey, where his métier would be the kind of offbeat stories he'd written for the *Argus* and the college's lit mag. Not exactly the *New Yorker*, but as ideal a first job as he could muster in a jittery economy, and he considered himself lucky.

Three weeks before Paul was to start at the paper, Julian Wolf, no longer teaching at Wesleyan but still in intermittent touch, called him with a proposition. He'd scored a deal for a narrative nonfiction book about the devastation wrought by supply-side economics and would be driving around the country for the next six months, interviewing and reporting. He needed an assistant to accompany him and later help organize the research and fact-check.

The job would be finite, the pay lower than the newspaper salary, no benefits. And there was always the chance the book might not come to fruition or, as befell most of them, be ignored upon publication. But the intangible upside, Julian promised, was formidable: Paul would learn firsthand from him how to tackle a "sprawling, ambitious" writing project, a skill that was hard to acquire anywhere else.

"I've only done smaller, quirkier pieces," Paul said. "I haven't worked on anything like this."

"Oh, man, you don't want to spend your whole career on cutesy human-interest filler," Julian told him. "That's not what makes the cover."

Cutesy human-interest filler as a descriptor of his oeuvre stung. Paul was very tempted to realize his freshman year dreams of becoming Julian's amanuensis and wingman—through a classic cross-country road trip, no less. And he recognized the truth of what his professor said, that the writing world rewarded seven-course banquets, not the petits fours he'd been daintily preparing. But he worried that the newspaper job—or any job—would no longer be there when he returned, and that he could waste a year on a project that might not lead to anything concrete.

Moreover, his father had just been diagnosed with prostate cancer, and Paul felt an only child's obligation to be nearby during the treatment. He told Julian he had to reluctantly decline the offer.

"Opportunities like this don't come around often," Julian said. "Don't you want to take a big swing?"

The baseball analogy recast his demurral from a practical, mature judgment into a marker of emasculation, the player with a small blister removing himself from the game to let the grittier athletes tough it out. But he stayed firm; he had to take the sure thing—the stable job.

He immediately liked his work at the Jersey paper, which tamped down any regret. His father's cancer was treated successfully and never recurred. Julian's prediction was correct; none of Paul's stories made the cover, but he didn't mind. He loved turning over rocks in his backyard, interviewing local eccentrics, spending two days at a landfill in hopes of finding something of interest. If you looked long and hard enough, inevitably you did.

He'd mostly put Julian's book out of his mind until two years later, when an advance galley arrived in the office. Paul flipped to the acknowledgments to discover that the research assistant, praised extensively in the first paragraph, had also been in his freshman year seminar with Julian. Paul hadn't thought of Tobias Forman as an exemplary student, and he wondered, with the envious imagination of a jilted ex-lover, if they, too, had had tête-à-têtes over beer after class. The salt in the wound: Tobias had been in the college clique of Manhattan-bred private school students.

Paul couldn't bring himself to read the book. A few months later it was greeted with slavering reviews and bestsellerdom, then enjoyed a tour on the prize circuit. Julian's career went stratospheric, and Tobias drafted off the title's success, vaulting forward as a journalist, eventually publishing acclaimed books in the genus he'd learned at Julian's feet: sprawling and ambitious.

Paul left the newspaper a year later and plied his small-beer trade in journals, making rent with scattered teaching jobs until he secured his steady gig at the college. Whenever he encountered the bylines of Julian Wolf or Tobias Forman, or their serious-sounding, slablike books inflated with fawning blurbs, the pain of seeing their names and not his was nearly physical; he thought of amputees describing the sensation of a phantom limb. Only in his case, the limb had never sprouted in the first place, stunted by his father's discouragement.

Paul had always taken snobby pride in hungrily emerging from his culturally barren household to become a college instructor and writer. But undercutting that self-esteem was the deeper anxiety that he could have become more than what he was—that he might currently be a tenured professor rather than a lowly adjunct instructor, be sought after by glossy publications and not have to supplicate himself before journals with modest subscription bases, have six books under his belt instead of just starting his first—had his parents been rich Yale professors who'd fed him well.

9

On Saturday, Mabel had a classmate's birthday party in North Slope. It was at one of the brightly colored pseudoeducational centers now pimpling the neighborhood, spatial video games charging extortionate rates to take your children off your hands. Clutches of parents sipped expensive to-go coffees double-cupped and wastefully ribboned in cardboard sleeves. Paul didn't know any of them and wasn't eager to discuss their kids' teachers and piano lessons and summer camps. He didn't do well at birthday parties, and he was already in a foul mood: sleeping on the couch had stuck a knife in his back.

"Do you want the parents to hang around," he asked the mother of the girl of honor, "or is this more of an independent-play party? Now that they're turning twelve?"

"Well, we'd love your company," she said.

He placed a contemplative finger on his philtrum. "The tricky thing is, I have to be home in half an hour to let in a handyman—we've got a serious bathroom clog." He'd intentionally scheduled the handyman to conflict with the party, and the clog was in the shower, not the toilet, and merely made the water drain slowly. "The landlord requires me to be home while he's working, a liability thing. I could run back here when he's done, though I'm not sure when that'll be."

The woman said that wasn't necessary, and Paul returned home feeling like a kid who'd wangled himself out of detention. If he'd had close friends in the neighborhood (he once did, before Mabel, before Jane—quite a few, but he had lost touch with them all as they moved on to families and the suburbs and more demanding careers), he might have made plans with one to meet up for brunch, maybe catch a matinee. But his only real social life now was sponsored by two colleagues in the English department who invited him to dinner parties every few months, Russ and Larissa Collier-Robinson (they had joined their last names at marriage, and Paul could no longer remember who originally had which).

Also, though he liked the food itself, he held in contempt the bourgeois frivolity of brunch, its stupidly long lines for seventeen-dollar eggs and five-dollar coffee and cocktails that no one drank at any other time.

He mashed up sardines and hummus on whole wheat toast, polished off Mabel's leftover diner pancakes, glanced at an academic jobs site before deciding he'd devote his full attention to it Monday, and read his weekend delivery of the *Times*. An above-the-fold front page article was devoted to the president's latest melody of dog-whistle racism. Buried in the middle of the paper was a shorter article about plans to hollow out the Department of Education's budget. Paul could feel a choleric simmering in his veins, as much from the newspaper's prioritization of coverage as from the administration's efforts. Respectable, Princeton-groomed accomplices to a criminal idiot.

Al, the handyman employed by his landlord, buzzed up. Paul positioned several thick books on his desk in the living room for show. He never felt comfortable in his own effete workspace when someone was engaged nearby in manual labor, a self-consciousness exacerbated, in this case, by their racial difference (though when the worker was white, he felt the class schisms more acutely—even if the average handyman was making more money than he was nowadays).

"The light in your stairwell's out," Al noted when he was done snaking the shower drain.

"Yeah, it's been like that for a week or so," Paul said. It had, in fact, been out since the spring. "I haven't had the chance to get a new bulb."

"I got some in my truck. I'll change it."

"You don't have to do that."

"Know my motto when something's broken?" Al asked rhetorically. " 'If I don't fix it, who will?' "

Though the stairwell was technically communal property and thus the responsibility of the landlord, Paul took this as an implicit rebuke of his own laziness. While Al was downstairs, he propped the door open to mitigate his white-collar relinquishment of the job.

"Thank you," Paul said, proffering a ten-dollar bill when Al finished the task.

"Tony takes care of it," Al said, referring to the landlord.

"I know. It's just a tip."

"Appreciate it, but like I said, Tony takes care of it."

Paul was left with even greater respect for Al, filigreed as it was by the white liberal's paternalistic and self-exonerating guilt of excessive admiration for a Black person's achievement. What a satisfying job title, to have *handy* attached to one's gender. A man who was handy, a man who, with his hands and a tool or two, fixed the broken world: unclogged drains, replaced light bulbs, installed smoke alarms, no Hamletian procrastination or dithering over another cup of coffee, outsize praise or extra remuneration not required. Things worked because of him and only him. Paul occasionally speculated about what would happen if everyone on earth somehow depended on him, with his limited mechanical, scientific, and mathematical competencies, to keep the whole operation running. No one had sufficiently broad knowledge to do it all by him- or herself, of course, but there had to be some polymaths out there—engineers, doctors, scientists, maybe even a few politicians—who could maintain a semblance of civilization. With him alone in charge, the entire system would immediately and catastrophically collapse.

What could he fix that, if he didn't, no one else would?

10

Two nights on the couch had twisted the blade deeper into his lower back, and Paul escorted Mabel to her mother's place between Seventh and Eighth avenues on Sunday morning with a hitch in his step. The accrual of the piddling insults of aging, each month a new minor complaint to track.

Outside Jane's bay-windowed brownstone sat a small pyramid of Amazon packages, their contents manufactured and transported by workers nearly as enslaved as the builders of the original pyramids. During their time together, Paul had successfully forbidden her to order online when she could procure the desired item from a local small business. Ever since she'd moved in with her second husband, though, their stoop was beset with fungal growths of corrugated fiberboard.

Steve Elster opened one of the Victorian double doors. He ran a space and satellite insurance company ("Disrupting traditional space insurance," its website trumpeted without irony) and paid for everything for Mabel, a source of funding Paul felt deep ambivalence about but for which he was ultimately relieved. He rarely saw the inside of the place, though the heavy oak portal alone was enough to instill feelings of inadequacy. His own building had an ugly metal door with a lock that didn't turn unless you jiggled the key just so.

Their garden duplex was generously sized for two adults and two children (Steve had shared custody of his ten-year-old son) and confirmed for Paul a cardinal desire in Jane he'd always suspected her of harboring: that, despite her work for a nonprofit that brought arts programs to public schools, what she'd most wanted out of life after a child was prime real estate. Paul had spent his twenties dining on tinned fish and canned soup. Jane's parents had liberally subsidized her until she'd wedded Paul, then a little less liberally afterward. A few years into their marriage, as she was reading in bed one night, she said, "Too bad you'll never write something my book club would pick." Her pessimism had nothing to do with subject matter or sensibility or even quality, but a tacit understanding that "bestseller"—the only consistent qualification for her group—would never be embossed on any book jacket of Paul's.

Steve was sweaty and mesh-shorted; Paul assumed he did CrossFit or some other form of optimized, programmatic exercise. He looked much younger than his age, his frame carrying a Tom Cruisian compactness. His hair was always neatly trimmed, though Jane had encouraged Paul to let his grow out when they were together—she much preferred the crazy-haired-dad look, or at least she used to—and was routinely cold for a few days after he was shorn. ("Men look like penises after they get a haircut," was one of her go-to lines.)

"Hey, kiddo," Steve said as Mabel skipped by.

Kiddo was a new pet name, but it spoke of a stepfatherly distance between them, a generic quality to whatever intimacy they'd cultivated for the two years he and Jane had been a couple. Steve probably called his son *buddy*, too.

The men said hello, and Steve told him Jane would be down shortly for their weekend debriefing. Steve's innate sociability meant he always loitered at the door when Paul would have been much happier to wait alone. There could be a hostility to gregariousness, a refusal to permit others their antisocial tendencies.

"Jane told me you wrote a book," Steve said, moving the boxes into the vestibule.

"Well, I sold it based on a proposal and I've been researching the last couple of months," Paul said. "Just starting the writing process."

"That's great. Who's publishing it?"

Paul told him the name of the university.

"Where's that?"

He named the small town in a distant state.

"So the college publishes books even if you're not a professor there?"

"Universities often publish nonfiction books that have more of a serious bent. The trade publishers put out the poppier, lighter stuff. The kind that book clubs pick."

Paul's literary agent had first submitted his proposal to twenty-one trade publishers, all of whom rejected it. She then sent it to thirty-two small and academic presses around the country. The university he'd wound up with had been the only interested party, which Paul attributed to the acquiring editor's childhood exposure to the Amish in Pennsylvania. The advance was a pittance, and their publicity, marketing, and sales apparatus was anemic in comparison to the New York houses, but the editor had promised him that everyone on the team loved the idea and would make up for it with enthusiasm.

"I've gotten into audiobooks for my commute," Steve volunteered.

Paul had never listened to a book on tape in his life.

"I actually just listened to a really great one by a guy Jane says you studied with. I forget his name. Julius, maybe?"

"Julian Wolf."

"That's it. Have you read it? About the CIA and the Sandinistas?"

"No," Paul said.

"Great book," Steve repeated. "I'd give it to you if it wasn't on my phone. What's yours about? Jane was a little vague."

"Modern technology, ways we can make things better." Not everyone was up for an in-depth takedown of the culture, people asked after your work only out of politeness, and any animus in his synopsis might be perceived later by Jane as an indirect attack on her gadget-happy husband who immediately upgraded his phone whenever a new model came out.

"And how it relates to the mess the president has made," Paul couldn't stop himself from adding.

Steve smiled, a show of reassurance that, despite his decidedly corporate rank—you couldn't get much more late capitalist than *space* insurance—they were on the same team.

"Oh, has he made a mess? I hadn't really noticed," he said, employing the toothless sarcasm that had become one of the standard modes of speech in their milieu for discussing the president.

"Yeah, right," said Paul with equal facileness and futility, and as the two men stood in silence, his restraint dissipated and he launched into a paraphrased passage from his manuscript proposal: the president wasn't the cause so much as the symptom of numerous problems that had been festering for years and were compounded by recent paradigm shifts; if the imbecile had any genius to him, it was in his exploitation of these changes, allowing him to succeed wildly in the two fields that had been possibly the most coarsening to our culture and collective decency, social media and reality TV; and his policies, while certainly destructive, were likely to cause less total direct human suffering than those of his Republican forerunners, but his unprecedented rhetoric had incalculably damaged the country—and, perhaps worse, his words had become all we noticed, hijacking our attention, causing us even to start talking *like* him, letting him frame everything through his rudimentary yet savvily manipulative linguistic prism.

Steve looked regretful for egging him on.

"Well, let me know when it's on audiobook," he said.

"Sorry," Paul said. "I get a little exercised on the subject."

"No worries."

"It's just, you know, when you start thinking about the effects on your kid's life . . . I mean, you're in the same boat."

Steve nodded, though his unperturbed face—and his pervasive *no-worries* attitude—suggested that he thought of his parental watercraft as more of an unsinkable yacht to Paul's patched-up dinghy.

"Well, what're you gonna do?" he asked.

Jane appeared, wearing the athleisure leggings Paul didn't know the name of but saw on the more fashionable Park Slope moms.

"Mind starting the kids' lunch?" she asked Steve on his way out.

"Already made tuna sandwiches," he said, squeezing her shoulder.

"Low mercury, right?"

"Wait, I thought they were supposed to eat the *highest* mercury. I've been giving them balls of mercury as snacks."

"Ha-ha," Jane said.

She asked Paul how the weekend had gone. He considered acknowledging the request for separate beds and Mabel's somewhat sulky attitude, but he wasn't in the mood for an interrogation.

"She had a good time at the birthday party. We watched *The Wizard of Oz*. Finished *Where the Red Fern Grows*. Got some worms. The usual."

"I heard you talking about your book with Steve. How's it coming?"

"Making progress."

"That's great." Jane smiled warmly. "I'm really happy for you, Paul."

There was an unavoidably patronizing note when someone said that, as though they were native-born citizens of the promised land of happiness and were glad you'd finally secured a thirty-day visa.

When Mabel was a year old, Jane had suggested they think about separating. Paul knew it wasn't a perfect marriage, from the start and certainly not after the introduction of a baby, but he doubted such a thing existed for him, and if divorce could be avoided for Mabel's sake, he was willing to do nearly anything. He suggested they try couples counseling and attempted to seal whatever leaks of his own creation he perceived in their marital dam. A few months later, as they were making some inroads, he published an essay he'd been working on for a full year. It was about his New Jersey hometown's sewer system and his ancestors who'd had a hand in its construction. He'd thought it was his most sprawling and ambitious work to date, and when the contributors' copies of the literary magazine arrived, he'd excitedly shown one to Jane. He did that with any new piece, but there was a stronger whiff than usual of a desire for approval, of trying to establish his worth as a writer, a last attempt to gum up the guillotine.

Jane said she was proud of him and that she couldn't wait to read it. "And I love the illustration," she added.

Paul glumly appraised the drawing opposite the first page of his essay. Jane was being charitable; the sketch of rhizomatic sewage pipes branching upward into a family tree was amateurish, as if doodled at the last minute by an intern with no art background.

"What's wrong?" she asked.

"No one's going to read this," he said. "Twenty-five pages about a sewer system in New Jersey? It's completely self-indulgent. I made two hundred bucks from I don't know how many hours working on it that could've been spent with Mabel."

She told him all the right things: that it didn't matter how others received his work or how much money he made off it, all that was important was that he express himself and be proud of what he'd made.

"Anyway, writing doesn't have to be your *job* job," she said. "It can be just for you. Like a hobby."

He'd begun crying at the well-intentioned but hurtful suggestion that what he'd been training for his entire adult life could be reduced to a leisure activity, like watercolors for a retiree looking to fill his hours. She'd cheered on his pursuit of his passion all these years, but he now knew that she'd only been humoring him, that his own wife didn't believe in him.

At their next couples counseling session, he'd told Jane that he agreed: they should get divorced.

"Thank you," he said at the door to Jane's brownstone. He made it a policy never to pick fights with her during pickups or drop-offs. "You look good, by the way. Haircut?"

"No."

"Something's different. I can't put my finger on it."

"I've been sleeping better lately."

His eyes roved around. "Definitely not your hair?"

She paused, clearly weighing the benefits of coming clean.

"Okay, I had a little Botox," she said. "Don't judge me, Paul. I can see you judging me. You never had a problem with me dyeing my grays when we were together."

"I'm not judging—" She knew him too well. "All right, I'm judging you a little. Why, Jane? You didn't need it."

"I'm forty-five years old and every woman I know does it. Sorry if you think that makes me weak, going along with the herd."

"I get it," he said after a moment.

"Do you really, or are you just saying that?"

"I really do. There are social pressures women face that I recognize I can't fully appreciate."

Jane laughed. "Did you just have a workshop at school on acknowledging your male privilege?"

"I'm a little annoyed that my empathy is being ridiculed."

"Sorry," she said. "I'll take it."

During his downhill walk home past the other handsome brownstones of her neighborhood, however, he reconsidered. It wasn't that Jane had gotten the Botox, nor even that she'd bowed to peer pressure; it was who her herd was in the first place. She'd made the choice to live among Brooklyn's elite, the people who could afford Manhattan (Steve had lived there before Jane had persuaded him to move) but found it a little too posh, too lousy with skyscrapers and chain drugstores, bankers and beggars—all the manmade and human emblems of the rigged capitalistic system they benefited from but preferred to ignore.

Park Slopers like Jane, who came from money and had (re)married into even more of it, could maintain some self-respect at their liberal jobs and liberal arts college reunions with a Brooklyn address. It bought them the illusion that they weren't part of the problems that had been festering for years. Problems that Paul would diagnose, maybe even help cure—as a published author, not a hobbyist—in *The Luddite Manifesto*.

11

Paul had drinks scheduled Sunday night at the Brooklyn Inn with a woman he'd sat next to at an event about James Agee hosted by the Forty-second Street library. His brief stint of online dating after his divorce had permanently turned him off the practice, with its callous reduction of people to statistics and traits and activities, the unfeeling matchmaker in the machine that coldly decreed a percentile of compatibility, not to mention the abasement of joining the militia of male suitors who, from what he gathered, made their slobbery propositions via misspellings and genital self-portraiture.

Subsequently, romantic rendezvous came along seldom, usually as setups from Russ and Larissa. He'd had one long-term relationship after Jane, with an ACLU lawyer. Mabel had been five when he'd met Catherine and six when they broke up, and it affected her more than it had Paul; she'd bawled for a day when he explained the ramifications. He hadn't introduced anyone else to her since.

He was surprisingly good on first dates; it was the second and third acts of relationships where he stumbled. A favorite accusation of Jane's was that he'd pulled the temperamental wool over her eyes during their courtship, initially presenting himself as having a catholic palate eager to sample all of life's flavors. He'd squired her to hole-in-the-wall tacos in Sunset Park and shabu-shabu in Queens, to readings in bookstores and bars, to parties where he'd been happy to talk with friends and meet new people. Museums. Galleries. Art house revivals she'd never heard of at the Angelika and Film Forum. Meanders through Prospect Park.

Much of this was novel and exciting to Jane, who'd lived as an adult only in Manhattan and rarely ventured off the island.

Then, over time, the radius of his social circle shrank, he could no longer summon the energy for interborough entertainment, he dreaded seeing yet another acquaintance publish yet another book while humorlessly describing the writing process, and what had been molten in him calcified.

"I don't see the fun in sleeping in a stranger's house and having breakfast with them hovering over us, asking a million questions," he'd said once when Jane had proposed a bed-and-breakfast in Vermont for a long weekend. "'Where you folks from? What are your plans for the day? Lots of great hikes around here!' And it's not the money—I'd happily spend the same amount visiting someplace interesting. B&Bs are for yuppies."

"First of all, nobody says 'yuppies' anymore," she said.

"*I* say it. It's a good word. It's been around since I was a kid."

"And it's nice to get away, to be in the country. It's nice to *do* something, period, instead of just sitting around the apartment, reading your back issues of the *New Yorker Review of Books*."

"The *New* York *Review of Books*, or the *New Yorker*. There's no such thing as the *New*—"

"Yes, I know, it was a slipup," Jane said. "So would you consider it? Or doing *any*thing?"

Paul considered the other activities Jane might suggest, such as seeing a dull, overhyped play or driving two hours to a scenic location overrun with mosquitoes and day-trippers. Whatever it was, they would have to expend a great deal of effort or money for something that wasn't worth it except to convince Jane that they hadn't wasted their weekend.

"I don't like doing things," he said.

"You don't like *doing* things?"

"I don't like doing things," he repeated, as if formulating a new philosophy for himself, one of maverick resistance to the trite performances the rest of humanity resorts to as a void filler.

The phrase eventually turned into a joke, often stated in a comically disgruntled voice, a card for him to escape from or verbalize distaste for destination weddings, meals with distant relatives, and other obviously unappealing excursions. But she also held it against him whenever his fundamentally inbent disposition overwhelmed her.

That outlook had bled into his writing, too. According to Jane, there was a specific moment she'd decided she wanted to marry him. A few months into their relationship, she had let herself into his apartment one night with her set of keys. He was in his room, listening to white noise on his Walkman—he didn't own noise-canceling headphones yet—with his back mostly turned to her as he typed. She could see, on the side of his face, a small smile like that on a pianist's as his fingers played across the computer keyboard. He was in the flow state, the wondrous condition of absolute concentration and immersive pleasure achieved, at its apex, by mathematicians devising breakthroughs in pure thought; at its nadir, by unblinking teenage boys sucked in by video games. She told him she rarely saw that look on him otherwise. His default appearance was impassive, a stern barricade allowing little ingress and barely any egress. It was the even-keeled demeanor she would later appreciate during the post-delivery scare over Mabel's heart, but at the time it had concerned her; she'd questioned if he were one of those perpetually saturnine bookish men with a constantly furrowed psychic brow. Seeing him light up as he wrote, she'd been reassured that he could experience joy, only his version was private, not public, and she'd accurately sensed that if they had a child together, he would feel what he was supposed to feel—maybe with even more intensity than the kind of father who dispensed his happiness wantonly.

Paul had sometimes wondered if what made Jane truly fall out of love—aside from his disinclination for doing things, the bedtime squabbles over who'd washed the dishes that degenerated into three-hour stalemates, the formerly endearing mannerisms that eventually drove the other person crazy, the clashing values that had chafed like a too-snug shoe, an endurable irritation at first until, by day's end, it had inflated into an obscene bubble of a blister—aside from all of that, if it was that his experience of writing had grown more rancorous, the essays becoming polemical cudgels rather than fine-point tools of inquiry. Subjects as seemingly apolitical as the history of streetlights in New York had turned into proxy wars through which he railed against the automobile industry's contribution to air pollution; an essay on

Hemingway's time in the Florida Keys had somehow shoehorned in an indictment of the gutting of welfare. His open curiosity in his twenties and early thirties had curdled—she'd claimed—into a wallowing, fanged righteousness that admitted no private smiles.

"You're happiest when you're complaining about the world," she'd told him more than once. "It's almost like you *want* things to be bad so you can sit back and criticize."

Some women might be attracted to a curmudgeonly crank at first, willing themselves to see a brooding charisma in any chronic malcontent. But no one liked being married to one. After the divorce, their coalition of friends, whose social upkeep Jane had been completely responsible for maintaining, made the not terribly agonizing decision to preserve ties with her over him. Outside of his time with Mabel, Paul retreated further into his habits, his sardines and hummus instead of brunch with peers, his solo moviegoing, his weekends scaling archival mountains of the *New York Review of Books*. If he did find himself at a party, he craved his armchair, his record player, a book, and a glass of peaty Scotch. He easily deflected the diminishing number of invitations that came his way with claims of childcare duties. He'd more or less achieved his goal of not doing things.

His date, Julie, was a history teacher at a public school in Midtown. They hailed from the same sociocultural slice of New York, cited recent articles they'd both read in not just the *Times* but also the *Times Literary Supplement*, entertained the assignation with a larkish, low-stakes air. She asked the bartender what IPAs he had on tap. Paul was quite certain she didn't have Botox and that few, if any, of her friends did.

He soon asked about cell phones in her classroom. She shook her head ruefully and said that, while her fellow teachers had thrown up their hands, she enforced the school's zero tolerance policy and took pleasure in confiscating them. Last semester a student had even had the temerity to listen to a podcast in class. Paul mocked the self-enamored tone of the few podcasts he'd heard (on his laptop), especially when two or more co-hosts batted around inside jokes in the argot of whatever niche area they'd colonized.

The more dyspeptic his venting, the more Julie laughed. For the first time in a while, he was actually enjoying a date.

"Do you go to events at the library often?" she asked.

"I've been there a lot this summer to do research, and if there's something interesting happening at night, I try to stick around."

"I've been going there for research most days, too. I'm getting this new course off the ground. Even days I don't need the archives. I just find I work better there."

"Being surrounded by books is great motivation," Paul said. "And it's quiet, which is more than I can say for any coffee shop."

"My students tell me they don't 'get' libraries. They think they can research everything on the internet."

"Young people now," he said, with enough presence of mind not to call them *kids these days*, "think you never have to leave your home for anything anymore. And they're essentially right, which is the problem. They don't have to see what's become of the world around them. In the old days, if you wanted to see a movie, you had to physically go to a theater and maybe pass a homeless person on the way in, then you'd have to buy a ticket from an employee making minimum wage, and then you had to sit in a communal space with other people in your neighborhood and figure out a way to socially cooperate with them. Now we just stay on our couches and pay a machine that tells us what we'll want to watch next, and we forget that society still exists. And whenever we *do* go outside, we stare at our phones and plug up our ears so we don't have to hear anyone else or, God forbid, our own thoughts."

Julie smiled politely. Two hectoring speeches in one day. *Professor Webb.*

"Sorry," he said. "I read that long interview in the *Times* with the moron in chief before I came here, and I guess I got a little 'triggered.'" The interviewer was, as Mabel had said, her classmate Hannah's father. Paul had counted three meaningful questions about policy in the entire exchange, all of which the president had galloped away from with his bottomless digressive stamina, and Hannah's father had let him go each time without a fight.

"I tortured myself by reading it, too. What an awful human being."

"Lately I find myself getting angry less at him and more at the paper for being so . . . placid about what's happening. It's what Chomsky says passes for liberal in the intellectual culture: highly conformist to power but—"

"Mildly critical," Julie finished with a smile of recognition. "I tell that quote to my kids."

Paul was impressed. It wasn't that well known a line.

"I've mostly adjusted to him," he said. "But once in a while I think, 'Jesus Christ, I still can't believe the president of the United States is—' "

"Oh, please don't say his name," she said. "In fact, can we not bring him up at all? I feel like I can't have a conversation without him being the center of it, and I just can't take it anymore."

Besides believing this approach to be wrongheaded—sidestepping discussion of the cancer was exactly what the tumorous president and his cronies wanted—Paul considered overly precious those people who censored others or themselves about his name (writing only the first letter of his surname followed by underscores, for instance, or referring to him by his numerical order among presidents).

But, given the circumstances, he mimed zipping his lips.

"I know I sound like a, what do they call it . . . a 'snowflake' who can't handle anything scary," Julie said, seeming to read his thoughts. "But you have no idea how many of my students ask me what's going to happen to them, how this is all going to end. Basically, if good or evil will win. And, honestly, I don't know what to tell them now."

"I guess I should figure out what to say to my daughter," Paul said. Julie noted the existence of his child with a smile that was either heartfelt or masking chagrin. "She's eleven, so she gets the gist, but I'm hoping he'll be out of office before she fully understands what's happening."

"And what do you think you'll tell her, if she asks? About what will happen to us?" Julie sounded as though she were not channeling Paul's daughter or her students, but asking for herself.

"What will happen—" Paul paused, savoring his provisional status as oracular sage. He considered what he privately thought and what he would tell Mabel after applying a parental filter for the disturbing facts, and hit upon a statement that rang true in both cases.

"Is what we believe will happen," he continued. "This chapter of history is ugly, but the next one is still unwritten. If we lose hope, we'll lose. If we think we can win, we will. Cynicism and idealism are both self-fulfilling prophecies."

"And you personally think things will get better in the next chapter?"

"I do," he said. "Not tomorrow, but someday."

"Not tomorrow, but someday," Julie repeated. "That's not a bad line. Mind if I borrow it for my students?"

"It's yours."

"I'll give it back when you need it." They'd returned to the joshing, first-date badminton that is as delightful to play oneself as it is insufferable to witness. "I wish I could be more glass-half-full about all this myself." She held up her depleted pint glass. "Speaking of which, another round?"

"Absolutely," Paul said, holding up a finger for the bartender's attention. "I think my very qualified optimism only kicked in after my daughter was born. A way to justify bringing her into existence. Otherwise, you know, why have kids if you think the world is going to hell?"

He'd given her another chance to mention any children. She didn't. Julie looked to be in her late thirties, making this sensitive terrain.

"Especially since I already felt guilty enough about adding to global warming by having her," he said. "Even if my ex-wife and I decided we wanted only one kid, to reduce our carbon footprint."

A clumsy segue, but these conversations were never smooth, and it was better than the blunt explanation two months from now that he wanted a committed stepmother for Mabel, not another half- or stepsibling.

"Right." Julie hesitated. "And was the carbon footprint thing more your wife's idea, or yours?"

"More mine," Paul said. "It's pretty important to me."

Neither of them spoke. The Sunday night crowd had thinned, and in the lull between songs it was quiet. The sun had set over the course of their date, and the atmosphere had similarly darkened from a playful encounter to a gloomy reminder of the fragility of democracy, the end of days, and more personal ticking clocks.

The bartender came over and asked if they wanted two more IPAs.

"Actually," Julie said, reaching for her backpack below the bar, "I should cut myself off. Big library day tomorrow."

Paul took the hint and paid for their drinks. He and Julie hugged briefly outside, said it was nice to see each other again, and split in opposite directions.

He stepped into a pizzeria, a post-date ritual that allowed him to salvage a lackluster evening with a shot of gustatory pleasure. The only other customers were two twentysomethings canoodling in Paul's view as he chewed a plain slice. They giggled and kissed despite their greasy mouths, mutually smitten the way only the young are, the grubbiness of their surroundings intensifying their ardor: they had little more than pedestrian pizza, but they had love.

The protein and carbs left him full and empty as he walked home. He was never bone-deep lonely, the way he'd sometimes been in his twenties before meeting Jane; a divorce and the responsibilities of part-time custody had cured that disease and fostered an appreciation for bachelor solitude. But still, there were times, not so much the downbeat ones but more the joyous occasions, when it would be nice to have someone to share his life with: when he'd sold his book proposal, for example, or how he imagined it would be the day *The Luddite Manifesto* finally came out, when he'd give a reading for his colleagues and remaining acquaintances, when everyone was congratulating him and asking him to sign their copies, when they'd celebrate at a bar, and then, after the last of them apologetically peeled off, when Paul would have to return to his fourth-floor walk-up, alone.

12

Paul spent the week emailing every department chair and academic contact in the tristate area. *Sorry, we're all filled up for the year; If you'd gotten to me a month ago, I might have been able to scrounge something up; [no response]; [no response]; [no response].*

He scoured employment sites for another job he could transfer his skills to—but what transferable skills did he have? The world did not much care for the talents that methodically ground out eight-thousand-word essays about Rhode Island outsider artists. His peers had stockpiled money over the past decade from nebulously titled tech-adjacent jobs that, he suspected, required scant sweat equity or legitimate expertise. Social media strategist, content consultant, director of digital operations—parodies of postmodern vocations. A superb editor he'd written for years ago at an award-winning academic quarterly was now the head of a heinous website whose stubby articles—squibs? listicles?—were accompanied by emojis readers could click on to convey their reactions. If he were hired at one of these places, he wouldn't be able to do even entry-level work, intellectually or ethically. And the highest-paying positions consisted of attending meetings at which nothing of note was accomplished other than vague directives to underlings. He'd never been the type to issue commands from on high; though he was in a field far removed from brute labor, he prided himself on earning every cent he made through visible toil, typing or grading papers or preparing a lecture. He didn't collect a paycheck just sitting on his ass in a conference room incanting buzzwords.

Adjunct instructors didn't receive health insurance, but Nathaniel had previously told him he could pay for COBRA to extend it for the time being, and that the individual departments would be voting during the semester on offering coverage to adjuncts for the spring; it was all but assured that the English department would support it.

When Paul investigated COBRA, he discovered that the premium would fall entirely to him, without any contribution from the college. Thanks to his higher salary from the spring—and the fact that Jane and Steve, not he, claimed Mabel as a dependent—his government subsidy for marketplace insurance went only so far, making even catastrophic coverage about twice as expensive as before.

So he'd go without health insurance for the fall, as he'd done for stretches of his twenties. He was in good shape; he'd just postpone any medical checkups until the new year.

He once again crunched the numbers dispiritedly. The after-tax salary for four classes over the four months of the semester would barely cover his rent.

"Hold on, Paul, I can't hear," his mother said after she picked up his call. She wore a hearing aid but had difficulty understanding Paul over the phone, forcing him to shout sentences two or three times. Her TV was on in the background, further scrambling their communication, and a clatter of plastic indicated she was reaching for one of the four remotes next to her armchair, at least two of which were never used. The volume at first went up accidentally before she lowered it.

"Hello?" she said too loudly, like someone with headphones on.

With diligent enunciation, he asked how she was. He infrequently phoned his mother, waiting instead for her weekly call. As her only adult blood relation, he should have been checking in on her more since his father's death. But the audibility issues strained him too much, and her apartment, in the Riverdale neighborhood of the Bronx, depressed him during his bimonthly visits with Mabel. His parents had moved there more than a decade ago, after they retired and decided a house was too much upkeep. Paul had lobbied for Manhattan or Brooklyn, but his father had wanted to save money and bought a two-bedroom in a high-rise eyesore near the Henry Hudson Parkway.

He girded himself. He'd run out of options.

"I have to ask you for a favor," he said.

"You have to what?" she asked.

"I have to ask you for a favor," he repeated, loathing every slow, loud syllable.

13

His mother's apartment was a twenty-three-minute walk from the northern terminal destination on the 1 train, but a two-minute hop to an express bus that departed for Manhattan half-hourly. His commute to the college would be long, though not all that much worse than his two-subway journey from South Slope. He could borrow his mother's car to pick up and drop off Mabel for her weekend visits. For the short term, it was *amenable*.

And free. His landlord, raring to get Paul out and jack up the rent, had allowed him to break the lease without a penalty. He'd save thousands of dollars while he searched for more teaching work and finished *The Luddite Manifesto*, and he'd be solvent enough to get his own place by January, February at the latest. A little detour he would someday laugh about, that semester he'd moved in with his eighty-six-year-old mother. Grist for a comic personal essay someday, maybe.

He put in storage his furniture, his bicycle, and all his books (housed since the divorce in stacks of wooden crates, which made moving them a snap), retaining just his clothes and what he needed to teach and write. He was generally proud of how nonmaterialistic he was, but seeing all of his worldly possessions fit comfortably inside an eight-by-eight-foot cell was a little sad, too. He thought about asking Jane to hold on to the terrarium, but he didn't like the idea of Steve's swooping in; it was his and Mabel's pursuit. He installed it in his bedroom in Riverdale.

The first night, he noticed a crack shaped like a lightning bolt in the ceiling directly above his bed. He pointed it out to his mother.

"It's fine," she said.

"Don't you want to repair it?"

"We had someone come in a while ago. He plastered it over, but he said there's a problem in the foundation and the crack would come back no matter what. Which it did, a year or two later. The only way to fix it would be to rip out the ceiling and start over."

"You're not worried about the ceiling caving in?"

"He said it would last twenty years at least. I don't expect I'll be here by then."

"You don't want to at least plaster it over again? Make the room look nicer?"

She surveyed the crack with a pinched face.

"Not worth the money," she said. "Why do you care? Are you worried about the value when you sell it after I die?"

"Of course not," he said, though the thought had crossed his mind.

He believed the expert's prognostication that the flawed foundation would maintain its integrity, but Paul still had trouble falling asleep that night. (It didn't help that the decades-old mattress wilted with a quicksand concavity and that the sheets were coarse relics from his childhood.) He opened his eyes at irregular intervals with a gnawing, childlike fear of the ceiling's collapsing when he was at his most defenseless. As he was finally drifting off, he startled himself awake with an anxious myoclonic jerk.

Cynicism and idealism were both self-fulfilling prophecies, he reminded himself, willing himself to think of the ceiling as structurally sound.

14

Cohabitation with his mother was tolerable if he kept to his room, which had its own bathroom right outside the door. She was out of the house often enough; spry for her age, she drove locally to run errands and had a weekly mah-jongg game with a group of retired women, whom she also saw socially at other times.

It was the living and dining rooms he had to avoid, and he couldn't justify skipping too many dinners, which were either bland dishes that had taken up permanent residence in the 1950s in his mother's culinary repertoire or mediocre takeout.

"Where's the *Times*?" he asked his first Sunday in her apartment. His parents had subscribed to the weekend edition once their New Jersey paper was no longer available to them.

"I canceled it," she said. "Your father's the only one who read it."

He reinstated his daily delivery; it was too cursory an experience online, the eye skating over articles it would have stopped at in the paper. Unable to bike his two loops around Prospect Park, he went for jogs in Van Cortlandt Park. Sometimes he escaped to a neighborhood coffee shop or diner to write. Unlike in Park Slope, he was usually the only person under sixty in an establishment here. Riverdale was just a few miles from Manhattan but halfway across the country culturopsychologically, its senior citizens sleepwalking around as if it were fifty years ago.

His mother's primary dialogue with him in recent years had been keeping him abreast of her acquaintances' children and grandchildren and inquiring about his own romantic life, usually by asking how Mabel liked Steve, a none-too-subtle setup to wondering aloud how she might take to a stepmother. Paul's deportment during these talks was steadfast neutrality. He treated them like a visit to the dentist; struggling while the sharp implement was against your gums only worsened the ordeal.

Otherwise, the apartment was a decent, quiet place to work.

A week into his move, he realized one morning that the shower in his mother's bathroom had been running much longer than usual. He knocked on her door; then, when he heard no reply, on the bathroom door inside her room.

"Mom?" he called several times. He cracked open the door and was hit by sauna-like steam. "Mom?"

"I fell off my chair," she said from behind the opaque shower curtain and through the thrumming water. She had a simple plastic chair designed for the elderly that fitted inside the tub. "I'm on the floor of the tub."

Thank God he was there, though he wasn't happy about what he would have to do.

"I'm going to come in and turn off the water. Then I'll hand you a towel and lift you back onto the seat. Can you get out yourself once you're there?"

She said yes. He stepped in and was able to shut off the water without looking at his mother. He gave her a towel and, once she'd draped herself, pulled back the curtain, moving to the other side of the tub so that her back was to him and raising his sight line for both their sakes.

"You need to put your arms out so I can lift you," he told her.

"The towel's going to fall off if I do that," she said. "I can't tie it from here."

He could do this. Other caretakers had to do much worse. They cleaned out bedpans, wiped asses, changed soiled underwear. Lifting his naked mother in the shower was nothing.

He bent his knees and, focusing on the top of her head, reached out and hooked his hands under the loose wings of her triceps. Her wet skin felt crepey and pruned from the hot water.

He hoisted her, trying not to touch any other part of her body while making sure she didn't slip. She didn't generate any lift herself, reminding him of Mabel as a toddler, when, as an act of passive resistance to wherever he wanted her to move, she would let her arms and legs slacken into dead weight, making any carrying job twice as hard.

With his lower back still tender from the fall off the scaffolding, he overcompensated with his arms. A needle jabbed his right rotator cuff.

"Fuck," he said.

"Please don't curse here, Paul," she said.

Through the acute pain in his shoulder, he gently lowered her onto the plastic chair and drew the shower curtain with the appropriate swiftness of a man terrified of seeing his mother in the nude. He told her he'd wait outside the bathroom to ensure she got out safely.

"Thank you, Paul," she said. "I don't know what I would've done if you weren't here."

"We'll buy you one of those alert buttons for the bathroom," he said, massaging his tender shoulder. "And a better chair."

15

He returned to his mother's apartment late one night, having spent the day first working at the Forty-second Street library. (He didn't see Julie, but her doppelgängers, as with anyone you're hoping to avoid, were around every corner.) Then he'd lingered at a pub over a burger and a couple of pints of beer—as a reward, but really to delay going home, the traffic-choked express bus ride, the muggy August walk, the gloomy sight of the dingy white-bricked complex, the chintzy faux marble lobby, the carpeted hallway that inexplicably smelled of roast beef, his mother's Nixon-era décor. If people listened to the same music at twenty-four for the rest of their lives, the same must be true for owning furniture at forty-four.

When he stepped inside he heard a commercial on the television. This was the first time it had been on since he'd moved in—his mother had never been much of a TV watcher, and Paul doubted she'd seen a movie this millennium. She wasn't in the living room, and the lights were all off; she must have gone to sleep and accidentally left it on.

He had to hunt for the remote, but before he located it, the program returned to a woman with eyebrows like grave and acute accents spewing invective at "the liberals." It was the cable network that was a de facto propaganda organ for the president. His mother had likely turned to it by accident, maybe when inaccurately aiming for the power button, and with her poor hearing hadn't realized it was still on.

Paul watched, captivated at first by the same darkly voyeuristic forces that gripped him when he sank into a toxic Twitter rabbit hole, the fascination that such banal evil existed in his own time, that millions of

Americans ate up this malevolent twaddle, that they couldn't recognize how obviously they were being conned.

His incredulous curiosity soon yielded, as it always did, to disgust and rage. These terrible people were demolishing innocent lives, the planet, all the progress humans had made. His daughter's future.

He zapped it off before his anger consumed him and led to a bad night of sleep. He'd learned by now not to read the news before bed.

16

Mabel made her first visit to Riverdale in mid-August, after missing his first two weekends because of Paul's move and an invitation to a friend's summer house. He picked her up in Park Slope, and the drive amid the Friday afternoon exodus from the city took an hour and a half.

"Grandma's car smells weird," she said.

His mother soaked herself in the same cheap perfume she'd used since Paul's childhood, a floral fragrance that was overpowering even in small spritzes. Despite the objective olfactory assault, he found it oddly comforting.

"You'll get used to it," he told her.

"The stitches are falling off the back of your seat."

"They're not real stitches. So it's not a big deal."

"What do you mean they're not real stitches?"

"The seats are pleather, not real leather. They don't even need stitches. They're just ornamental. For show. It's actually called a 'skeuomorph,' when something new uses a design feature of an older technology even though it's no longer necessary."

"Why would they put them on if they don't do anything?"

"It makes it look like real leather," he explained. "In general, skeuomorphs make the new version seem more authentic, and not inferior or strange. Like how on computers, the icon for saving something is a floppy disk. People like having a reminder of how things used to be."

"What's a floppy disk?"

"Exactly," he said.

They visited the Wave Hill public gardens on Saturday, rambling about the greenhouse and the grounds overlooking the Hudson River, stopping by a class on seeds for children. Mabel had wanted to be a botanist ever since she'd learned what it was, and Paul hoped that ready access to the estate, Van Cortlandt Park, and the New York Botanical Garden would alleviate the doldrums of these next few months. But she slumped through the outing as if it were a compulsory field trip.

Paul retied his shoes before they departed. His back and shoulders still hurt from the scaffolding fall and the bathtub event with his mother, and the mattress in his room left him sore every morning, so much so that he researched new ones. But he couldn't justify the cost for what he hoped would be just a few more money-saving months.

As he crouched by Mabel, some skin peeked out below her T-shirt. He lunged with his mouth and gave her a spluttery zerbert.

"What the *heck*?" she said, recoiling.

"C'mon," he said. "I used to do this all the time."

Her miffed face signaled no recollection. It couldn't have been that long since he'd done this—two, maybe three years. She'd squeal happily every time, shrieking *Daddy!* over and over.

He tried it again to jog her memory.

"Stop it!" she screamed, pushing his head away before he could make contact and pulling down her shirt.

Other adults and children gawked. Paul momentarily felt like a predator, as though no one would believe he was really Mabel's father.

"I'm sorry," he said.

"Just don't do it again," she said.

They'd eaten an early dinner in Park Slope on Friday before driving back to Riverdale, but Saturday they were stuck in the Bronx. Mabel and her grandmother had a labored, somewhat formal relationship, as if newly meeting at each encounter. They ordered in pizza and Paul tossed a salad.

"What's your best subject in school?" his mother asked as Paul distributed slices, a question she must have posed dozens of times over the years.

"Science," Mabel answered politely.

"Mabel's been doing a lot of botany projects at her camp this summer," Paul said. "Botany's the scientific study of plants."

"I *know* that," his mother said. "I'm not an idiot." She turned to Mabel. "That's good. There are lots of jobs in science. When your father told us he wanted to be a writer, I says to your grandfather"—*I says*, it made Paul cringe even more as he got older—" 'Well, I hope he knows what he's doing.' "

"Mabel's eleven," Paul said. "She has plenty of time to figure out her career. And whatever she wants to do, her mom and I will support her."

"It's still important to think about a job where you can make a steady living," said his mother. "Look what's happened to you."

His temper rose, but Paul had long ago resolved never to bicker with his mother when Mabel was present. Furthermore, she had no clue about the normal vicissitudes of a writing and academic career, that in a year he'd have a manuscript on its way to the printer and a CV with a whole new subsection.

"This is temporary while I finish my book," he said.

Mabel stared at the slice on her plate, its mottled cheese puddled with oil. "Can I just have salad?" she asked.

"But you love pizza."

"I just feel like salad," she said firmly.

She'd never been a picky eater; aside from tater tots, she gobbled down almost everything. He shifted her slice to his plate and served her salad.

After dinner his mother asked Mabel if she wanted to watch TV. "I signed up for all the channels," she said.

Paul and Jane had agreed that Mabel could have an hour of screen time per weekend day (family movie-watching being the loophole), and, as it was the first moment she'd looked happy in Riverdale, he gave his permission. She expertly navigated the streaming onscreen menu, sliding the cursor around the alphabet of the search box with dexterous familiarity, and selected a sitcom set in junior high. Paul watched with her, as a bonding activity and out of curiosity. The show was predictably hammy, the actors all telegenically coiffed and spouting implausibly precocious dialogue penned by Hollywood hacks three times their age. His daughter was rapt, her eyes glowing like the screen itself. But what bothered him most was how enmeshed the internet and phones were in its story line. Nearly every scene pivoted around provocative posts or texts, direct messages that shouldn't have been sent or "likes" that betrayed crushes. The plot of the episode couldn't have existed a mere ten years earlier. Their fictional lives without these technologies were unimaginable.

Not a single character on the show was rebellious in the slightest, either, as the classic young heroes of his era typically were; they all unconsciously swallowed the capitalist ideology around them like fish in the ocean. Childhood was no longer what it once was, a secondary gestation period in which developing humans could remain cocooned without too much materialistic interference. It had been severely abbreviated, while adolescence had elongated like taffy on both sides by years, all in the interest of companies who preyed on those with the noncommittal, faddish lifestyles of teenagers and the disposable income of adults.

It would take a heroic effort for Mabel to withstand the shallow depredations of American youth culture—which was now American culture writ large. She had a few years left before the damage was irreparable.

"Oh my God, do you, like, think Justin's going to, like, ask Tricia to the dance?" Paul asked in a Valley girl voice that was decades outmoded in its satirical affect.

"*Dad.*"

"No, seriously, I, like, can't wait to see."

"I can't hear—you're ruining it."

"But I want to see if he asks Tricia or Vanessa."

"It's *Nessa*, not *Va*nessa."

"OMG, are you Team Nessa? Because I'm Team Tricia."

"Stop," she said, though it looked like she was holding back a smile at his usage of these contemporary bits of terminology. "I'm trying to watch."

He quieted down for the rest of the show, not pushing his luck, but remained by her side; if she was going to consume this pabulum, he wanted to be part of her experience.

"Okay, no more TV," he declared immediately after the episode ended (Justin, Tricia, and Nessa wound up going to the dance together, a platonic ménage à trois that satisfied all parties). He ushered her into his bedroom. "What do you want me to read to you tonight?"

"I'm getting a little old to be read to," she said.

He'd known their arrangement couldn't last, but he'd feared this day for a long time. They had only so many activities they did together, reading and the terrarium chief among them.

"You sure?"

"I'd rather just read on my own. It's faster."

"Okay," he said stoically. There was a better chance she'd miss it if he easily consented to its banishment.

"Steve showed me a new way to make the bed," she said. "I can teach you if you want."

"I've told you my philosophy. I don't see the point in making it when I'm just going to unmake it later in the day. Others are free to waste their time on it."

He brushed his teeth, and when he returned she was leafing through a catalog.

"You should be reading a *book*, Mabes, not—" He peered at the cover. "The Sharper Image? This still exists? Why do you even have this?"

"Comes to the house."

He grabbed it. The mailing label was addressed to Steve. Of course he'd be the type to get this—to actually *buy* this crap.

"Electric *s'mores* maker?" he said, turning to a page at random. "Glow-in-the-dark floating target game? Heating/cooling beverage base with wireless phone charger?" He would have laughed if he weren't so appalled that Jane's husband had exposed their daughter to these products. "It's like someone got stoned and came up with inventions for rich idiots."

"What's 'stoned'?" Mabel asked.

"Drunk," he said. "Let's do the hydrocortisone."

He retrieved the tube from the bathroom and did her back. "Other side," he said.

"I can do my stomach," she said when she turned over.

"You know the rule. Not till you're twelve."

"I'm *almost* twelve."

Twelve was an arbitrary cutoff, decided upon by him and Jane a few years back. "Fine. I have to watch to make sure you don't use too much."

"I've been watching you do this forever." She squeezed a pea-sized amount onto her finger and reached under her shirt.

"Lift up your shirt so you can see the spots," he told her.

"I can feel them," she said as she dabbed herself. "There's a big crack on the ceiling, you know."

"I know. Don't worry about it."

"It looks like it's going to split open."

"It's not."

"How do you know?"

"A ceiling specialist told Grandma."

He glanced at another page of the catalog.

"Lighted wine bucket and speaker," he read aloud. "Once humans destroy ourselves, the alien anthropologists sifting through our remains just need to read this catalog to figure out what went wrong."

"Once humans destroy ourselves?" Mabel asked. "I thought you said scientists will fix global warming before it happens?"

"They will. It's a figure of speech. It doesn't mean anything. Read a book. Okay?"

She nodded and returned the ointment.

"Good night, my little dumpling," he said. "I love you."

"Love you," she said.

He chucked the catalog in the kitchen trash can, where Mabel wouldn't see it again and would be neither tempted by its preposterous wares nor reminded of his doomful prediction. He had to be more careful these days with what he said around her.

17

He received an email with the intro-to-writing syllabus the department had assembled. It listed no books, just essays and articles. There was some wiggle room for teachers to assign texts of their own choosing, and a few of the weeks later in the semester were labeled TBD BY THE DEPARTMENT. Elementary stuff a second-year grad student should have been handling, but he could do this for a semester or two.

He couldn't stomach another spiceless boiled chicken and rice dinner that night with his mother, however. He worked and ate at a diner on Johnson Avenue, took a walk through the wealthy, leafy section of Riverdale, and returned just before ten o'clock.

The TV was on, providing the only light in the living room. It showed a commercial featuring a hale sixtysomething couple with pastel sweaters looped around their necks enjoying outdoor activities, doubtless for some geriatric pharmaceutical. His mother noticed him as he came in.

"How are you?" she asked, fumbling at buttons on the remote that did nothing.

"Fine. You don't have to turn it off for my benefit."

She kept pressing fruitlessly as the program returned. It was the right-wing cable network from the other night, and centered on the screen was the blocky, self-satisfied face of Colin Mackey, a sadistic phys ed teacher in another life, in this one the star host of the program *Mackey Live*.

"Coddled college students in California are protesting a campus visit from a conservative author," he sneered. "Whatever happened to free speech? Does the First Amendment only count when it's speech you agree with?"

Text floated behind him on a big screen—MACKEY'S FINAL COMMENT—as the set went pitch black save for a spectral spotlight on him, as if he were handing down the Word of God.

"The First Amendment also protects the right to peaceful protest, you idiot," Paul said to the screen as Mackey continued to bark. "Why are you watching this shit?" he asked his mother.

"I was just flipping channels." His mother finally located the power button. The room went silent and dark.

"I came in the other night and this crap was on, too," he said.

She was quiet for a moment.

"Fine, I was watching it," she said. "And don't curse, please."

"Why would you watch *this*?"

"I don't know. Curious what he has to say."

"You're curious what *Colin Mackey* has to say? I can save you some time. Liberals—sorry, *the* liberals—are evil. Minorities and immigrants are criminals and rapists. And the president is God. That about sums up his worldview."

"He doesn't just say that," she said.

"So you watch him regularly?"

She paused. "Yes. Not around you, because I knew what you'd say."

"Jesus." He looked back at the TV, as if it were the culprit. "Did *Dad* watch it with you, too?" He couldn't imagine his father, who revered FDR above all other politicians for steering the country out of the Depression that blackened his childhood, tolerating this buffoon.

"I didn't watch it when your father was alive. I'm sure he would have disapproved as much as you."

"And with good reason! Have you actually listened to what this guy says? He's a crypto-fascist. No, that's too generous—he's just a fascist."

She didn't respond.

"Don't tell me you watch the rest of this revolting channel, too."

"Sometimes," she said.

"Jesus, Mom," he repeated. "I just don't know what to say. I can't believe this."

Aside from her age, in the sweet spot of the channel's viewership, he wouldn't have ever pegged her as a fan. She had lived a hermetically sealed life in their predominantly white New Jersey township that, over the years, had welcomed a sprinkling of upwardly mobile Indians and Asians, toward whom she'd always professed an open-minded attitude. Paul had thought of her as apolitical; the rare times he and his father had discussed current events or government leaders, she'd hardly ever joined in. She'd even seemed to like the previous president and his "beautiful daughters."

"You're right about one thing," he said. "Dad would be appalled."

"Well, your father never let me speak my mind," she said, turning on the lamp by the chair. The light revealed an angry, determined set to her jaw, as though it were ready to snap with decades of stored-up grievances. "He never asked me what *I* thought about anything. You neither. And whenever I *did* speak my mind, you both made fun of me."

Paul had no defense. He and his father had had a habit of condescendingly smiling at her opinions or mocking them outright.

"I'm sorry about how we treated you—really, I am—but *that's* why you're watching this asshole? As an act of rebellion against your son and your dead husband, by allowing an even more overbearing man to speak for you?"

"I don't have to explain myself to you. Good night." She pushed herself up from the arms of the chair and shuffled off to her room.

Paul absorbed the revelation, motionless and stunned. Then he turned the TV back on. Mackey was still in the portentous chiaroscuro of his "Final Comment" segment.

"Words matter," the host said. "Words become ideas, ideas become actions. Words can change the world. And the liberals know this, my friends. So it starts with canceling a provocative speaker. Soon they're canceling newspapers, magazines, books, websites, TV shows—maybe even this one. Until, eventually, they achieve their ultimate goal: canceling *your* voice."

Mackey bullied the camera with a pointed finger. "But we have an ally in our war against these tyrants—the president. His willingness to step into the ring and stand up for American values when no one else will is proof of what Thomas Carlyle wrote about in 1840. He called it 'the great man theory': 'The history of what man has accomplished in this world is at bottom the history of the great men who have worked here.' Certain strong, virtuous, and courageous individuals are the ones who shape history. Let's thank God we have this president—this great man—shaping the history of our country as he takes on the vicious radical left, going with his killer instinct for the jugular."

A haughty smile at this final, tortured metaphor of violence, the only linguistic frequency his audience could hear—the eldest among them daydreaming of bygone American military supremacy, the younger ones raised on first-person shooters, F-16 flyovers at the Super Bowl, and action movies ending in orgiastic bloodbaths.

"I'm Colin Mackey, and this is my final comment," he said.

Paul turned it off, repulsed yet amazed at the gall: to venerate *this* unscrupulous ignoramus, who had failed upward over and over in his gauchely charmed life, as a "great man." And Mackey, a reactionary simpleton unqualified for any respectable news organization, surely thought of himself in those terms as well. Utter mediocrities so convinced of their own excellence that they'd bamboozled their benighted flocks—and now Paul's mother—into believing in it, too.

18

Paul didn't remark on his mother's news consumption the next morning as she puttered around fixing tea and scrambled eggs and reading a paperback mystery. He wanted to believe it was somehow a misunderstanding, a phase, that she wasn't a terrible person. That was how he now viewed these people, whose former leanings could, in their most magnanimous interpretation, be traced to self-sabotaging ignorance but who could no longer offer any partially convincing rationalizations.

But after dinner she went straight to the living room and, apparently emboldened now that her secret was out, turned on the network. Paul, reading in his room, heard it through the walls, distracted by his awareness of the poison she was pouring in her own ears. During a commercial break in Mackey's show, he confronted her.

"Are you actually listening to what they're saying?" he huffed, standing over his mother's green velvet armchair they'd owned since his childhood. He spoke about how the network scapegoated minorities and blamed "liberal elites" for the country's ills to hoodwink its viewers—so-called real Americans—into thinking it was on their side, that they lied pathologically and whipped up anger and hatred all in the name of low taxes and power. It was obvious, comprehensible to a child—in fact, he'd first lectured Mabel about this a few years earlier, and she'd gotten it.

"You have your opinion, I have mine," his mother told him.

"Everyone is entitled to her own opinion," he said. "Not her own alternative facts."

Mackey reappeared and introduced his guest, a lackey in the administration who appeared to have goose-stepped onto the set from a Klan meeting.

"I can't believe you want people like this in your living room," Paul said.

"If you don't want to see it," she said, "you can go to your own room."

A maddening heat had been kindling in his chest during their conversation, manifesting in a desire to throttle his skeletal mother into grasping common sense and logic. He'd last felt this urge with Mabel as a recalcitrant young child.

Before he could get further worked up, Paul did as she suggested, storming off with blustery, dignified scorn. Then he lay down on the twin guest bed, a grown man sent to his room by his mother, and simply felt pathetic as he looked up at the crack in the ceiling.

19

After another extended Friday afternoon drive from Park Slope to Riverdale, Jane asked Paul if he would consider picking up Mabel on Saturday mornings instead. At first he emphatically refused, insisting he have his rightful complete weekend with her. But when he took into account that he, too, had to fight the traffic, leaving them time only for a grim dinner with his newly extremist mother, more sounds of mastication and utensil scraping than speech, he relented. It would leave him more time for *The Luddite Manifesto*, at least; the move and his futile job searches had disrupted his writing rhythm. The school year was starting, too.

In his habitual opening-day monologue to the first of his freshman writing classes, he told them how they were barraged with more stimuli in one day than the average person in the eighteenth century saw over a span of years.

"As a result of this information overload, we usually focus solely on what's right in front of us, what's shiniest and loudest," he said. "That's what corporations, politicians, celebrities, the media are trying to make you focus on—to part you from your money, but also to convince you that the system is working for you, not oppressing you. It's the job of the writer to turn away from these distractions and make the reader pay attention to the dark, quiet corners of the world and ourselves that we've been conditioned to ignore. And if you do it well, you not only help the reader see things with new eyes, you give her an entirely new language to describe them in."

A boy in track pants yawned silently and scratched his neck. A girl wearing what looked like pajamas doodled. A car alarm outside progressed through a discordant overture of carnival sounds.

Paul's speech in his latter three classes—Nathaniel had mercifully scheduled all his courses for Tuesdays and Thursdays so that he didn't have to trek to campus the rest of the week—also failed to elicit a reaction from the students, whose lackadaisical manner suggested they hoped this mandatory course would result in an easy B plus or a not too arduous A minus.

"Why does Ralph Ellison use the second person throughout the essay?" he asked for the fourth time that day. Then, because they were freshmen and this was a middling college, he added, "By writing 'you' throughout instead of 'I,' even though it seems clear he's relating his own experiences as a child?"

For the fourth time no one answered until, on the edge of the room, a boy with close-cropped hair raised his hand. (Why did all these male college students nowadays have such short hair? Their last time to defy the strictures of bourgeois society, and they all voluntarily looked like middle-management-penises-to-be.)

"Because he was talking to me," he said. "It was my experience. I'm the one who went through it. I'm the kid in the essay."

Everything about the boy's appearance spoke of landscaping, horseshoe driveways, Range Rovers.

"What's your name?" Paul asked.

"Jason," he said, wearing the same incipient smirk he'd had all class. There had always been students like this—invariably fitting Jason's description—but they seemed to be popping up much more the last few years, keeping pace with the college's overinflated tuition.

"I assume you're being facetious, Jason. But you got at something about the essay, even in jest. What might that be?"

Paul waited, rephrased the question, and waited again. He was about to supply a response when a girl in the back row, the hood of her zipped-up sweatshirt encircling her face and black hair, raised her hand.

"For experiences that readers who aren't Black may not be able to understand, or want to understand, he makes us identify with it by using 'you,' since it sounds universal," she said flatly. "And the emotions of a child he describes might feel too simple if it was in the first person, but they sound more complex like this, because it's like the adult writer is speaking to his younger self."

"Nicely put," Paul said. He tried not to favor the good students too much. "What was your name again?"

"Elena," she said.

Elena, he committed to memory, the only student of the day he'd given that private honor, and moved on to the next question.

20

On Thursday, the express bus pulled away just as he and another woman hustled up to the stop. The woman cursed; the next one wasn't due for thirty minutes. Paul would be late to his first class of the day, and the subway would delay him even more. He could return home for his mother's car, but then he'd have to pay for tolls and a garage, in which case he might as well spring for a cab into the city—except no cabs ever ranged this far north.

The woman opened a ride-sharing app on her phone. Car icons crawled over the map of proximal streets like ants in tunnels.

"Sorry to bother you," Paul said. "I don't have a smartphone, but I'd gladly split the fare with you into Manhattan. I can pay you up front in cash." He took out a twenty-dollar bill.

The woman scrutinized the trustworthiness of his face; not owning a smartphone now was itself cause for suspicion. "Here's where I'm going," she said, showing him the address, which was close enough to school. "It'll be around forty-five with tip."

He gave her the twenty plus an extra five.

Paul had never been in a ride-sharing car before. It was a modern sedan, outfitted with miniature bottles of water and two phone chargers, pulsating with lyricless nightclub music, redolent of a pine-scented air freshener (one of his favorite smells, though not from this artificial source). There was no conversation; the woman plugged in earbuds, and the driver didn't speak except to confirm her name.

That night, Paul looked up how much profit the drivers made and how much the companies skimmed. The most prohibitive costs of being a driver were the sunk ones—the car and the insurance—and they were covered by his mother, though he would have to put his name on the latter. She seldom drove now that Paul handled the grocery shopping. All he'd have to pay for was gas.

And a smartphone.

21

Paul bought the cheapest smartphone he could, a several-iterations-old used model off the internet. He took pains not to flash it around people he knew, as he had a reputation for his clamshell phone; the prologue to *The Luddite Manifesto* still included the boast about his Stone Age device, and he'd once been referred by not one but two people to a *New York Times* journalist hunting for sources who were "smartphone holdouts." (He was glad when the paper deemed his language too salty to be quoted; it had turned out to be a fluffy trend piece for the Styles section.) When Russ finally noticed it one day in the faculty lounge, Paul claimed that his phone had broken and the company had all but forced him to upgrade.

"Watch out for the slippery slope," Russ playfully warned him. "Soon you'll be making unboxing videos."

"Boxing videos?" Paul asked. "I don't get it."

"*Un*boxing. Milla's into them. Don't look them up, they're horrific."

After completing the application process to be a driver and giving his mother's car a deep clean, he took it out for his first fare on a Friday night, from a large Spanish Colonial on a quiet cul-de-sac in Riverdale down to the East Village. The passenger was a high school girl who pecked at her phone the entire ride. They hit a bottleneck on the FDR, but with the fare amplified for surge pricing, he pocketed around forty dollars after fees. He grabbed a few more pickups in Manhattan, then, when he was ready to call it a night, waited until he had another fare with a destination closer to home, in Harlem. He followed the lead of the driver he'd had and didn't talk aside from saying hello and goodbye.

At the end of the night his take-home pay was more per hour, when he factored in prep work and grading and commuting, than teaching. He would have to refill the gas tank soon, but if he did this a few days a week, on top of not paying rent, he could recover a chunk of his lost income.

Before bed, he turned his phone off and charged it in the living room. He found it depressing how many people admitted to looking at their phones just before sleep and first thing upon waking—a cold, flat substitute for having a partner in bed to whom you said good night and good morning.

22

His mother now left the TV on the cable channel most of the day, even when she wasn't watching. The words themselves didn't penetrate the walls of his bedroom, but elsewhere in the apartment he had to hear the braying, corrosive misinformation of its hosts and guests, all peroxided former beauty pageant contestants or bloated men who should have been grazing on a golf course.

Paul had initially planned to take fares only when he was through with his work for school and unmotivated to write *The Luddite Manifesto.* But to escape the right-wing din of the apartment he began driving more often, occasionally for a long shift, other times just to snag a ride or two around the Bronx and have an excuse to miss dinner. He'd munch on trail mix and listen to WNYC during lulls, politely suspending both activities when he had passengers. They always said a quick thanks or bye when leaving, but that was it for conversation. The cabbies of his youth had been expected to be garrulous, the streetwise wits of the city. The frictionless economy was also soundless.

Charmless, too. Taking a cab late at night in his youth had been a cheap urban thrill, the adventure of hailing a stranger's car, hoping he knew the way, an atom kinetically bouncing around the city alive with possibility; you might end up anywhere, doing anything, with anyone. But when you pressed a screen to flag down your driver and the route was predestined with GPS, the data archived in some server, the magic was negated. Just another high-efficiency delivery system of a product.

One Thursday night, after a day of teaching, his fares led him from the Bronx all the way to Midtown, where he immediately received a pickup request for a nearby address. He pulled up to a plaza behind which loomed a forbidding skyscraper, its vertical stripes of concrete between narrow windows resembling prison bars. He averted his eyes from the hideous facade until he heard a tap at a backseat window.

"For Lauren?" a fortysomething woman asked as she poked her head in. He confirmed it.

She settled into the car with a deflating sigh and tapped furiously on her phone. Lauren had the look he often received for pickups in this neighborhood, a sleekly blow-dried black mane and flattering but subdued corporate attire. Ten minutes into their drive to the Upper West Side her phone tinkled with a Madonna song.

"Yeah, I know." Her voice had an appealing rasp. "Tell him to go to Keith if he has a problem with it. This is not my jurisdiction. It's Keith's."

One of the perks of the job, playing off Paul's journalistic curiosity for other people's lines of work, was eavesdropping on the flotsam and jetsam of his passengers' days, the intra-office dramas with their supporting casts.

Lauren *uh-huh*ed her way through the conversation.

"Did he say something to him?" she asked as they approached their destination, a luxury building off Columbus Avenue. "Well, guess fucking what: it's Colin's show. He makes the call."

Paul took notice of the name plus the word *show*, though she could have colloquially meant any kind of production, televised or not, run by someone named Colin.

She hung up and unbuckled her seat belt, but before she could open the door, her phone rang again.

"Jesus Christ," she muttered, then answered while stomping to the building's doormanned entrance.

Paul googled the address of the pickup. It was the headquarters of the cable network; he somehow hadn't noticed any insignia or promotions on the building. He'd passed by it many times in his life but had forgotten it was there, that he lived not too far from the locus of televised evil.

Then he searched for his passenger's first name and "Colin Mackey." One of the first hits was a LinkedIn page. Lauren Davidson had graduated from Boston College nineteen years earlier, with a degree in, surprisingly, biology, and had held positions on a variety of television programs over the years. For the past dozen years she had rotated through several different roles, currently as a senior producer, on *Mackey Live*.

To think he'd been that close to someone who, a few minutes earlier, had probably been that close to Mackey himself as he'd filmed his terror show.

23

They were rich, Russ and Larissa, certainly not from teaching at the college, though they were tenured and drew good salaries, but unacknowledged family money on her side. They lived just within the upper-bounded range of their peers so as not to be ostentatious; like Paul, they shopped and worked at the Park Slope Food Coop. In addition to their North Slope three-bedroom, they owned a modern, winterized country house in the Berkshires set a quarter mile into the woods. (Paul had been, just once, years ago.) Their two children were in top-rated P.S. 321 for now but would attend an obscenely expensive private school after fifth grade, and every summer they went to a sleepaway camp in Maine that cost seven thousand dollars apiece (he'd looked it up), during which time the parents rented a villa in the South of France. (Paul had never been.)

Needing to keep up with their crowd but loath to spend too much of his adjuncting wages, Paul bought an eighteen-dollar Malbec with a fancy-looking label. Your age divided by two minus five, he calculated, was the minimum dollar amount you could get away with on wine for a dinner party.

Larissa kissed his cheek at the door, and Paul, not thinking to respond in kind, instead proffered the wine like an ungainly teenager pinning his prom date's corsage. It had been a while since his last dinner party; he was getting rusty with yuppie customs.

She brought him into the living room, where Russ and three couples from the college he didn't know well or at all nibbled demure slices from a slate cheese board chalked with the names of the four varieties.

Typically they invited one or two other stragglers so that he didn't feel quite as much the anomalous bachelor, but not this time.

The conversation soon zeroed in on budget cuts at the college. "My travel plans were completely scotched," said one of the men, a medievalist. "I've already canceled two conferences."

Others one-upped him with tales of disappeared research funds, unpurchased computers, and ignominiously paying out of pocket for a visiting writer's dinner.

"My health insurance was taken away," Paul announced with a victorious grin.

"How is that legal?" asked the medievalist.

"I'm an adjunct instructor now, after eight years of being a senior lecturer. They can do whatever they want."

"So you don't have *any* insurance? What will you do if there's an emergency?"

"I'm looking both ways when I cross the street and hoping my appendix doesn't burst."

He let his cavalier acceptance of potential catastrophe linger in the room like flatulence no one could bring themselves to comment on. A reminder that someone they personally knew was uninsured would also help swing any undecided voters in the English department when the measure came up later in the semester.

"Shall we?" Larissa asked, motioning toward the dining room.

A caterer, no longer present, had prepared the dinner. "I would've cooked myself, but this week was a mess," Larissa said with an embarrassed look after she identified each dish.

The medievalist asked if anyone was watching a new series about a serial murderer. One of the couples was a fan.

"The *Times* gave it a mixed review," said Larissa. "Is it actually good?"

"We hated the pilot and despised all the characters at first, but it gets better after that, and you start to like them a little despite themselves," the wife said. "Though it really doesn't get good till episode four."

"Five," her husband corrected her. "When they go to Bermuda."

"Right, right. The fishing boat scene."

"'Is that a shark?'" he said.

The couple giggled as if privately reminiscing over an anecdote from their own subtropical vacation.

"Let's give it a shot," Russ said to Larissa. "We need something new to binge."

"I'm jealous you get to watch it for the first time," the husband said. "You'll thank me when you get to the finale. It's incredible. It's worth getting through the season just for the end."

"Yeah, the show's unwatchable until the very last second," Paul piped up. "But it's worth it. It's an amazing second."

Jingling laughter from the room. On the infrequent occasions his parents had hosted dinner parties when he was growing up, deep laughs had boomed upstairs to Paul's room from the participants; either it was a misperception of childhood, or the adults he knew weren't laughing as boisterously anymore. Regardless, he was glad he'd found an opportunity to contribute here; he had mutely smiled through countless conversations like this the last decade or two, pretending to understand what others were nattering about. Massive cultural artifacts had passed him by, TV shows about dragons and dark antiheroes, movies with spaceships and superheroes, kids' fluff with wizards, and then of course the whole of popular music, which he'd stopped following well before Mabel was born. It was all aimed at thirteen-year-old boys, but the rest of the country had come to embrace these adolescent spectacles about post-9/11 American exceptionalism, disavowals of collective action and an ensuing overreliance on saviors—on a "great man"—to rescue us. And they were created and consumed in ignorance of the tragic reality that America was now the global supervillain itself, at the whim of the darkest antihero of all backed up by his army of sycophantic dragons. It was one thing for kids to get hooked on this stuff, but now his peers—professors with PhDs who had devoted their lives to fourteenth-century literature—were addicted.

He missed the get-togethers of his twenties and early thirties. Schedules that didn't require weeks of advance notice, the unforced conversations, the bawdy jokes, drinking to excess, no one worrying what time they had to wake up—the sheer *fun* of being twenty-three, the limitless potential of a night with good friends and exciting strangers and improvised adventure. But forty-six: another staid evening with colleagues at which food was the main event, cut off by the deadlines of babysitters and morning soccer. Though it wasn't just the shackles of children; responsible adults became responsibly boring over the years, stripped of their ancillary passions, their weirdnesses, afraid of revealing themselves, petrified of a two-day hangover. Did anyone even want to be at these things anymore, or did they just worry that not going was damning proof of a moribund social life, and by talking so much about television, they were confessing to their true desires of spending another night at home in front of a screen?

One of the men asked if anyone had seen the president's tweets earlier, initiating a fifteen-minute armchair diagnosis of his suspected pathologies. They did impressions of his trademark locutions, mocked his superfluous exclamation points and capitalizations, derided the most recent mutant shade of his skin. Paul didn't speak.

Russ and Larissa had taken their kids to a protest the previous weekend at the president's flagship building. "Jack and Milla came up with their own cute signs," Larissa said. She passed her phone around the table so the guests could see her children holding up placards that said WAKE ME UP WHEN THIS ADMINISTRATION IS OVER and CANCEL THE PRESIDENT. The others cooed over their adorableness and praised their political conscience.

"I wonder if these protests do more harm than good," Paul murmured as he held the phone—a jarringly large device, twice as big and heavy as his.

"Why's that?" Russ asked.

"Never mind."

"No, I'm curious."

Paul wished he hadn't said it, but now that he was forced to elaborate, and fortified by his second glass of wine—a good Rioja the hosts had provided—maybe it was worth it.

"Well, is this really the most effective way to demand change? A demographic that isn't themselves being targeted shows up on the weekends, very respectfully, making"—he was about to say *cute signs*—"not too much of a disturbance. It's sort of like bringing toothpicks to a tank fight. And then putting pictures of your toothpicks on Instagram."

The guests suddenly seemed interested in their plates. Paul drained his glass as a rash speckled his chest. He was rarely contrarian or churlish at gatherings; he would certainly have these thoughts, but he'd encountered enough holier-than-thou dinner party boors—almost all looking just like him—to know he should keep them to himself.

"You've got a point," Russ said diplomatically. "Though I still think it's better, on balance, to show up than not."

"You're absolutely right," Paul said. "And before any of you do it, I'll cancel myself." Their friendly chuckles—less for the callback quality of the tame joke than his use of the verb, which had lately become a source of amusement edged with nervousness (one day, they all probably feared, they also would be canceled for a tossed-off, imprudent comment in class)—relieved him, as did the fact that Russ hadn't challenged him about whether *he* was causing any kind of disturbance. Since attending various campus actions at Wesleyan and going to protests intermittently in New York in his twenties, Paul hadn't been to one in years. He disliked crowds, never felt any solidarity or identification within a group, and was self-conscious joining chants, in large part because so many of the sentiments were inapplicable to him and felt fraudulent to declaim. ("Whose streets? Our streets!" especially discomfited him; as a middle-class white male, he found it more imperialistic than revolutionary.)

Larissa gracefully swerved the talk to their children's schools, and he made an effort to be more agreeable for the rest of the dinner. After dessert, he trailed Russ into the kitchen, where he was racking the dishwasher.

"Sorry about that comment earlier. I honestly think it's great your kids are politically engaged." Paul raised his wineglass. "Can I blame it on the Rioja?"

"You can," Russ said with a no-harm-done chortle. "The sequel to *Blame It on Rio*."

"I think you may need to rinse that one off a little more," Paul said. Russ had wedged in a trout-encrusted plate.

"This dishwasher's shockingly powerful. You hardly need to rinse anything."

How much water and energy must it consume to clean a plate that dirty? Paul had gone without a dishwasher his entire time in South

Slope, and when lugging his laundry bag up and down three flights and carrying it two blocks through freezing or rainy or humid weather to the laundromat, he sometimes considered how easy it was for Russ to clean his clothes. The other, more extravagant perks of his friend's lifestyle came to mind when he saw him and his wife side by side. Russ bore a resemblance to seventies-era Robert Redford, and he had alluded one time, with what sounded more like shame than bragging, to some catalog modeling he'd done in his grad school days. Larissa was a few years older and considerably plainer, and though Paul tried not to read into the aesthetic mismatch, aware that such disparities with the genders reversed were commonplace, it had always struck him as slightly suspect. (That Russ had once also referred to having "made out with guys in college" at Oberlin, then never mentioned it again, fueled Paul's dubiousness.)

"How's Mabel?" Russ asked.

Milla was a year younger than Mabel, and Russ was the one father with whom he traded notes and confidences. He had thought he'd find more intimates over the years, but at every new stage of his daughter's life—playground, daycare, school—he failed to connect with the other dads, who were a different breed from him: relentlessly jovial and energetic, hokily game to join sing-alongs and make-believe exercises.

"I think she's having a reaction to my move to Riverdale," he answered. "She's been a little standoffish."

"Could also just be her age, no?" Russ said.

"Maybe." Paul drank some wine. The Rioja was excellent, far superior to his Malbec, of which no one had asked for a refill. "I don't know. I sometimes feel like the innocence of childhood is over."

"Right. The end of tickling and tucking into bed is nigh."

"Not just *her* childhood—childhood in general. Like it's been co-opted by other forces. Kids are on their phones and computers constantly, they're not allowed to go anywhere by themselves, their pictures are all over the internet by their first birthday, they're terrified of climate change and school shootings. It feels like another planet compared to the way we were raised."

"I'm not sure about that," Russ said as he forced a ramekin between dinner plates. Paul knew him to be an inefficient packer at the Coop. The richer you were, the less practice you had consolidating objects into tight spaces. "The world changes, but kids are still kids. Think about what we went through. Every night in bed, I was afraid Russia would launch a nuclear missile right at me—in Newton, Massachusetts, clearly the top target in the Cold War. And for some reason I was convinced a kidnapper would come through my window."

Paul laughed with the pleasure of connection over a long-forgotten detail. "I was obsessed with them, too. I used to put my blanket over my head and hide until I could barely breathe."

"Me, too! There must have been a rash of TV shows with kidnappers back then."

"Yes. Lots of episodes about the very common experience of climbing through a second-story bedroom window in a suburb and stealing a child. I think your kids are safe here on the third floor."

"We didn't mention it tonight, in case it doesn't go through, but we're actually about to put in a bid for a townhouse, so Larissa and I can each have our own office," said Russ. "And their rooms would be on the second floor. So, incrementally riskier."

Sobered up by the drive home, their genial exchange left Paul feeling worse for what he'd said earlier. What an ungrateful jerk, to criticize not only his hosts but also their children—and for protesting, of all things. When he'd been married to Jane, he'd resented her reproachful lectures about any faux pas he might have committed at an outing, but it was probably good for him to have a monitor.

He could still taste the Rioja's tart cherry on the tip of his tongue, a hint of coffee. He took pleasure in reading about blind taste tests that revealed snobby oenophiles to be connoisseurs in the emperor's new clothes. But this was better than anything he'd drunk in a long time. They lived well, Russ and Larissa.

Too well. Protests aside, they were part of the problem, in the comfortable-as-a-Jacuzzi tax bracket that would sacrifice for others only up to the point that it made them a tad chilly, people with far more to lose than gain in any revolution, who casually remarked—to a friend with no health insurance—about the prospective purchase of an entire townhouse as if it were a candy bar.

Echoing in his head was the handyman Al's motto: *If I don't fix it, who will?*

Then Steve's even more rhetorical question to him: *Well, what're you gonna do?*

And he realized, as he pulled in to the garage of his mother's apartment complex in her eight-year-old car, that he was, for the first time in his life, wholly on the other side of the fence, with more to gain than lose.

24

Jane called. His cell reception in the apartment was spotty, so he phoned her back on the landline. Mabel was invited to another sleepover on Saturday and said she didn't want to schlep to Riverdale on Friday after school only to turn around again within twenty-four hours, so could she skip this weekend altogether?

Schlep was Jane's word, not Mabel's. He wouldn't put it past her to have planted this idea in their daughter's mind.

"I was already down to one night a week," Paul said. "Now you're asking me to go to fortnightly."

Jane snorted.

"Sorry—'fortnightly,'" she said. "Look, I know. It's not fair to you. But she's at the age where she's having more social plans, and she's making friends at her new school. It's a good thing."

It was his fault for living so far away. Though the total conscious time spent with her hadn't been cut too drastically by shifting his pickups to Saturday morning, the halving of their nights together was symbolically meaningful, and Paul missed her company on Friday evenings. But more than anything else he yearned for their little life in South Slope—the early bird specials, the old movies, the aimless jaunts through the park. It would be a long weekend at home alone with his mother.

"Can we limit sleepovers to Fridays and every other Saturday, then? I don't want to get in a situation where I'm going three weeks without seeing her. And she should also be cleaning out the terrarium regularly."

Jane paused, as if considering how to handle a difficult child's unreasonable request. Paul felt needy and weak, especially for the terrarium ploy; he could easily take care of the basic cleaning himself.

"Okay," she said. "I'll talk to her."

Right after he hung up, the landline rang. He never otherwise picked it up, as all the calls were for his mother. "Jane?"

"Hello? Who's this?" came a loud, hoarse answer.

"I'm sorry," Paul said. "I thought it was someone else."

The man asked to speak to Paul's mother.

"She's out right now. Can I take a message?"

The caller coughed several times, a hacking so violent Paul moved the phone from his ear.

"Tell her Marvin called."

When his mother returned from a dental appointment, Paul relayed the message, though not the peremptory tone of the caller. She nodded as she arranged a platter of cold cuts.

"Who is he?"

"A friend." She examined the contents of the fridge for a second time.

"I've never heard of him before. Was he a friend of Dad's?"

"No."

"So how do you know him?"

"If you must know," she said, "I've been seeing him."

"You mean . . . in a romantic context?"

"Yes."

"For how long?"

"A few months."

"Why didn't you tell me about it?"

"I was going to," she said. "At some point."

Her husband had been dead for twenty-seven months. She was eighty-six, with a few decent years left, and certainly entitled to companionship in her dotage. But her instinct for secrecy was perceptive. It bothered him. He'd never been cheated on, to his knowledge, but this felt like what he imagined it to be, albeit as a transitive and Oedipal infidelity.

"If you're willing, I'd like you to meet him," she said. "We could have him over for dinner."

He was living there rent-free, and he was forty-six, not a solipsistic teenager. He could get through a dinner.

25

When Paul opened the door after the second staccato plonking of the bell, a lean man with a fringe of white hair haloing a liver-spotted pate was there, holding a bottle of red wine. He looked a bit like he could have been the brother of Paul's father.

"Marvin Belfer," he announced, extending his free hand.

"Paul." He never stated his full name. In his professional circles, the only people who did that were egotistical writers who were well known, or wanted you to think they were, and it had turned him off the custom.

Marvin walked in before Paul could invite him. He found Paul's mother in the kitchen—he seemed to know his way around the place—and kissed her on the cheek. Paul bristled. His parents had never been publicly affectionate with each other.

As Paul's mother finished preparations in the kitchen, Marvin eased onto the living room couch with a glass of wine as though it were his apartment. "So," he said, slapping his own thigh. "You're the writer."

"I am," Paul said.

"Your mother told you I'm writing my memoirs?"

"I don't believe she did."

"I've got quite a story," Marvin said. "Raised in a one-bedroom apartment in the Bronx during the Depression with three siblings, kid brother had polio, made me want to become a doctor. Spent a year in Korea, went to City College then med school at Einstein, had three beautiful daughters, ran my own cardiology practice in Yonkers for forty-seven years."

"I look forward to reading it," Paul said. That was what everyone who'd heard about his own book deal had told him, unconvincingly. No one looked forward to reading anything anymore, let alone by a person they knew.

"No complaints."

"What's that?"

"The title. *No Complaints*. My motto from day one. Everyone else in the world loves to whine. 'Oh, life's so unfair, Mommy and Daddy didn't pay me enough attention.' I had plenty to whine about. But I didn't. I worked my tail off, and look at the result."

A self-made man from an era when that was still feasible, who couldn't possibly imagine that the odds were now steeper, the margins of error thinner, that of the more than one hundred billion humans who'd ever walked the earth, nearly all under nasty, brutish, and short conditions, by pure chance he'd been born in the most opportune time and place and, what's more, into a body that permitted nearly all his purportedly meritocratic achievements, a lottery jackpot of a life.

"What's your book about?" Marvin asked.

"It's called *Complaints*," Paul said, but Marvin was distracted by the announcement of dinner.

Paul let him ramble on through the meal, forcing half-smiles at his horrible jokes ("This is terrific king salmon. Much better than queen salmon"). Loneliness was a great motivator for coupling, but he was baffled as to why his mother consented to be with Marvin, who steamrolled over her conversation and didn't listen to anyone. His father hadn't been this bad—had he? Paul's memories of him were already growing fuzzy, his understanding of the man narrowing to a few mannerisms (the way he put his hand on the back of the passenger seat when backing up the car, his up-and-down *Hell*-low? as he answered the phone) rather than a comprehensive survey.

When Marvin's mouthful of salmon created a small opening, Paul asked if anyone had heard what the president said at his press conference that day.

"I don't pay attention to any of that," Marvin said. "It doesn't matter."

"I think his rhetoric matters to some people," Paul said. "People who are affected by it—if not necessarily in policy, then in the way others start talking about the issues and about them. I'm sure what he said today matters to a lot of Mexican immigrants."

"Well, if they want to come here, they should be prepared to be talked about. And they should come in legally. My grandparents came to this country through Ellis Island, not under a fence."

"What do you think *you* would do if—"

"Please don't talk politics at dinner," Paul's mother chided him. "Let's be civil."

So Marvin had been the catalyst for his mother's Mackey fandom. At least there was someone to blame for it.

Dessert was angel food cake, his mother's lifelong specialty. She sliced through the chocolate frosting and fluffy sponge with a long serrated knife. Her hand trembled as she cut, and she got some frosting on her fingers. Paul handed her a napkin without comment.

"Judith used to call that a 'serenaded knife,'" Marvin said quietly, a far-off look in his eyes. "Even after I told her it's *serrated*. It became our little joke."

"Judith was his late wife," Paul's mother told him as she laid her clean hand on Marvin's shoulder.

Paul nodded respectfully. It was hard to hate people like Marvin completely, once you learned more about them. Nearly everyone had a vulnerable side.

26

His mother's justifications for going out a few nights a week no longer required what Paul realized had been white lies about seeing friends.

"Where's your ring?" he asked one night at dinner. She'd continued wearing it after Paul's father died.

"In my drawer," she said. "It was getting loose. I have to resize it."

Her ring finger remained bare, however. Observant enough to see that her son and Marvin hadn't clicked, she didn't invite him over again, but she started to sleep over occasionally at his place, a fact neither of them discussed except for her obliquely commenting that she'd be back in the morning.

Paul took the car out one of these nights, determined to rack up a big score. The evening was indeed profitable, and he stayed out much later than usual. At two A.M. he picked up a young couple outside a Williamsburg bar for an Upper West Side drop-off, a good waypoint on which to conclude the night.

The schlumpily attired man and leather-miniskirted woman stumbled inside, both apparently drunk enough that when he banged his head on the roof it elicited only hysterical laughter. They didn't strap on their seat belts, and within seconds they were making out, something that hadn't yet happened to Paul in his driving history—though, to be fair, he'd done it several times in his younger days as an inebriated passenger and had never given much thought to how the driver must have felt (in his case: uncomfortable and emasculated). He put on the radio to drown them out.

As they crossed the Williamsburg Bridge, there was shifting in the backseat followed by the sound of an unzipping fly. A glance in the rearview mirror revealed that they were now supine and prone on the seat. In a cab with a transparent divider's sham veil of privacy, he could maybe imagine this happening, but they weren't really doing this with him inches away—were they?

They were. More noises that cut through the classic rock station: lewd friction from the pleather upholstery and the woman's skirt, bodies contorting themselves, then what he assumed was her underwear coming off.

They couldn't have sex in his car—his *mother's* car. He had to say something. He could tell them it was too dangerous to drive with them lying down. Or he could just kick them out; that's what an old-school cabbie would do.

But an old-school cabbie wouldn't be vindictively penalized as a consequence of standing up for himself. They could give him a low rating, or even file a complaint with the company. He couldn't hazard this source of income.

He pretended to be unfazed as the passengers had sex without attempting to obscure it. Their clumsy copulation lasted most of the ride, ending—prematurely, it appeared—with a squeaky curse from the man. Neither participant seemed postcoitally embarrassed by Paul's presence.

After Paul parked in Riverdale, he noticed the backseat had a dark oval in the middle. He went upstairs, grabbed a roll of paper towels and a glass of soapy water, and spent ten minutes scrubbing away the stain and the mushroomy odor.

27

The next day, his driver rating wasn't lower, but the couple had stiffed him on the tip. He hated not only that he hadn't stopped them, but also that *he* was the one who'd felt ashamed. And when his mother returned from Marvin's late that morning with no mention of her overnight absence, he flushed with the further shame that, along with everyone else, his octogenarian mother was having more sex than he was.

28

The first week in the curriculum labeled TBD BY THE DEPARTMENT was arriving, and Paul received a set of links to personal essays, most published on websites with which he was unfamiliar. They were all brashly vapid, with logorrheic headlines like I Broke Up with My Toxic Boyfriend and It Was the Best Thing I Ever Did and My Family Body-Shamed Me at Thanksgiving. I Had the PERFECT Response. (The one targeted at male students: How to Successfully Hang with a Bunch of Bros When You're the Only Non-Bro.)

This wasn't literature; it was narcissism sluiced through an internet router to generate social-media-trendy verbal automatisms ("I felt seen," "the struggle is real") classed up with pseudoacademic jargon ("discourse," several more instances of "toxic masculinity," anything with "spaces") that disburdened both writer and reader from having to think through the idea at hand. And he would be enabling their intellectual laziness by feeding them this processed, preservative-laden junk.

Paul knocked on Nathaniel's office door and asked if the links were perhaps a mistake.

"Nope!" Nathaniel replied in a chipper tone. "We're incorporating more of what the students have been asking for in recent years. Punchier, more contemporary writing."

Paul gave him a skeptical look.

"I know it's not Proust," Nathaniel said. "But this is the kind of writing that sells nowadays. We have to cover our bases."

"Don't you think that sometimes it's worth fighting against what 'sells nowadays'?"

"Of course, Paul. But not when we're losing this much enrollment, which means losing even more of our budget. We're just trying to stop the bleeding."

They'd predictably chosen money over their core mission of properly educating students, and all they were teaching them, in turn, was how to make more money (or, given the field, how not to make less). Nothing he could do about it now; he'd formally outline his complaints at the end of the school year.

The department, in tacit acknowledgment that this was not what its instructors had trained for in graduate school, later sent along questions for class discussion, which were as simpleminded as the source material.

"How does the writer grab your attention with the headline?" Paul asked in his last class of the day about the first essay, which was titled Sorry Not Sorry: I'm Addicted AF to Selfies.

No one spoke, just as they hadn't in the first three classes. This was beneath them, too.

"It's direct, it uses slang, and the tone is confrontational," Elena finally answered, bailing him out, as she often did.

"Thank you, Elena." He read the next question: "Do you agree with the editorial decision to include the author's selfies in the essay?"

Again there was silence. He sighed loudly. "C'mon, guys. Does it help or hurt the essay to have her photos?"

"It helps," Jason said. "'Cause she's hot, but the kind where you can tell she's a little crazy."

A few boys laughed.

"Anyone have a response that doesn't play on an insidious cultural stereotype?" Paul asked.

After another lull, Elena slowly raised her hand with an expression of pained sympathy for Paul.

"It's relevant to the subject and it attracts attention, but I think it gives more attention to her appearance than the writing."

Paul nodded. "Anyone else agree or disagree?"

He didn't hold their church-like quietness against them. He gave up and recited the last question: "Is the tweet that links to the essay good?"

This time, before anyone could respond, or not, he said, "Jesus Christ. 'Is the tweet good?' They're not even trying with this bullshit."

The class perked up at their teacher's show of insubordination.

"Should they have paid to have a Kardashian retweet it?" Paul said mockingly. Some of the students giggled. "Is the essay 'lit'? And if so, is it 'lit AF'?"

Their tentative chuckles swelled to real laughter. Even Elena, normally stone-faced, was giggling in her hooded sweatshirt. This was the first moment he'd connected with them, but it was cheaply earned, the type of pandering-to-the-kids act he'd always disdained in his own aging teachers who'd referenced lines from whatever popular sitcom they'd watched the previous night.

"Let's move on to the next one," he said, and he read the questions without inflection or pointed commentary for the rest of the class.

29

As his mother watched in the living room, Paul listened outside his bedroom door for how Colin Mackey would address the issue.

"What happened today is a tragedy," Mackey said at the top of the show, after catching viewers up to speed on the event in question. "And it's a preventable one. Our mental health system has failed us. The man's unstable behavior had raised red flags for years, yet no one in the state, stymied by lenient laws and the red tape of bureaucracy, did anything to stop him."

Some facts Mackey conveniently left out about the assassination of the Democratic representative from California: that he had criticized her several times in the past month on his show; that the "man" was, more specifically, a gunman who had gotten hold of an assault rifle, which he turned on himself after shooting the representative at the groundbreaking for a new public housing development; that the representative and the president had become embroiled in a vicious Twitter feud that week, likely instigated by Mackey (the two men were said to speak often by phone); and that one of the president's online attacks, after warning his followers that she was rumored to be gathering support for a "totally bogus" congressional investigation against him, read, KNOCK HER OUT!

Years earlier, Catherine, the ACLU lawyer Paul had dated, had taken him to a work function at which the representative, then a state assemblymember, had spoken movingly about her upbringing in Leimert Park in Los Angeles and its influence on the criminal justice reforms she sought. He met with her for a few minutes. Her warmth and approachability didn't come off as the oleaginous charm of a politician, and Paul thought she was the rare officeholder who might not compromise her ideals as she rose in power. Afterward, he told Catherine that he could see her becoming the first female president—a historical null set he'd (shamefully) never given much thought to until Mabel was born.

"No, she's too good a person to be president," Catherine said. "This country doesn't deserve her."

And now she was right.

Paul waited until the show was over before ambushing his mother.

30

Satisfied?" Paul asked his mother just as "Mackey's Final Comment" wound down. "This jerk and the president finally got someone killed."

"*They* didn't shoot her," his mother said. "A crazy person did."

"His 'craziness' isn't the issue here."

"Of course it is. He killed himself, too. That proves he was unstable."

Mackey had used this argument earlier in the program.

"That doesn't prove any—look, they put the idea in the guy's head with their words. You think he'd target *this* woman if not for them? If he hadn't tweeted, 'Knock her out'?"

"He said he meant 'knock her out of office.' "

Paul clapped his palm on his forehead. "Don't tell me you're so gullible that you believe that ridiculous lie."

"They're allowed to criticize a public figure. She was doing the same thing to him. It isn't their fault what unstable people do."

Paul regarded this woman whose home he shared. She'd been a decent mother to him as a child—if not quite loving or supportive enough by modern helicopter-parent or even Boomer standards, at least certainly not cruel or withholding; perhaps a little dotty and meek, an understudy who never quite took to the role, mired in the stultifying thought patterns, rigid behaviors, and emotional austerity of the grueling decade in which she'd been born.

"I'd be less upset about this," he said, "if I thought the two of them had a shred of private remorse about contributing to the death of a person. But they don't. They think of her purely as an enemy combatant who needs to die so they can live. That's all life is to them. Another person's loss is their victory."

She recycled Mackey's and the president's talking points and clung to the notion of the assassin's "unstable" psyche as the real problem.

"They could literally have *me* killed, and you'd still be repeating what they say," Paul said. "You've been fucking brainwashed by this asshole."

"I've asked you many times not to curse in my home," she said. "And if I've been brainwashed, then so have you. You think the newspapers and magazines you read, the radio shows you listen to, you think they're not telling you what *you* want to hear? And you're not repeating what they say?"

His white-haired mother in her decaying armchair watching television, a Whistler portrait of regressive America. She was no different from the people he'd read countless Midwestern-diner profiles of by reporters trying to make sense of their politics of senselessness.

"They're telling me facts that are empirically based and testable," he said. "Not conspiracy theories and blatant falsehoods and contradictions. And then I carefully think through their ideas to determine whether they hold water. When someone tells me two plus two equals five and up is down, I've got enough brains to know they're either wrong or lying. This is what you worked your whole life for—to give up your mind to *these* people? Are you seriously that stupid?"

Now it was her turn to glare at him with scorn.

"Don't you *ever* call me stupid," she hissed.

"Okay, sorry. I misspoke. You're not stupid. You're deeply misinformed."

"You didn't misspeak. You've always looked down on me. With your degree your father and I paid for. You think I wouldn't have liked to go to college? I had to work from the time I finished high school. So did your father. *After* he almost got killed in Korea. What've you had to deal with? Never had to serve, no Great Depression, no World War Two, no nothing. And all you do is mope around. So don't you talk to me about what I've worked my whole life for when you've never had to work hard for anything."

He had no worthy response to the personal or generational attacks. For a moment he could identify with where she was coming from.

Perhaps the bulk of her reactionary turn, aside from Marvin's influence, was an elder's natural contempt for the privileged perch of her juniors; he certainly understood that. Only he saw the groups on both chronological sides of him as the entitled ones ruining the country—along with his genteel contemporaries like Russ and Larissa, politicians, the media, the internet, corporations, the entire system. His mother wasn't completely wrong about who was to blame, but she'd chosen the very worst of saviors.

"A forty-six-year-old man who lives with his mother," she went on. "And you think I'm the one who has a problem."

31

He left the apartment to make some money. While waiting for a fare in Kingsbridge he opened his phone's web browser, which he'd thus far avoided doing in idle moments; he considered it a surrender. He located an article written for what he had in mind: fact-based information to send to misguided relatives who supported the president. It enumerated, in simple, nonjudgmental language, various ways the president was damaging the country and enriching himself. He texted it to his mother.

Two hours and four fares later she still hadn't responded, so he found something written in a more vituperative style, on a site he hadn't seen before, and sent it to her.

While parked—demand was much lower in Riverdale than Manhattan—he read more of the site, called RealNews, whose monomaniacal coverage of the president was apparently unconcerned with libel laws. The writing was several cuts above the usual internet sludge, though, with scathingly worded pieces about his cabinet's incompetence, his eldest son's borderline racist tweets, his latest gaffe that had his aides scrambling for ludicrous explanations. It was infuriating to read in aggregate, yet inspiring to see others documenting it all, equally outraged, convinced that comeuppance was nigh—it *had* to be—for this fool's-gold-plated grifter. If only the mainstream media acknowledged what they were up against and adopted this pugnacious tone.

He read RealNews for an hour, rejecting a couple of fares. It kept recommending he download the app for a better reading experience, so he did. He'd never written a comment on the internet before, but after seeing a few and coming up with retorts in his head, he created a username: TheLuddite.

He also misspelled "Pustulant" as "President," he posted on an article about a misspelled tweet from the president. It appeared right away, and a shot of satisfaction coursed through him at the small instantiation of public resistance.

He received a fare request, felt guilty for ignoring his side gig, and drove for another hour before returning home. He didn't have it in him to read one of his dense research texts for *The Luddite Manifesto*, so he disconnected his phone from its charger in the living room and scrolled through RealNews in bed.

He was drifting off when his phone vibrated with a notification: Your comment has received a like. He hadn't realized he'd signed up for alerts—it must have been automatic—but he pressed it and saw the proof: another user had indeed endorsed his comment with a thumbs-up.

The pleasure he'd felt from posting it earlier multiplied, an adrenaline crest on the endorphin wave. He'd published essays and articles before, of course, but there was no immediacy to them—his newspaper tenure had been before the internet's prevalence, and his essays had required months and sometimes years of work, there was an arduous editorial process, they had to wait their turn in the queue, they reached a paltry audience, and without any social media presence, he'd had minimal online engagement. But now he had come up with a quip, it appeared on a nationally read website seconds later, and other people (or at least one other person) had read it—and approved.

The comments that had the most likes, numbering in the thousands, rose to the top of the pile, nearly as visible as the articles themselves. They had attained their popularity through either algorithms boosting users with more seniority and previous acclamation or, less commonly, because the site's editors had recommended them.

He clicked on a different article about the president's delaying a speech for 9/11 survivors in order to extend a TV interview with his favorite cable network.

He's a last responder, Paul wrote, smiling when he saw it transfer from his phone's text box to the website.

He woke at five in the morning. Rather than try to go back to sleep, he checked his phone. Three people had liked his new comment.

32

Paul was obligated to hold individual meetings with all his students, an exercise he had welcomed at the beginning of his teaching career, when he'd been eager to recreate the sort of mentor-mentee relationship he'd had in his own undergrad days with Julian. He'd never found one that came close to their level of intellectual compatibility and camaraderie, however, and over the years the encounters had devolved into uneasy five-minute conversations—across his desk and lately with the classroom door wide open—for which neither party wanted to be present. Paul somnolently detailed their performances on the first essay, requested that they contribute a bit more in class, and inquired, in an avuncular manner, into their academic plans. Not only was none of his current students interested in majoring in English, hardly any wanted to be in the humanities. The smartest were on the computer science track; the shrewdest, headed for professions that exploited the computer scientists' ingenuity.

In his youth, his peers would have scorned the ambition to be a technocratic entrepreneur as that of a soulless materialist. But he couldn't really blame this lot. They'd grown up in the long shadow of a recession, terrified of the prospect of another, now captive to the drunken skipper at the helm of the economy. They saw plainly who the winners and losers were, and there seemed to be no middle ground left. You were either a corrupt opportunist, like the president and his henchmen, or you belonged to the great mass of chumps. Society, as far as they could tell, was made up solely of billionaires and paupers, the beautiful people and the untouchables, the internationally famous and the invisibly obscure.

His mother and her ilk didn't believe anything anymore, convinced the authorities were lying to them. But these kids didn't believe *in* anything—other than the mercenary dictates of capitalism.

Except for Elena, whose essay had received the only A out of the seventy-two he'd graded. She remained the lone bright spot at the college for him, the one thing he looked forward to when he trudged up the mechanized steps of the express bus Tuesday and Thursday mornings. While everyone else had written a personal essay, the option requiring the least research, Elena had undertaken a piece of real journalism, interviewing half a dozen custodial and cafeteria staff at school for an exposé of the college's dehumanizing treatment of its workforce. It wasn't perfect—she was still a raw writer, prone to sermonizing and overstatement—but the scope and empathy impressed him.

"Thanks," she said, with as little emotion as she showed in class, when he complimented her work during their meeting. Was she depressed, or just reticent? In the past he might have delicately probed as to whether anything was bothering her in her personal life—this was an area where he felt he could provide a little comfort or insight—but he'd shied away from gestures of intimacy in recent years; the risk of its backfiring was too high.

Was she Latina? Or Latinx, a word he was still unsure how to pronounce? Her olive complexion and black hair could go either way, as could "Elena" and her surname, Martin. He'd never made a strong connection with a minority student before—not that he had all that many to pick from at this school for (primarily) rich white kids who had no shot at Columbia or NYU. It had always felt like a personal failing, that from all the altruistic motives he could ascribe to teaching, he couldn't legitimately count the dismantling of white supremacy as one. The last several years, as he'd watched others crusade with justified fury and bravado for their rights, Paul had often felt he'd missed the invitation to a rollicking party everyone else was attending. Through Elena (possibly) he at least had a chance to be an "ally," though the term felt dilute at best, and other white men who proudly took on this mantle seemed suspect to him, like skulking backstage techies aiming a spotlight on the diverse ensemble cast while concealing an ulterior motive—either basking in the reflected social status of the stars or gaining access to a peephole in the girls' dressing room.

"Are you interested in pursuing writing as a career?" he asked.

"I'm not sure. My academic adviser told me it's a dying field."

"Well—and I don't say this often—I think you have the talent to make it. I'd be happy to be an informal mentor, if you're looking for guidance from someone who doesn't reflexively pronounce the form dead."

"Okay," she said with a shrug, but he thought he detected an iota of excitement in her eyes.

"And I think, with a little more polish, you could submit this to the student literary magazine. I could even send it in for you—the editor took a few classes with me."

She looked dubious. "Don't bother. They'll just reject it."

"If they do, that's part of becoming a writer, getting used to rejection, not letting it stop you." She appeared surprisingly crestfallen at his pessimism, so he upgraded his prediction. "But I've got a pretty good feeling, if you work with me on this, that it'll get accepted."

"When would we work on it?"

He'd missed the express bus that morning and had driven his mother's car to school, hoping a few fares after classes would exceed the garage's criminal rates. He could hold off for a couple more hours.

"How about now?" he suggested.

33

They sat perpendicular to each other at a table in the mostly empty, fluorescent-lit student union as they drank coffee and Elena edited her essay on her laptop. Paul went sentence by sentence, proposing minute adjustments to her prose that he'd let go as he'd graded it, cutting superfluities, requesting physical details, fine-tuning the diction. He had always loved this part of writing, the finessing of a structurally sound piece. It made him feel like a true craftsman, someone who worked with the material of words as a carpenter did with wood.

"I'd go for an em dash here," he said. "Some writing books tell you that an em dash clutters up the prose and disrupts the sentence. But it can reflect a mind interrupting and refining itself, one that's able to hold more than a single thought at the same time. Think of it as a fork in the sentence's road, creating tension for what comes next."

Elena seemed to be sponging up the scraps of instruction. She'd probably never received this level of academic attention in her life. This was a big part of the problem with literary pedagogy today: an overemphasis on feeling and the primacy of personal subjectivity at the expense of the nuts and bolts of phrasing and syntax, of treating the language and form with reverence. Then there was the permissive attitude toward "experimental" writing that was typically little more than untutored, masturbatory scrawling.

"They also tell you not to start a paragraph with 'but,' but I'm a fan of it," he said, pointing to an onscreen sentence with his pen. "I didn't mean to say 'but' twice in a row. I'm not obsessed with buts."

He laughed. Elena smiled.

"Anyway," he said, "it's a strong transition, no wishy-washiness. Just make sure the sentence has a muscular tone."

"A . . . muscular tone?" she asked as she copied his advice.

"Yes, forcefully worded." He laughed again. "With a muscular and toned *but*."

She typed that along with a few other tips he'd dispensed. As she read over the sentence he'd targeted, she absentmindedly tugged the zipper of her hoodie down, the teeth slowly unnotching like the anticipatory groan of a roller coaster ascending to its peak. She stopped when it was halfway open, revealing a low-cut shirt that, from his three o'clock vantage, exposed a swath of hitherto hidden flesh. He averted his eyes; then, as if having judiciously shied away from watching an eclipse, he felt an instinctive pull to stare at her sternum despite the damage it might do. He did, for a fraction of a second, catching a flash of her cleavage before resolving not to look again.

"Speaking of em dashes and forks in the road," he said, atoning for his wayward eyes with more academic wisdom, "you ever read the Robert Frost poem 'The Road Not Taken'?"

"In ninth-grade English. And our class president read it at graduation."

"I'm guessing she or he said it was about the importance of blazing your own path even when it's unpopular, that kind of thing?"

"They."

"Excuse me?"

"They said the two roads were a metaphor for identifying as nonbinary. They said some days they wake up in the morning and they feel like a girl, and sometimes they wake up and feel like a boy. Those are the two roads in the woods for them."

It had taken him years to reverse the conditioned order of "he or she" without feeling self-conscious, and at times he felt incapable of navigating this new linguistic landscape, with its cryptic atlas of pronouns and initialisms and acceptable terminology that was redrawn weekly in lines too fine to be legible for anyone over forty.

He pulled up the Frost poem on his phone and returned to the more tranquil waters of poetic exegesis. "Anyway, Frost's real intention is actually the exact opposite of bravely going the unpopular route. Here's how he describes the second road, the road that's supposedly untaken: 'Though as for that the passing there had worn them really *about the same*.' They're equivalent, despite first appearances. So when the speaker says at the end, 'Two roads diverged in a wood, and I—,' that em dash sets up a tension. Will he admit that both roads were actually the same and it made no difference which one he picked, or is going with the myth that he was a maverick? The em dash is the *real* fork in the road as he decides what kind of person he fundamentally is. Then he says, 'I took the one less traveled by, and that has made all the difference.' He went with the self-aggrandizing legend."

"It sounds like he's a fundamentally cynical guy," Elena said. "To say that it doesn't matter what we choose because it all ends up the same."

"Exactly," he said with a big smile, a smile he used to make more often while teaching, joyful at seeding ideas in young minds and watching them flower on their own. "But cynicism and idealism are self-fulfilling prophecies. If you're idealistic at heart, maybe the decision at the fork in the road, at the em dash, *does* somehow make a difference, even if things still appear the same."

Before she could respond to his uplifting conclusion, an employee announced that the union was closing in ten minutes.

"There's a coffee shop I like a few blocks uptown, if you want to finish up. I'd say we've got an hour of work left," Paul said. The place was on the way to the garage, where he had an hour and a half remaining until he'd be charged overage fees.

"Sure," she said, zipping up her hoodie.

34

Manhattan's Thursday nightlife was shifting into first gear, restaurants filling up, revelers packing sports bars for the starts of games and the dregs of happy hour. The destination of a public space, stripping Paul and Elena of their school titles, and approached under a black sky, made them both shyer. Neither spoke for half a block as he struggled to come up with something that didn't sound like a dad making stilted small talk as he drove the babysitter home.

"Are you writing anything now?" Elena asked.

"A book," Paul said, glad she'd broken the ice and given him the opportunity to mention his project. She asked what it was about, and he gave her a thumbnail description, tamping down the curmudgeonly crankiness.

"My friend's mom's a book editor," she said, naming her and her workplace at one of the New York imprints. "Do you know her?"

"No. I elected to publish with a university press. For nonfiction, they generally handle the more serious work. The New York houses are more into flash than substance. Though I'm sure your friend's mom is good at what she does. Is your friend into writing?"

"No, but my roommate's a poet."

"That's great. It's important to have peers when you're learning your craft. I had a close circle of writer friends in college." All except for him had given up on writing within a few years of graduating, and all were, last he heard, thriving in their respective nonliterary professions.

"She's been posting her poetry on Instagram since middle school. She says if I don't build my brand now, I'll be irrelevant."

"Not to put down your roommate, but writers like that are never taken seriously. They're the ones who are ultimately irrelevant."

"She has over forty thousand followers," Elena said.

Paul had never written anything forty thousand people had read.

"Writers are supposed to keep some thoughts private," he said. "Otherwise your brain will shift to thinking about what will result in maximum popularity. And you'll start employing the debased language that others are using. Words matter—" He caught himself. "If you use their language, their internet-speak, instead of coming up with your own formulations, you'll inevitably think like everyone else."

They'd reached the coffee shop, but the employee inside signaled through the glass door that it was closing.

"Should we go back to the library?" Elena asked.

"The problem is, my car's in a garage, and my time runs out in an hour and change. If we go back to the library, I don't know if I'll get to it in time."

He couldn't take Elena to a bar. If they went to a restaurant during the peak dinner hour it might be too loud to work comfortably, and since she couldn't drink, he'd feel obligated to order food for both of them—and foot the bill or else reveal himself as a member of the precariat, an affiliation unbecoming for someone taking on a protégée.

Elena fidgeted with her backpack straps, looking to him for a decision.

"I suppose we could work in my car," he said, thinking aloud the only solution he could devise.

"*In* the car?"

"I know it's not a writers' colony in the woods"—Paul had been rejected by Yaddo and MacDowell more times than he could remember—"but if we push the seats back, there should be enough room to be comfortable."

She looked down at the sidewalk and ran a fingernail over her bottom teeth.

"Okay," she said.

They set off, again silently.

"Writers like your roommate are enterprising, and you do generally need some careerist ambition, some hustle, to make it as a writer," Paul told her, picking up the thread from before and piggybacking off a passage he'd recently written in *The Luddite Manifesto*. "But they're also predatory. They see that as physical communities break down and trust in institutions corrodes, people are looking for order and meaning, to be told what to think by authority figures. They want to be literal 'followers,' as if they're members of a religion. Or, worse, in a cult. And the cult leaders, like your roommate, are happy to be the dictators of their own little kingdoms, seizing the power that accrues more than ever to certain individuals, bullying people into thinking like them, even though that's inimical to the notion of what writing and reading are supposed to be about, which is to explore a subject with humility and encourage your reader to ask further questions. Not to mention that they cheapen the language, tossing carelessly written words out like pennies at a wishing well, just to see what happens. If you're a real writer, you should treat your sentences like precious gems."

Elena nodded as they waited for the walk signal. He was satisfied with his lecture and stopped speaking. She understood. Not everyone in her generation aspired to be a bubbleheaded influencer. If they raised Mabel right—if *he* raised her right—then even as the world continued its downward slide, maybe she'd turn out to be like Elena.

"But the writing world's the least of it, of course," he said when the white walking figure lit up, as though it were telling him to keep at it, that this was a chance to explode his young student's mind beyond the provincial parameters of her experience. "We've already had the first movie star president, now we've got the first reality TV president, and soon enough we'll get the first internet president, some troll who's made his name—or his pseudonym—through the cesspools of social media and fringe forums. At that point we won't be too far off from an artificial intelligence leader who rules by algorithmic decree. So think about that next time your roommate suggests you 'build your brand' to stave off irrelevance."

His speech had gone off track, but before he could make an apologetic joke about getting carried away and calling her roommate a cult leader—he'd really been doing that a lot lately, turning into one of those bores who took their writing a book as license to speechify—they were at the garage.

"My car has over an hour left," Paul told the attendant loitering at the entrance. "Could we just go in the car and wait out the rest of the time?"

"You want to wait *in* the car?" the attendant asked.

Paul chuckled. "Strange request, I know. It's just for a quiet place to work."

The attendant's eyes shifted between Paul and Elena.

"We have to be the ones to bring the cars out. It's an insurance thing."

"I wouldn't be driving it out. We just need to do some schoolwork, then I'll let you drive it out when my time's up."

The man said he would check if that was allowed and disappeared inside.

"We don't have to do this if it's a hassle," Elena told Paul.

"No hassle," he said. "I've got the time now, but I won't have much over the weekend."

She nodded while pursing her lips.

"Okay, as long as you don't drive it out," the attendant said when he returned. "Follow me."

Paul entered the dark maw of the garage. Elena stayed behind, examining her phone.

"Coming?"

"My roommate texted," she said. "She's locked out. I have to let her in."

"She can't crash with one of her forty thousand followers?"

Elena didn't smile. He had a stab of apprehension that he'd gone too far in excoriating the girl earlier.

"Just joking," he said. "But can't she kill time for an hour?"

"She did this for me when I lost my keys last week. I'd feel bad making her wait."

It occurred to Paul that Elena might have misinterpreted his suggestion that they work together in his car inside a garage.

"Of course. My car's probably not the best office space, anyway. Send me the revision when you're done with it and I'll pass it along to the editor."

She thanked him and turned heel.

Paul took fares for a few hours, still anxious that she might have considered his workplace suggestion a proposition, or that she'd caught him peeking—nearly against his will!—at her cleavage. But he'd made a good-faith effort to find a suitable public location, and the garage had clearly been a last resort. He'd have to be an idiot to attempt to seduce a student inside a garage—surely she knew that.

His fretting didn't abate until he arrived home late that night to an email from Elena, with her revision attached and a note thanking him for his help. It was all right, this episode and more globally. There were still some students out there who appreciated a dedicated teacher, who wanted to become real writers, who recognized that someone like Paul had wisdom to impart about literature and life—that, for the most important things, he was and would remain decidedly relevant.

35

Paul had been canvassing job boards all semester, each unsuccessful round widening his geographic (New Jersey, Connecticut, Rhode Island) and institutional (community colleges, adult education centers, private high schools, and, most reluctantly, online classes) radii. No one needed or wanted him. He was saving money this semester in Riverdale, but he couldn't sign a lease in Brooklyn until he had more work lined up. This was the fate his less successful peers had feared, and so, as their portfolios lay fallow, they had ceaselessly posted their way into hey-remember-me visibility on a bounty of integrity-depleting platforms while he had stubbornly refused and become, as Elena's roommate had predicted, irrelevant.

He was skimming nonacademic positions when one caught his eye: an "evening hours social media producer" at his mother's favorite cable network. He imagined the recent college graduates who would sign up, the ignorance, cynicism, rage, or abject desperation that would compel them to shovel out the company's bullshit on the graveyard shift. He could see several of his own students—especially the baseball-hatted boys—happily enlisting, obedient foot soldiers eager to secure health insurance at the expense of daylight. Maybe most of the company's employees started off feeling uneasy about what they were doing there, and over time that crumbled into ambivalence, and finally apathy or a full-fledged embrace; people always wanted to convince themselves that they were good. The old cliché that Hitler thought he was serving a higher purpose, that the architects of the War on Terror—the religious fundamentalists on both sides of the trench line—believed they were combating, not causing, terrorism.

Except this president and Mackey didn't even have that warped pretense to altruism. They knew full well they were serving themselves alone, and they laughed about it behind closed doors. The rot had to infect everyone in their administration and the network.

It would be satisfying, at least, to land an interview and ask whatever functionary he talked to how they could sleep at night.

He was completely unqualified for the job. He applied anyway. When he checked the next week, the position had been filled.

It made him think of something else.

36

Paul's car idled near the headquarters at ten o'clock on a Monday night. He was parked behind a string of black sedans he presumed were for the more senior employees, judging by the predominantly white-haired or balding men who entered them. People churned in and out of the revolving doors—still, late at night, the machine never stopped. A wraparound digital banner on the building circulated a farrago of the day's quotidian and harrowing news: Dow Jones +1.1% . . . President says even if global warming "real thing," could be good "because no one likes being cold" . . . Monday night football score . . .

A security guard soon forced him to make room for other black cars, so he looped the block, flicking away requests from passengers as he waited. But by midnight he hadn't gotten what he wanted and he drove home, having wasted two hours of gas and potential fares.

He repeated this procedure on Tuesday, again to no avail. On Wednesday night at eleven he was ready to call it all off when the name he was looking for appeared on his phone. He immediately accepted the ride and waited outside the building.

"For Lauren?" she asked again in her husky voice as mid-October air gusted in the open door. Once more she sat with the kind of sigh that seems intended primarily for the benefit of the sigher herself, audible proof of her own struggle in a harshly indifferent and taxing universe.

"Long night?" he asked.

"Uh-huh."

She tapped her phone as Paul piloted north and west.

"You know, I think I may have had you before," he said after a few blocks. "Do you often hail cars from that area?"

She again mumbled in the affirmative.

"It probably sounds weird without context for me to remember you," he said. "This isn't my real job—I'm a professor. I'm writing a book about technology, and I'm driving as research for a chapter on the gig economy. I sometimes take notes after rides if the person is talking on their phone about work. You must've been talking, if I remember having you."

She continued holding her phone but wasn't looking at it. "What're you saying in your book?"

"Oh, I don't want to bore you."

"I wouldn't have asked if I wasn't interested."

"Well," he said, "it's called *The Technophile's Manifesto.* The central thesis is that technology is expanding so many new avenues of commerce and improving life in so many ways that it should be less regulated, to give entrepreneurs more freedom to innovate."

"And what have you learned about the gig economy?"

"I was initially a skeptic. Mostly because that's all you see in the news, that it exploits drivers and delivery workers, that sort of thing. But it's the free market at its finest. Ride sharing cuts into the taxi and limousine commission's monopoly, which is obviously full of bureaucratic inefficiencies. And it opens up a bigger part-time labor pool and eliminates corrupt unions. I don't understand why anyone would think this is unfair to the drivers. It's a great disruption for people who are willing to work hard." He paused. "And now I'm rambling. Sorry—you're actually the first person I've revealed myself as being 'undercover' to."

"No, it's interesting. Where do you teach?"

He told her. On the faculty website he was still listed as a senior lecturer, and to someone unacquainted with the pecking order of academe, the two words might sound more impressive than being just a professor.

"How about you?"

She said the name of the network but not Mackey's show. "It's probably not very popular with your colleagues."

Paul contrived a knowing laugh. "They don't quite share the same political persuasions as I do. I don't watch it myself, but that's just because I'm not much of a TV person."

"I try not to tell people in New York where I work. They assume I'm a wacko evangelical or something. They don't understand the employees aren't like that."

"I get it. For a political affiliation that brags about their tolerance and diversity, most liberals I know are deeply intolerant of everyone else and don't want real diversity of ideas—just appearances."

"Well said."

"The hypocrisy I encounter among my colleagues as a professor is absolutely staggering. You wouldn't believe some of my stories."

He didn't know what a senior producer's duties were but figured Lauren had to have some hand in picking guests, and an ostracized conservative professor in New York City willing to rat out his co-workers might be catnip for Mackey. He'd found a clip online from *Mackey Live* that had aired years ago in which a prankster, dressed for the role in a brass-buttoned navy blazer and with neatly parted hair, had convinced the show's bookers that he was a young conservative leader on the rise. Thirty seconds into the interview, he made a volte-face, chucking insults at the network's blinkered, bigoted, aesthetically unappealing viewers (he'd used less elegant language). To his credit, Mackey had verbally sparred with him for a minute before cutting his video feed.

The impostor's error had been his juvenile mode of attack; beyond taking offense at his show of disrespect, anyone watching would have written him off as an unserious thinker reduced to middle-school jeers, his goal nothing more than currying approval with those already on his side and generating attention for himself. If Paul managed to gain an on-air, in-person interview to talk about the disingenuous virtues of liberal academia, he, too, planned to change gears without warning. But instead of resorting to crass antics, he'd speak elevated, cogent truth to power against Mackey, the network, and the president, leaving the audience out of it in hopes of giving them a wake-up call. Most would still write him off as a crackpot, of course—his repeated failures to win over his mother had grounded his ambitions—but maybe he could enlighten a few thousand clueless viewers. The advance publicity for his book wouldn't hurt, either. If his speech got traction, perhaps a trade publisher would make an offer to him and his academic press to buy the rights for orders of magnitude more money. He could move back to Brooklyn, stop driving at night, have better standing to secure a tenure track job.

Lauren didn't respond. He'd been too obvious. Telling a news producer that she wouldn't believe his stories was the equivalent of what strangers, upon hearing he was a nonfiction writer, had always said to him: that *they* had so many crazy stories, and Paul should really write about them.

"So, am I in your book?" Lauren asked when they reached her building.

"What do you mean?" he asked, momentarily forgetting about his made-up book and thinking she was referring to *The Luddite Manifesto.*

"Are you quoting me? What did I say on the phone?"

"Oh—I don't remember what you said, but I'd never directly quote someone without their permission, anyway, even on background. I'm not in the business of pushing 'fake news.' "

He spoke the phrase with a grin to signal that he wasn't too much of a "wacko," either, but that they were members of the same reasonable micro-tribe.

"Thanks for the ride." She looked at her phone for his name. "Paul."

"You're welcome"—he needlessly consulted his own phone—"Lauren."

She gave him five stars and a healthy tip.

37

Mackey's show aired live Mondays through Thursdays (Friday's show, he found out, was prerecorded, but he didn't know at what time). Reencountering Lauren too soon would look peculiar, so he delayed swinging by the headquarters until Wednesday. There were no requests from her. He returned the next night, circling the block for ninety minutes until her name appeared on his phone. He raced to the pickup spot.

"Well, hello again," he said.

She looked amused as she took her seat. "You stalking me?"

"How'd you guess?"

"Seem like the type. One of those sketchy professors doing 'research for your book.' "

"You got me. No, I've just been driving in this area a lot. High concentration of media people. A lot of them freelancers, so it's relevant to the gig chapter."

The Madonna song again played from her phone. It sounded like another work matter, and she spoke more discreetly than she had the first time. Paul drove as slowly as possible, worried she'd still be occupied when he let her out. He sufficiently delayed their arrival so that she hung up a block in advance.

He couldn't keep picking her up at her office; one more time and it really would look like stalking. There was an alternative path to seeing her again and planting the idea of booking him on her show, but he doubted he'd be able to pull it off. Lauren was conventionally attractive, though not a type he ever went for—or, more germane to his purposes, who ever went for him. The few business-minded women he'd dated before Jane had sniffed out his deficit of world-stomping ambition and deemed him an unsuitable mate for power coupling. There was no point in trying.

"Thanks again," she said as he pulled up to the curb.

Opportunities like this don't come around often, he could hear Julian Wolf warning him. *Don't you want to take a big swing?*

"Would you like to meet again? Outside of this car, I mean?" he asked. The nerves that suddenly jangled him came not from the standard fear of romantic rejection but the anxiety that his designs would be scuttled, with all his stakeouts for naught.

A corner of her upper lip minutely arched as she held open the door. "Is this an interview request about the gig economy, professor?"

"If you like," he said, stepping into the character of a suave academic accustomed to seducing women with his virile intellect, the kind of man Paul had met scores of times and instinctively despised. "Or it could be dinner."

38

He made reservations for Saturday—Mabel had another sleepover, despite Jane's promises to spare those nights for Paul—at a high-seating-capacity Italian restaurant near Lauren's apartment whose internet review was stamped with three disconcerting dollar signs. The bill would exceed profits from a full night of driving, but based on her job, building, and clothing, she'd expect a certain degree of indulgence.

He arrived first, told the server that tap water was fine, and ordered himself the cheapest glass of wine on the menu, which he nursed until Lauren showed up fifteen minutes late.

"Sorry," she said. "A work thing came up."

He clucked empathetically. "So, what exactly do you do there, that they're bothering you on a Saturday night?"

"What?" she asked, cupping her ear. He repeated the question, projecting his voice above the crowd with some effort.

"Everything," she said. It was not the first time he'd heard someone boastfully complain about overseeing every single detail at their workplace. He waited for her to elaborate, hoping she would mention that she was in charge of booking guests, but she stopped at that.

"And which show do you work for?"

"*Mackey*," she said. People who had held positions of authority for years had a tendency to dispense skeletal information, out of an assumption that their interlocutors shared their comprehensive knowledge base or as a power move that forced subordinates to own up to their ignorance.

Paul pretended to be confused, though he'd spent hours recently researching the man. What he'd found was depressingly predictable. Mackey had grown up in a comfortable New York suburb, been an accomplished wrestler in college, made his bones in regional radio and then TV assailing Democrats and defending Republicans, and become a national force in the past decade by espousing farther- and farther-right views—whether from his true beliefs or cynicism, it was hard to say. Along the way he'd banked tens of millions of dollars for himself, divorced his first wife and remarried a former intern with whom he had two young children, and now lived in a gated compound on Long Island from which he choppered into work, where he feigned to be the populist defender of the working class.

"*Mackey Live*," she clarified. "Colin Mackey's show."

"Oh, right," Paul said. "I haven't seen it, but I know who he is, of course."

He had to be patient, not to appear hungry, to present as a professor too immured within his mahogany library to be all that aware of, let alone impressed by, her sphere of mass infotainment.

He'd been on enough dates over the years—and was a practiced enough shoe-leather journalist—to keep the conversation flowing when he was motivated to do so, lightly peppering Lauren with questions about her biography, evincing curiosity (he asked to see pictures of her much-adored niece and nephew), rephrasing her statements with teacherly eloquence to demonstrate he was listening, disclosing just enough personal data that he not come off as an interrogative vulture who picked her clean while giving nothing of himself.

Lauren had grown up in suburban Westchester and lived in Manhattan since shortly after college. Her parents were both doctors nearing retirement; her "genius" younger brother was "a literal brain surgeon" in Los Angeles. (Paul's joke, "Does he also do figurative brain surgery?" went unlaughed at.) She vacationed yearly in Paris and spoke decent French, and she remained tight with a group of women from college who had all migrated to the suburbs.

"You were in a sorority?" Paul asked.

"No fucking way," Lauren said. "What do I look like to you?"

She described herself as Mackey's "right-hand woman," though she was irked that she'd been continually passed over for the brass ring of executive producer, the job going to "one incompetent guy in his fifties after another."

Paul claimed that he had recently moved to and lived alone in Riverdale to be near his elderly mother. Otherwise he was able to hew closely to the truth; it helped that his companion didn't ask for many details in return. She whipped her phone out several times during dinner to dispatch notifications, behavior that, were it a real date, would immediately be disqualifying to him.

Lauren ordered a seventeen-dollar cocktail to start, then a glass of equally expensive red wine, each request a dagger to Paul's wallet. She pecked at her arugula salad, ate a minority of her side of roasted brussels sprouts, and finished only half her salmon entrée without asking for it to be wrapped up. To Paul's relief she turned down dessert when the waiter recited the options—but, far worse, asked to see the dessert wine menu instead.

He wasn't sure if she actually liked him, given how little they had in common. But whenever he mentioned his work, she showed more interest.

"It's refreshing to meet a professor," she said over her twenty-five-(!)-dollar glass of Moscato d'Asti. "I'm used to dating TV and finance guys who only talk about ratings or money."

"And"—he smiled, a show of good-humored confidence—"how do I stack up in the ratings?"

"Well, you're definitely not a douche," she said. "Which is what most of the guys I meet are—media douches and banker douches. And which is what I used to go for. My therapist would approve of you."

"Good. I'd have a hard time seeing my daughter tomorrow and thinking I was a douche."

He'd already mentioned his daughter, but his intent wasn't the customary one about declaring himself finished with procreation. In case she had any vestigial desire for noncommittal cads, he wanted ironclad justification for why he wasn't one; he could masquerade as a conservative, but not as that. Moreover, Lauren was at the age and in a hard-driving profession that might make the prospect of someday becoming a stepmother appealing. A pang of sadness followed the reference to Mabel, though. Not only was he not with his daughter as he deceitfully tried to woo this woman, he didn't know whose house she was sleeping at, what she was doing—what she was feeling. Her life, after just eleven years, was becoming opaque to him.

"And my parents would love what you do for work," Lauren said. "To make up for my profession."

"I'm sure they're very proud of what you do," Paul said, unsure whether she meant her overall field or her job for Mackey specifically.

Lauren blew a raspberry.

"They're very proud of my brother. My dad and him both went to Harvard, and my mom went to Wellesley. They take a lot of pride in being intellectuals."

Beneath his automatic silent grammatical correction ("My dad and *he*"), he now understood why Lauren, though she seemed like the kind of person for whom money and power were two of the most important metrics when considering a mate, had consented to go out with him: a craving for parental approval, even in her early forties.

The check obliterated his last two nights of driving. He waited a moment when it landed, hoping she might propose going Dutch, but she sipped her wine and gazed around the room.

This was typically when, after a date of obvious incompatibility, he'd say goodbye, record a small withering of his soul, and hightail it to the nearest pizzeria. Instead he offered to walk her home.

"How chivalrous of you," she said. He couldn't tell if it was flirtatious or sarcastic or some combination, a line from a woman who'd gone on hundreds of dates over the years and had found that barbed guardedness was her best defense against both creeps and vulnerability. The short walk, with minimal conversation, didn't yield a definitive answer as to whether she was attracted to him, either. Paul could feel his opportunity slipping away with each wordless step.

"This is me," she said when they reached her building, and Paul kissed her before she could say anything else. He usually required much more encouragement from a woman before initiating any advances (especially in recent years), but it was easier to act boldly when you had no real emotional investment in the outcome. Presumably that was how many men had been functioning for eons: desensitized and therefore assertive.

She reciprocated. It had been a while since he'd done this with anyone, and though he'd assumed—and hoped—that he would be numb kissing a woman for whom he felt nothing, he became hard immediately. Aside from nocturnal and early morning erections, he couldn't remember the last time he'd even been aroused; the drive that had dictated so much of his youth had nearly vanished in the last few years. Animal instinct took over as he gripped her ass.

"Aren't you full of surprises, professor," Lauren said when she pulled away. "Maybe you've got a little douche in you after all."

It was normally repellent when a person fetishized you for a trait or skill they didn't fully understand, or had a favorable misreading of your character that endowed you with attributes you didn't actually possess ("douche," certainly, but also "professor"); not only did it prove they didn't know you, it invalidated their judgment.

But Paul felt his erection grow stronger nonetheless.

"Maybe a little," he said.

39

The editor of the school's literary magazine gushed over Paul's submission of Elena's essay and wanted to publish it in their winter issue.

Rather than forward the email to her, Paul decided to tell her in person. After the next class, he asked her to stay.

"So, the editor of the lit mag read your piece," he said with a deadpan face and voice. "And, well, as I said, part of maturing as a writer is getting used to rejection."

Elena's face dropped—she did care about this, her blasé mien notwithstanding—and he apologized for the good-natured deception.

"Are you messing with me?" she asked after he read aloud the email.

"Nope. I told you it was good. And it was worth spending that extra time on it."

Her incredulity gave way to a small, embarrassed smile.

"So it'll be on the internet?"

"And in print. They make a really nice-looking journal." She appeared additionally pleased by this, which warmed Paul's heart. This generation, or a small part of it, could still appreciate the value of physical artifacts over a snazzy website. "The editor will be in touch with copy edits. And he'll probably ask for a bio."

"What do I do for that?"

"It's just a few sentences about where you're from or what you're studying, that kind of thing. Maybe something about your background."

"What do you mean by my background?"

"You know, where you come from, or your family. Geographically or whatever."

Elena didn't say anything.

"Just don't say, 'She enjoys writing about herself in the third person,'" he advised her. "Everyone makes that joke."

"That's considered a joke?"

He laughed. "Congratulations, Elena. Your first publication."

She beamed again, almost in spite of herself.

"You should celebrate tonight," Paul said.

"Yeah, maybe."

"Seriously—it's important to commemorate milestones. When my first essay got into my college lit mag, I went to a bar with some friends and my writing professor—he helped me get it published—and it was one of the more fun nights of my life. Although, to be honest, I didn't remember much of it the next day."

"I'm too young to go to bars," she said. "And I have a lot of work tonight, anyway. But thank you again for your help."

After she left, he imagined her bio, in which she paid a little tribute to him.

Her professor, who worked tirelessly with her on revising this piece, told her—with a sigh—not to say she enjoys writing about herself in the third person, he envisioned the final sentence.

40

Since the shower incident with his mother, he'd developed tenderness in his right shoulder that ached when he raised his arm, making it harder to drive, an activity that now consumed four nights a week. Likely as a consequence of the pain below his neck, twisting it hurt often enough that he needed to rotate his trunk to look backward. He'd never been skilled at any sport but he'd always been in good shape, having settled upon cycling in his early thirties as his primary exercise (excellent for cardiovascular health, low-impact on the joints, solitary), and though his body would, of course, at some point decline, he didn't think the deterioration would be this rapid and this soon. A demoralizing idea: the best he could hope for in the future was to chase a receding, increasingly infirm version of the past.

He sometimes thought of Elena's piece on the college's workforce during his shifts. Everyone entered his car with their phones out—they'd needed it to monitor his approach—and almost all continued to engage with it during their rides. Just a few had initiated conversation; otherwise, he never spoke, fearful of saying something that might damage his rating. Tips were variable and seemed uncorrelated to his performance, only the level of the passenger's innate generosity or guilt.

Despite the shoulder twinges, he had to keep at it. He needed to move out of his mother's apartment and see Mabel more than one night a week. He was at risk of losing her if he didn't.

The shoulder issue grew bothersome enough that, despite being uninsured, he broke down and made an appointment with the cheapest sports medicine doctor he could find.

Paul was somewhat discomfited by the location of the office (near the nebulous border of Brooklyn and Queens), the illustration on its window (a stick figure orbited by a football, a basketball, and a baseball), and the informality of its signage for DR. ANDREW "ANDY" TWEEDY.

He further regretted his choice when the doctor, a decade younger than Paul, his hair gelled into a bed of short spikes, bounded into the examination room accompanied by a force field of musky cologne.

After Paul described the sites of pain, the doctor asked when it had started. He mentioned the initial backache resulting from the scaffolding incident.

"You in construction?" the doctor asked as he twisted Paul's arms from behind him at different angles and swiveled his head. "You don't look like it."

"No, I was just trying to make my daughter laugh by climbing it," Paul said, thinking he would find this amusing.

The doctor didn't react.

"How about the shoulder?" he asked. "It gradually got worse? Or was there a single episode you could point to, where you felt a shooting pain right after?"

If he told him about his mother and the shower, he could see the guy being disgusted, thinking of Paul's lifting a naked grandmother up from the bathtub. And it might be revealed that Paul lived with her, an even more mortifying admission.

"Nothing I can think of," Paul said. "My mattress isn't great, so that may be a factor."

"It's probably just bursitis," the doctor said when he was done examining him. "I can write you a script for an anti-inflammatory, but I should take X-rays first to rule out any structural issues."

"Can't you do it without the X-rays?" Paul asked, anxious about the cost.

"I'm looking at a forty-six-year-old male with severely limited range of motion whose glenohumeral joint is fucked." Beyond the anonymity assigned to him and the arcane anatomical vocabulary, the casually deployed expletive unnerved Paul; it would have been more palatable if he'd even added *up* to the end of the sentence. "There's a good chance it's because the back pain from when you fell made your posture worse, and that's why you also have the shoulder pain, plus all the driving doesn't help. But there could be underlying problems that the script won't do jack shit for, and if the real reason is your shoulder's structurally fucked, we're back to the drawing board, only three weeks later when things have deteriorated and you're feeling even shittier."

It seemed like he was offering him a choice, in between all the gutter talk.

"What if I'm pretty sure there are no structural issues? I've never had problems before I fell and drove this much."

"You said there was no precipitating episode, right? No single thing you did that hurt your shoulder?"

"I'm sure there must have been something," Paul said, still hesitant to disclose what had happened with his mother.

"Trust me, you'd know immediately if something did this," the doctor said. "It's my shoulder, I'm getting those X-rays. You want to be one of those old guys who can't have a catch with your boy?"

"Girl."

"What?"

"I have a daughter, not a son," Paul said more loudly. "Remember when I said I was climbing the—"

"Whatever. One of those old guys who can't fucking braid his daughter's hair."

Though he hadn't braided Mabel's hair in years—he'd never been any good at it, his fingers deft on a keyboard but clumsy everywhere else—the doctor had a point. Mabel had at least a few more years where she might be interested in outdoors activities with him. Before he left South Slope, he'd planned to start taking her on long bike rides with him in the fall. And Steve was phenomenally fit; he couldn't let her see him as the physically inferior man.

He said he'd do the X-rays but didn't ask about the charge, not wanting yet another imprecation thrown his way. "My father-in-law's a radiologist, so I've heard my share of lectures about the importance of X-rays," he threw in. The doctor might give him a professional courtesy discount based on his (former) relation to Jane's father; it had happened before.

After taking X-rays with a technician, Paul waited for the doctor and googled the probable out-of-pocket cost. It looked like it would be a couple of hundred dollars. Steep but manageable.

"Good news," the doctor said when he returned. "No structural issues in the shoulder or spine. I'm writing you a script for diclofenac."

"Thanks," Paul said. "I'll tell my father-in-law I went with the X-rays."

"Make another appointment in three weeks if you're still in pain," the doctor said. "And don't climb any more scaffolding. You're too old."

"Should I do any exercises?"

"Once you can handle it, push-ups can build up the serratus anterior, which will reduce shoulder impingement."

"What about stretching or something in the meantime?"

"Nah," the doctor said. "Stretching's bullshit. Just take the fucking meds."

Paul waved to the receptionist on his way to the front door.

"One minute, sir," she said. "We require payment upon leaving."

She handed him a printout. Under a slew of cryptic line items, the bill was exorbitant.

"This must be a mistake," Paul said, holding the sheet out for her to review. "It was just X-rays."

"You had X-rays of multiple locations, plus a first consultation with Dr. Tweedy, with no insurance discount. The bill is accurate."

The half hour he'd been there had cost the equivalent of weeks of teaching a class. He handed over a credit card in defeat.

Paul had no insurance company to whom to appeal. He had no excuse, either; he'd been charged for what turned out to be an unnecessary service and hadn't checked the price beforehand, mostly because a man with more circumstantial authority had sworn liberally, and he'd been afraid to contradict him.

41

He read RealNews and, though he rarely drew more than a few likes, commented on his phone whenever he was waiting on a fare. He now took out his phone elsewhere, too: the faculty lounge (he didn't care anymore what others thought), at breakfast, on the toilet. The fact that he was doing what he criticized in *The Luddite Manifesto* wasn't lost on him, but he considered it research, not escape; he was more plugged in than ever to politics' interplay with technology.

He was reading and posting in bed until three or four in the morning after driving (and not sleeping all that well, thanks to that god-awful mattress), and hadn't touched his book in weeks. In class one day, as his students slogged through a writing exercise, he nodded off at his desk, snapping awake to a murmur of laughter.

He made an appointment with a sliding scale psychiatrist in Ditmas Park who, he learned from an internet forum, held a lax attitude toward dispensing sleeping pills. After writing Paul a prescription for Ambien and finding out what he did for a living, the man asked if he'd ever considered Adderall.

"A lot of writers I see are on it," the psychiatrist said when Paul demurred. "They say they can't imagine doing their jobs without it."

Paul thought of the sports medicine doctor's exhortation: *Just take the fucking meds.* The American panacea. Everyone else was doing it to seek an edge, from schoolchildren to suburban moms to pro athletes. Why not him?

He obtained the Adderall on the cheap through an online coupon service. Though he'd never had any attention span issues, he wished he'd discovered it years ago. The sustained influx of mental energy, like mainlining rocket fuel into his skull, the desire to attend single-mindedly to the topic at hand, the sense of psychic invincibility—it was a wonder drug, casting him back to his college days, when he could read or write for hours without interruption. So what if it was artificially sponsored: what a joy to return to the flow state.

The same drug the president was rumored to take, he mused. So that's how he found the energy for his Fourth Reich rallies.

The diclofenac was ameliorating his shoulder pain, too, while giving him a pleasant bonus buzz in the muscle. A nice one-two-three punch: Adderall by day, then a hit of diclofenac before bed chased by Ambien, whereupon he'd float into oblivion on a tingly pharmaceutical cloud.

His fervor for *The Luddite Manifesto* was back, the ideas and paragraphs snowballing. When he was sleep-deprived and facing a day of teaching, he upped his dose of Adderall before class and was fine, maybe even better than he'd been before. He'd finish the manuscript by next semester. If they scrambled, it could be in print in a year's time; he could apply to schools with a published book out; he could get a real teaching job. He'd have his life back.

42

Lauren's work schedule—Monday through Thursday, roughly eleven A.M. to ten thirty P.M., often stretching both ends, then saner hours for the pretaped show on Fridays—and Paul's Saturday nights with Mabel made coordinating another date difficult, so they couldn't meet up until Friday night.

They again had dinner near her apartment, and once more she sampled fractions of her multiple courses and made no effort to chip in for the punishing check. As was the previous restaurant, this one was loud, a trick aimed not only at bringing customers in, as the South Slope waitress had said, but also shuffling them out faster and goading them to drink more since they talked less. He supposed diners like Lauren now preferred this, the restaurant positioned as arena-based spectacle rather than communal haven in which to break bread and discuss the day. He projected with some labor—he had a naturally low voice that didn't serve him well in the classroom, and he'd be hoarse tomorrow—and, as usual, trained the conversation on her. Somehow he managed to elide the president, Mackey, and her network's mendacity.

She invited him over for a nightcap. It baffled him that someone would spend as much as she did to live in a building like this one, a characterless tower whose elevator odyssey and hallway warrens took minutes to negotiate. Once inside she immediately turned on her massive TV. It played a reality show about kept, confrontational women. "Whoops," she said, zapping it off. "Force of habit. You're not supposed to know I watch this shit yet. I swear I read a lot."

Her furnishings were tastelessly opulent: black full grain leather sectional couch, white shag rug, burnt-orange walls, gaudy chandelier, oversize glass coffee table. It was probably the creation of an interior decorator who had been granted a hefty budget and free rein within an unimaginative aesthetic, and the resulting atmosphere was like the waiting room to that decorator's office.

Lauren fixed vodka gimlets from a bar cart. "I always wanted a cart with liquor in my living room, like they have on *Mad Men*, but I thought they were only for men and it would look like I was an alcoholic if I had one," she said. "Then one day I was like, fuck that, I'm being gaslit."

Was that even the right use of the now ubiquitous *gaslit*? It wouldn't matter if he disputed it. Prescriptive definitions barely counted anymore, not when the identity of the speaker had complete authority over the words themselves, when a bill that allowed the government to spy on its own citizens was almost tauntingly called the PATRIOT Act, when drone attacks on foreign civilians were considered part of its ongoing war "on," not "of," terror, when the country's leader could claim that day was night and his lieutenants would have to reconstruct his meaning from the ground up with mealymouthed statements that began, "What I think the president was trying to say was . . ."

Paul examined her bookshelf, stocked with the kind of popular political treatises he would never read, authors for whom writing was nothing more than a vehicle for a talking-head slot and the speaking circuit. To his surprise, they ran the gamut of mainstream ideologies.

"You have quite the fair and balanced library here," he said.

"I told you I read. Gotta keep up in my job." Lauren brought the gimlets over to the couch and coquettishly tucked her stockinged feet under her thighs. "So, we hardly even talked about you tonight. How's *your* book coming?"

"Dribs and drabs," he said, taking a swig to get off the topic. "I forgot to mention, I was at my mother's place last night and watched your show, and I saw your name in the credits. It was kind of exciting." He really had watched the show, albeit the next morning online. Interspersed between Dear Leader encomia were tirades against Mexican immigrants, a progressive elementary school that had eliminated European history from its curriculum, and a Democratic senator's speech supporting victims of sexual harassment—the regular hodgepodge of hate and dissembling.

"For the first month I worked in TV, I thought that was cool. Then I realized, that's how these assholes hook you, when you're new to it. They work you to death and underpay you for the honor of seeing yourself onscreen for a split second," she said. "Not even yourself—just your name. And it's not like it is for *you*, when you write something with your name on it and everyone sees it."

Paul nodded as if he were used to widespread name recognition.

"Mackey—Colin—he really has some strong opinions," he said.

"That's why they pay him the big bucks." Lauren was full of shopworn lines from TV. It was as if, like a resourceful foreigner, she'd learned to speak English from watching sitcoms.

"It made me wonder, does anyone with a Latino background work there?" A dicey subject to raise, but he had to broach it at some point. They'd barely touched politics beyond that initial conversation in the car, and if she were as cruelly reactionary as her boss, he wasn't sure he could keep up the act for long. "Because I was trying to imagine what they'd be thinking about some of the things he says."

"Sure, a few. But he's clearly just talking about illegals."

The cavalier, dehumanizing repurposing of the adjective as noun.

"Right. It just made me think, when the president watches, whether *he's* grasping all that."

Lauren gulped her gimlet wearily. It looked like she was about to make a speech she'd recited many times to people appalled at her line of work.

"Look, I know Colin can come off like a bully on the show. But he's a truly decent guy. He personally pays every employee a Christmas bonus—even the cleaning staff. He's polite to everyone on the set, which is more than I can say for a lot of other talent I've worked for. When my dad had prostate cancer, Colin sent him a handwritten letter and referred him to his doctor. He's definitely not a racist or anything—one of his oldest friends is Black. And, obviously, he doesn't mean *every*thing he says. He's a normal, old-school conservative. Plenty of what he says is just to rile up the audience, get them on his side for the issues he cares about."

"Come on," said Paul, unable to hold back. "Maybe he exaggerates a little for the viewers, but he wouldn't just say things on a TV show he outright doesn't believe in."

"How naïve are you? Do you have any idea how cable news works? Or politics?"

The accusation made Paul feel like a child in an adult world.

"Everyone does that," Lauren said. "Both sides. Tell people what they already want, in words they understand, and they'll start wanting the other things you tell them that they don't understand yet. Ninety-five percent of people, even the smart ones, are sheep who need to be told what to think by other people they trust. Why do you think the president won? It's not the economy, it's not racism or sexism, it's not even immigration, all the reasons the economists and political scientists come up with to explain why working stiffs in Michigan worship a New York billionaire who shits on a gold toilet. It's how he talks. He talks like them, so they listen to him, and he makes them feel good about themselves because they think he's listening to them and that he's on their team. Then they vote for his tax plans that fuck them over."

Paul's most cynical instincts were vindicated: it really was all a game to these people, one played out with Nielsen and approval ratings, the homes and communities and overseas villages they devastated relegated to afterthoughts. As long as they raked in advertising money and won elections, annihilated lives were just collateral damage.

"I'm sure Colin can separate his private beliefs from his public ones, but I don't know about the president," Paul said.

"Colin says he's way more strategic than people think."

"I imagine he doesn't care about abortion or if someone's gay, but don't you think he generally thinks like his supporters do?"

"Not the insane stuff. Their nickname for his base is 'the idiots.' "

"Seriously? 'The idiots'?"

"That's what Colin told me once. Maybe it's 'the morons,' I can't remember. He might've been fucking with me. Don't tell anyone I told you that, okay?"

"Of course." He remembered his mother's defensiveness when he'd called her stupid. Deriding the president's followers as selfish or racist didn't faze them—some were proudly so—but to be considered patsies by the people they trusted, preyed on for their feeble intellects, was psychologically intolerable.

"Remind me," Paul said, "what exactly does a senior producer do? I know you said 'everything,' but what does that mean in practice?"

"I guide the editorial content of the show and make sure the trains run on time."

"That's it?"

"*That's it?*" she echoed disbelievingly. "It's a hell of a lot. Especially for a live show."

"No, I know," he said. "It sounds like a challenging job."

She looked as though she were about to make a disclosure of life-defining shame.

"My original plan was to go into medicine. But I bombed the MCAT. Twice. My grades in bio were okay, but I didn't get into any med schools. Not even the crappy ones abroad. I was living at home and didn't know what I was going to do with my life. Then a friend from college who worked in local TV news hooked me up with an entry-level job. I liked it, one thing led to another, and I stayed in the industry." She snorted. "You probably have no clue what I'm talking about. I'm sure everything with writing has come easy to you."

Paul shrugged.

"My therapist says ambitious people think if something comes too easy to them, they assign it a low value, so we choose the harder thing even if it's not the right fit for us. And that I'd be happier if I just came to terms with the fact that being a doctor was hard because it wasn't the right fit for me."

"Well, it seems like working in TV is a good fit for you."

"I get the medium. I'm good with people. I know how to bring something to life." She traced a fingernail over the couch and, finding a blemish in the grain, licked her finger and rubbed it. "But sometimes, when I'm walking through the cubicles, I feel like I'm a rat in a maze trying to find a piece of cheese. And I don't think my brother or parents ever feel that way at the hospital."

Paul nodded sympathetically, docking her points for where those cubicles were but also picturing her coming home close to midnight four days a week, from antiseptic office building to more antiseptic apartment building, seldom venturing out in daylight, her constant companions one domineering man on television and, at home, a pack of querulous women also onscreen. She had money, she had a high-status (if reprehensible) job, she had friends, she had looks—but it was a life void of authenticity and meaning, cold and desolate as her living room view of neighboring skyscrapers inhabited by other rats recuperating with takeout and top-shelf alcohol from their gilded mazes. Most observers would rate his own contingent circumstances as more dismal, but Lauren's was the truly tragic existence: a person with all the trappings of material success who was a spiritual failure.

He should make an excuse to leave and abandon his mission. It was unlikely to succeed, and this arrangement with Lauren under false pretenses not only made him feel morally compromised, it was depressing.

"You wouldn't think it, but you've got this sexy vibe going on, in your own way," Lauren said, snapping back to her seductive rasp, as though embarrassed by her lapse into openness. "I bet all the girls you teach have crushes on Professor Paul."

As far as he could tell, none ever had, but he again felt the stirring of an erection. He lunged forward for a kiss, and, after some grappling on the couch, they proceeded to the bedroom. She had a few photos of her niece and nephew on her dresser and a painting of a Parisian street on the wall, but there were no other homey touches. The carpet beneath his bare feet was so soft and thick that he nearly wanted to remain standing—until he got under the silky, caressing sheets of her king bed. It felt more like a hotel room than someone's bedroom: sumptuously impersonal, existing outside of quotidian life, a space not built for the seven A.M. agony of wiping the crust out of your eyes and making coffee. It was a room made for midnight, for raiding the minibar. For fucking.

Once more, his carnal desire surprised and even disheartened him. He'd always considered himself less superficial than other men, not swayed by physical beauty alone, certainly not by money or status. But, as they had missionary sex, he was powerfully aroused by Lauren's taut body, by the liquid sensation of the sheets, by her erroneous exaltation of his position within the academy, by the notion of himself as a spy penetrating (literally) the opposition's ranks, and, most shamefully, by what her job was.

"That was really fucking good," she said when it was over.

"It was," he said.

43

Rather than take public transportation the next morning to Riverdale only to drive all the way south again to Brooklyn with the vodka gimlet boring into his brain's right hemisphere, Paul got on the subway, retrieved Mabel in Park Slope, and shuttled her from another subway back into Manhattan to the express bus, which they would ride up to the Bronx Zoo.

"This is taking for*ever*," Mabel said as the bus slogged through the Upper East Side. "And the seats smell like . . . I don't even know what."

The upholstery did have the unplaceable nauseating odor endemic to long-distance buses. "Sorry," he said. "I just couldn't find the car keys and didn't want to be late. I'll drive you back tomorrow."

They'd never been to the Bronx Zoo before; their zoo was the one in Prospect Park, though they hadn't made a visit in a couple of years.

"Amazing how clumsy they are on land, but how graceful they are in the water," Paul said as they watched the sea lions. "It must be strange to feel so at home in one environment and so inept everywhere else."

Mabel kept watching but didn't respond. She used to dart around the zoo, intoxicated by the sight of each new animal.

"Want to see the gorillas?" Paul asked, though he wished he hadn't proposed it when he found out it cost six dollars extra for each of them.

They entered the Congo forest exhibit and parked in front of a transparent wall, waiting for a primate to appear. One finally did, emerging from behind a massive tree with a regal deliberateness to its lumbering gait. It stopped a few feet from them, eyeing Mabel.

"Wow," Paul said quietly.

He peeked over, expecting Mabel to be similarly awestruck. Her eyes were watering.

"Mabes, what's wrong?"

"He's trapped here," she said.

"Well, yes, he's in captivity. But at least he doesn't have to worry about hunters or finding food or anything."

Mabel shook her head. "He's still trapped. And he didn't want to come here just so he could be entertainment for people. Everyone just stares at him all day."

Paul was trying to think up another reason for her not to mourn the plight of the gorillas. Perhaps she was communicating some identification with them, a sensitivity he should encourage rather than squelch.

"That's a very empathetic reaction," he said. "I'm proud of you. If you want to leave now, we can."

She swallowed and nodded.

They'd been there only an hour, having spent about fifty bucks for the privilege, with a lot more daylight to eat up. It was temperate for early November, so Paul suggested they eat a late lunch in Van Cortlandt Park on the way home to his mother's apartment. He hailed a car with his phone, feeling a guilty lordliness being on the passenger side for once. They ordered sandwiches to go from a restaurant near the periphery of the park and took them to the interior.

The sun was well into its bronzed descent, toasting the undersides of the clouds crimson, though the tops were a brilliant white. The grass was no longer lush but still abundant enough beneath their crossed legs. A gust of wind washed over them. Paul loved autumn, the sense of the world's hunkering down into itself as it prepared for hibernation.

Would Mabel be able to enjoy an experience like this in thirty years with her own child? A picturesque day, green grass, no interfering devices, relative peace and security around them. It could still be any previous century, an oil painting of picnickers.

He couldn't let himself think like this, ruining every good thing with dire premonitions.

"Not bad, huh?" Paul said. "Eating good sandwiches in a nice park with a cool breeze as the sun goes down on a fall day. These are the moments you've got to take the time to appreciate. You have to notice beauty in the world, to really look for it, or else it's easy to forget it's still there."

Mabel chewed.

"Look up," he said, thinking of his laptop's advice to himself. "Check out how the clouds are dispersing. Really study them closely. It's too bad that describing them as cotton-candy clouds has become such a cliché, because cotton candy is what they look like more than anything, you know?"

He paused, hoping she might contribute.

"These are the things the GDP—the economy—doesn't measure. And they're not what people really care about as much these days," he went on. "You know the saying, 'The best things in life are free'?"

"The sandwiches weren't free," she said.

"Well, sitting here is free. Being together is free. Dad and Mabel hanging out."

Daddy-Mabel time, they used to call it when she was young and he was trying to stir up excitement around her weekends in his custody. He'd forgotten that.

"Parks cost tax money. Someone from the park department gave a talk at school."

"Fine," he said. "Everything has a price. There's no such thing as a free lunch or a free park. You're absolutely right."

Another breeze frisked the trees' remaining foliage.

"I guess the breeze is free," Mabel said.

Her contrarianism—up until that last, mollifying sentiment—had activated his sardonic reflexes, and he wanted to crack a joke about how the Republicans would steal the breeze if wind energy were more profitable and popular with their base. It was a fine line, teaching her about the ills of the world without snuffing out her faith in human goodness, her willingness and capacity to notice its beauty. Cynicism and idealism were self-fulfilling prophecies.

"That cloud looks like the batter for Grandma's angel food cake," she noted. "An angel food cloud."

"You know, it does," he said. "Very good visual metaphor."

44

Enfolded in a leather wingback chair in the faculty lounge before classes on Tuesday, Paul reread the syllabus's second batch of internet essays. (The most submoronic geyser of undigested text this time: Not Gonna Lie, I Love Lying to My Followers about My Lifestyle.)

Russ came in and trickled a cup of watery coffee out of the urn. Beyond shop talk around the department, they hadn't socialized since the dinner party. Paul wasn't sure how much it had to do with his truculence that night; he'd apologized again for his comments in a thank-you text, Russ had said he had absolutely nothing to be sorry for, and he thought the matter was over. Usually he would have been invited to do something else with him and Larissa by now, and, despite his modus operandi of not doing things, he could have used it in his Riverdale exile. Maybe they were just busy; their bid for the townhouse had been accepted and they were overseeing renovations before they moved at the end of the year. Paul had looked up the place. At his current salary and course load, he would be able to afford it after a mere two hundred and eighty-six semesters (pretax).

"How's the book coming?" Russ asked.

"Not bad," Paul said. "Been on a little tear lately." He'd never reveal to Russ his pharmaceutical experiment. Antidepressants were fine in their world, even slightly admired as proof of the complexity of one's interior life, but taking Adderall suggested your prefrontal cortex, the most valorized part of the brain in academia, was deficient, an incompetent CEO. Another reason those allegations about the president stuck.

"So you're not using my method of years of agonizing teeth-pulling?" Russ had authored three books of modernist literary criticism, none of which Paul had read. For the publication of the last one, he'd thrown himself a party at the National Arts Club, where Paul had made a dinner or two of the passed hors d'oeuvres and vomited at home.

"I'm trying to figure out ways to create some buzz around it when it comes out," Paul said, tactfully casting a line in case Russ had any media connections he didn't know of or might offer to underwrite another book party. "I'm a little tired of the things I write being dead on arrival."

"Even if it doesn't make a huge splash," Russ said—a little too pessimistically—"it should be helpful in applying for tenure track jobs."

"Hopefully." Paul looked around; no one was coming into the lounge. "Though I've been feeling the same way about teaching lately."

"How's that?"

"The usual laments of the disaffected academic," he said, nearly calling himself a "professor" but swerving at the last second. "What I'm teaching doesn't matter to these kids in the slightest, in one ear and out the other. And the school is mostly an overpriced diploma mill that's part of the bigger scam of higher education, and I'm an accomplice."

Russ's forehead dimpled.

"You never think like that?"

"Occasionally, of course," Russ allowed. "But there's one kid in just about every class that I'm able to reach. Not a lot, but it's something."

Paul was reaching Elena, at least. But helping a handful of young people a year when their leaders were incinerating the lives of billions was like bailing out the ocean with a leaky bucket, its greatest beneficiary the helper himself for fooling himself into thinking he was making a real difference.

An older Victorianist, Leslie, came in and said hello, halting their conversation. All three read, settling into a collegial silence. People reading printed text in a room together in quiet. It seemed unlikely that Mabel would ever come to know this small, civilized pleasure.

"Jesus," Leslie said after a few minutes as she looked at her phone. "He's just so horrible." It was obvious whom she was talking about; nearly every aghast reference to "he" without an antecedent now meant one man in the world alone. She informed them that their wonderfully enlightened president had just, by tweet, compared a female reporter's appearance to that of a barnyard animal.

"I saw him on the news the other day, blustering in front of a bunch of soldiers, all of them carrying rifles," Russ said, "and I was thinking, 'This guy's around people with deadly weapons all the time, at least some of whom must hate him, and somehow no one's shot him yet.' Even if just for the notoriety."

"They must screen everyone close to him with a gun for any signs of mental instability," Leslie said. "Anyone in their right mind knows it would just cause a civil war."

"And if it were a soldier or the Secret Service, I suppose there'd be conspiracy talk about the Deep State taking him down, and his followers would get even crazier."

Paul put down his reading with a pronounced rustle of paper.

"Yeah, we should just throw our hands up and do nothing," he said. "Let him do whatever he wants. Let him pronounce himself president for life, let him install his kids as the next rulers, let the country turn into an authoritarian dynasty. Just so long as we don't offend anyone."

"We're talking about assassination, not giving up," said Russ.

"One person—with the assistance of moral invertebrates and ignoramuses—is ruining the world, but you don't think it's a good idea if someone 'knocks him out,' to use his phrase, because his already vile supporters, who will never listen to reason anyway, will get more upset?"

"Yes, frankly. Their version of getting upset is inciting more violence."

"Even if that's true—and I think most of them are ultimately more interested in sitting on their couches, watching TV and looking at their phones like the rest of us—the violence they'd stir up is peanuts compared to the violence he's inflicting daily in office. And what if it's not true? Isn't it worth trying? Wouldn't *you* do it?"

"But it *would* happen," Russ insisted.

"That's not my question. If you had the opportunity to kill him, and you knew for a fact it wouldn't incite further violence but would instead save the country, would you do it?"

"You're asking if I would assassinate the president myself with—miraculously—no political repercussions?" Russ asked with a laugh. Paul nodded soberly despite the question's dorm-room tenor. "And what would happen to me?"

"You'd go to jail for life or be executed. But you'd rescue the country from self-destruction. And the world, most likely."

"It's an absurd hypothetical," Russ said, making clear, to Paul, his embarrassment over admitting that he couldn't do it. "We're better off voting him out."

"Maybe *you're* better off, because nothing he's doing is directly affecting you in the short term. And if we do somehow vote him out, there's no way this guy's going to live out his twilight years golfing. He'll still be pulling all the strings of the traitors in government and his cult. He's going to be terrorizing us until the day he dies. If he stays alive, he's going to turn this country into Nazi Germany."

Russ gave him the knowing, indulgent smile of a parent soothing a child frightened by a ludicrous monster of his own creation.

"Come on, Paul," said Russ. "We're not turning into Nazi Germany. And even if you killed him, someone else would take his place. Just like if Hitler had been assassinated."

Paul shook his head. "That's what they always say, but I don't think it's true. Hitler had a grip on the people like no one else. Same with this asshole. A shameless, tacky charisma and celebrity that plays perfectly to what the culture has conditioned us to be mesmerized by for years." He recalled Mackey's praise of the president. "It's the great man theory of one person shaping history. Only this is an awful man deforming history."

If there had been an abstractly philosophical note in his voice before, one tentatively open to parlor debate, it had now devolved into acrimonious hectoring intent on quashing dissent.

"But I suppose you, in your townhouse in Berlin, would argue that assassinating Hitler would only ruffle the feathers of a lot of sensitive Nazis, so we should just calmly wait for the next election for someone nicer to defeat him," Paul said.

He was winded by his peroration. A frosty silence overtook the room, the taut vacuum of speech after an offensive joke. Leslie coughed.

"I'm sorry," said Paul. "That was uncalled for."

"It's okay," Russ said with a dismissing wave. "We all get worked up over this stuff."

The three of them returned to their respective reading, and Paul left sooner than he needed to. He had the presentiment, as he said goodbye to Russ, that there wouldn't be any dinner party invitations in the offing for a long time, maybe forever. He had to watch his tongue; these were his colleagues, his friends, not conservative trolls spoiling for a fight in the RealNews comments.

But it was a form of complicity *not* to speak up at these moments, even among so-called allies. *If I don't fix it, who will?*

Still, he was glad Russ hadn't asked him if he'd assassinate the president. He would have said yes to save face, but he'd have been lying. Aside from not relishing lethal injection or lifelong solitary confinement, to do that to Mabel, to burden her with the legacy of a father always referred to by his first, middle, and last names, would be unconscionable.

45

Paul had planned a trip to the New York Botanical Gardens for Mabel's next visit, but after they arrived in Riverdale it began raining. He presented a choice of board games, a movie from his collection, or reading.

"Can I watch TV?" she asked.

She'd plopped herself in front of the television each visit so far, but just after dinner, and part of the reason he'd permitted it was so that his mother wouldn't be tempted to turn on the cable network (though she'd also consented never to do it while Mabel was present). The promise of semi-unfettered screen time also seemed to be the only allure Riverdale held for her, and Paul didn't want to give her another reason to skip her partial weekends. Even in the past, when they'd had a better time together in Brooklyn, he was aware that there was an inescapable disappointment to an only child's visitations with her divorced bachelor father, that they formed a diminished family unit with two thirds the fun, two thirds the life (a charitable estimate in Paul's case). Some single dads compensated domestically, spearheaded arts-and-crafts projects and baked cupcakes and learned to braid properly. That wasn't his skill set.

"Only for an hour," he said.

"But it doesn't mean an hour less of watching after dinner, right?"

"No," he said, dismayed and impressed by her shrewdness. "I suppose not."

It rained all afternoon, so he permitted her to watch, for two hours, yet more atrocious tween programming. For dinner she shot down his offer to make her pancakes and requested salad. It was counterintuitive to be displeased that his daughter was selecting the healthful option over the sweet one, but it registered as another step away from carefree girlhood and toward miserable adult asceticism. Afterward he said they could watch any of his movies or another half hour of TV of her choosing. She opted for the latter. When it was over, he insisted she read in the bedroom.

"I can do it all myself," she said when he brought out the tube of hydrocortisone.

"You can't reach all the patches on your back."

"My back's not itchy tonight."

He swore she'd been clawing her back while they'd watched TV, but he didn't want an argument, and supervised her as she applied the steroid under her shirt.

When he returned later to say goodnight, she'd fallen asleep under the sheets with the lamp on, a book about spiders splayed open by her side. He smiled at the tableau. Still an inquisitive reader and nature lover at heart.

He lifted the blanket to tuck her in and felt something hard beneath it. She'd stashed an iPad there. He ran his fingers over its smooth corners, furious that Jane had bought this for her without asking him first. It was probably Steve's doing.

He replaced the device under the sheets—he didn't want her to know he'd found it—and picked up the cordless in the hall to phone Jane. Before he could dial, he heard Marvin's voice. He was about to hang up and use his cell, but when Marvin said, "It would be unnatural if you didn't," he listened in.

"I feel guilty," said his mother. "Not about him. You."

"Don't worry about me," Marvin said. "I'm a big boy. You *should* miss your husband. It took me four years after Judith died to wake up feeling normal. And it's still not the same, it's never going to be the same, but that's okay. Things change, you adjust, life goes on."

Paul's mother wept softly.

"It's okay, sweetie," Marvin said. "Let it out. Don't bottle it up."

Paul hung up, hot with the adolescent shame of witnessing a parent's vulnerability in a private moment, even at both their advanced ages.

Remembering his mission, he reverted to his previous emotional state and called Jane on his cell, pacing the living room as it rang.

"How could you let her get an iPad?" he asked when she picked up.

"What?" she said. "I can barely hear you."

He moved to a spot in the apartment where the reception was better and repeated his accusation.

"I told her not to bring it over," Jane said.

"Well, you've been found out."

"She needed one for school. All the kids do their homework research on them now. They're easier for them to use and carry around than computers."

"You know what's also easy to use and carry around? *Books.* Which she barely reads anymore. Probably because in between her training to be a technocrat, she's looking at who knows what on the iPad and playing idiotic video games where you dice up various foodstuffs." This was the one game he was familiar with, having spied on many a subway rider spellbound by the childish graphics and gameplay.

Jane laughed hard.

"Various foodstuffs!" she said between fits. "Oh my God, Paul. I've got to start writing these down."

"It's not funny, Jane. Her brain is still developing. I don't want her ruining it."

"I know." It took her some time to calm down. "I'll tell her not to bring it over again. I know you disapprove, but the school basically mandates it. What do you want me to do? It's not a phone, I monitor her usage, we put parental controls on it, we take it away before she goes to bed, and at least I can see her using it. If you go on one of your crazy rants every time, she's just going to rebel."

"They're not 'crazy rants'—they're well-reasoned arguments that are informed by numerous studies." Maybe she had a point, though, about the potential for rebellion. He'd had an acquaintance in college who watched TV around the clock, and Paul had learned later that when he was a boy, his parents had banned it from their house. "But as long as you really do monitor her usage, in terms of time and content, and don't let her take it out of the house except to school, I guess I can live with that."

"Deal," Jane said. "How was she otherwise? Does she seem all right there?"

He was peeved by the insinuation that Mabel might not be happy staying with him. "Yes, she's perfectly content."

"What did she eat?"

"She ate . . ." Paul had always had a hard time keeping track of the survival units of his child's existence that Jane always committed to memory—what she ate, naps, vaccination schedules. "Oh, salad. At her request over pancakes, you'll be happy to know."

"Shit," Jane said.

"'Shit'? Salad's a great sign. She's eating healthier."

"It's not a good sign when an eleven-year-old girl wants salad."

"How is that not good?" he asked, not believing that Jane was as dejected as he was by their daughter's descent into responsible eating.

"Mabel is starting to have body image issues."

"She's eleven years old. She doesn't have body image issues."

"Jesus, Paul," she said. "You can be so unobservant about other people."

A relatively benign slight in their generally amicable co-parenting partnership, but it still needled him. He prided himself on that very skill, observation, or at least on paying close attention to things for a long time and with unflagging concentration. He wrote thirty-page essays in which he *observed* the often unnoticed nooks and crannies of the world: Civil War reenactors, minor league baseball teams' concession stands, the unsavory ecosystem of Atlantic City pawn shops. And he believed he'd imparted, by nature and nurture, his talent for patient observation to Mabel, who could spend hours in Prospect Park watching ants go about their work.

"And what, exactly, have I not observed?"

A loud sigh on Jane's end.

"First of all, she's a little . . . chubby. Which is fine, I certainly never comment on it, but she's clearly starting to pick up on it."

Paul conjured up an image of Mabel. He hadn't seen any of her peers for a while and didn't have a good frame of reference for the average body type of an eleven-year-old girl.

"She might have a few extra pounds, but that's just baby fat that'll disappear when she gets older."

"And *second* of all, most girls have body image issues no matter what they look like. Please don't argue with me. Just recognize when you're out of your depth."

"Maybe if she didn't spend so much time on the internet on her iPad, she wouldn't have these issues. Or if her mother didn't get Botox. You ever think of that?"

"Yes, Paul. You win. It's all because of the iPad and my Botox, which, by the way, she didn't know about. I'm a terrible parent and role model."

He didn't want a protracted contretemps, particularly one he was losing. "You're not a terrible parent or role model," he said. "I'll keep an eye out for any eating problems. But I'd also appreciate it in the future if you told me about developments like the iPad, instead of having me find it hidden in her bed."

"Fair enough," she truced.

He retired to the couch. It only now dawned on him why Mabel might have wanted to apply the steroid herself under her shirt. He'd have to pay closer attention to her behavior. There were things about being a young girl he didn't understand—Jane's comment about his being out of his depth in this department was more accurate than the one about being generally unobservant—and he didn't have a female partner by his side to help translate for him.

46

In the morning, Mabel had cereal and orange juice, nothing out of the ordinary. He studied her over the opinion pages of the *Times*. She was a bit thicker than he'd realized, likely because her plumpness had always been only adorable to him—more to squeeze and pinch, a soft decadence. He'd felt sorry for parents with rail-thin children; they were missing out.

Paul had been slightly overweight around her age before he'd slimmed down. That period of time had been so brief, memorialized in just one paunchy, prepubescent photograph of him at a Jersey beach, that he'd forgotten about it until now. Jane had been an ectomorph her whole life. If the genetic fault lay with anyone, it was him.

His little daughter: the years of torment possibly awaiting her, the wasted energy, the self-loathing and insecurity.

"What are you *look*ing at?" she asked.

"Nothing," he said.

On the drive to Brooklyn he heard manic scratching in the backseat.

"Try not to scratch, Mabes." It was a sentence he'd uttered thousands of times.

She stopped, but minutes later was stealthily sawing her skin with the edge of the seat belt strap. It was terrible to listen to, to know your child preferred the grating pain she was inflicting on herself to the unstoppable itch coming from her own body.

"You don't have any social media profiles, do you?" he asked when she was done.

"You have to be thirteen," she said.

The indirect answer wasn't reassuring, and he didn't completely trust Jane's "monitoring" of her iPad use.

"You know, those sites make it seem like they're all about having fun, bringing people together, but they really exist to make money off you," he told her. "They convince their users to upload content for free so they can get your personal information to target you for companies that advertise. And they're not really free, even if there's no financial cost to use them. They take over your time, and they colonize—they take up space in your brain that could be used for better thoughts. They all encourage you to see others, and ultimately even yourself, not as three-dimensional human beings, but as an image and data on a flat screen. Do you understand that idea?"

"Yup."

"Then, to make it seem attractive to the rest of us, a few celebrities get paid to post things. They're the only people who actually benefit, at least economically."

"Influencers," Mabel said.

"But beyond all that—"

"Or content creators."

"Right," Paul said. "But beyond—"

"Also sponsored content."

"Yes, that, too." It was unnerving how conversant she was with the subject. "Beyond everything else I said, the people who are popular on these things promote a very materialistic and narcissistic view of life. You know what that means?"

He turned his head at a red light on the West Side Highway. She looked as apathetic as his students.

"It means their values, the things they care about, aren't very meaningful," he said. "Instead of caring about the planet and other people, like you do, those sites reward people who only like taking pictures showing them having a good time, buying expensive stuff, going on fancy vacations, looking cool. And we don't care about those things, right?"

She nodded without conviction and stared ahead at the road.

"But we're all susceptible—we're all easily fooled by these sites, so the longer you spend on them, the more you start to adopt their values. And their values are just based on trends, not on more enduring ideals. For instance, until the twentieth century, it was considered fashionable to be . . . heavier, because it implied you were rich enough to eat well and not have to work."

She didn't reply. He shouldn't have made that last, ham-fisted point, whose inverse would only make her feel worse.

"So what do you think, Mabes?"

"Light's green," she said.

He hit the gas and repeated his question. She tugged the seat belt slack and let it snap back a couple of times.

"Is it that you don't care about those expensive things," she asked, "or just you don't have them, so you don't like it when other people show them off? Like with Sharper Image?"

"That's a fair question," he said. "Sometimes people do resent the things they don't have. But I decided a long time ago that expensive things, or looking like you're successful according to what other people might value, aren't what matter to me in life. What matters to me is being a good person and trying to make life better for others. And I think that's what matters to you, too. Right?"

He turned again, and she gave him another placating nod. He hoped she wouldn't challenge him on how exactly he was making life better for other people. He supposed he'd have to fall back on Russ's statement from the faculty lounge about teaching.

From what he'd seen—*observed*—the past few months, she was fast becoming captive to consumerist youth culture. At her age, he'd devoted plenty of hours to *Star Wars* and baseball and Saturday morning cartoons. But at a certain point he'd put down those childish things, because the culture back then, for the most part, demanded you do so or be left behind by your maturing peers. Now there was little incentive to grow up, not when you could narcotically reside in an adolescent bubble for decades alongside an army of eternal, self-obsessed teenagers, forty-year-olds still enamored of comic books. Especially when their president acted like a petulant brat himself.

She might not outgrow it, especially if he didn't intervene. But he was just one man attempting to fill her reservoir with nourishing beliefs that the world was intent on draining for profit.

"So try not to go on those websites," he said. "Even if your friends do."

"None of my friends go on the sites."

"Really? Good. I'm glad to hear that."

"They just use the apps," Mabel said.

47

Lauren invited Paul to join her and some friends from the network for a dinner on Friday. He dreaded meeting the company she kept, but an appearance would help solidify their relationship, maybe provide an in to a different show. Part of him looked forward to the aftermath, too.

The restaurant was a cramped spot in the West Village for which the group used their connections to secure a reservation (one of them booked chefs for a morning show). It was even louder than the locations of their previous dates, and Paul, the oldest of the ten-person party crowded around a circular table, could hardly hear anyone.

Aside from Lauren's closest co-worker on *Mackey Live*, Kelsey (the network's platonic ideal of a female staffer: early thirties, boringly pretty in her lissome blondeness, the mildest of Southern accents), the others, onetime *Mackey* colleagues, were now employees of other programs on the network who had dinner reunions twice a year. They were camera-ready to a person, though all but one worked behind the scenes. None struck Paul as notably conservative. They weren't even uniformly white; one man was Black (and gay), and there was a Japanese American woman. They didn't touch politics, not out of tact but apparent incuriosity. Instead they gossiped about industry personalities and jobs, TV shows, scandals. If their phones weren't in their hands, they were face up on the table, their incessant flashing notifications a hazard for the photosensitive epileptic. Paul said little as the group recklessly ordered alcohol and barely eaten, heavily photographed sides; he felt as if he were at a table with a pack of wolves without appetites.

"Would you mind passing the beet salad?" he asked the sharp-elbowed (literally; she'd knocked him twice without apology) woman next to him. She was scrolling through Instagram, blindly bestowing hearts on every picture, and didn't hear him. Paul had to reach over her plate, but she didn't even notice that.

"Who's coming to my place after this for our toke sesh *biennale*?" asked a man who covered hockey for the network's sports arm, the sole on-screen talent in the gang, confusing the temporal measurement and stroking the side of his neatly shorn cranium as if it were a well-loved pet. "I have to tell my guy how much."

"I'm in," said the woman next to Paul.

"You're *always* in," said the hockey man. "Nothing stops you."

"Oh, I'll cut a bitch," she said, snapping and slipping into an ethnically ambiguous and likely offensive accent. "I'll cut a bitch to get what's mine."

"I know it. Your middle name is Cutthroat."

"No, it's my first *and* last name. Cut Throat."

The teasing barely concealed a fundamental truth about them all: they were just like Lauren, mercenaries lacking any coherent convictions, sellers to the highest bidder regardless of its fascistic inclinations. Paul wasn't sure if they were worse than the network's true believers.

Most of the group—not Lauren, thank God—expressed interest in heading over to the man's apartment.

"Please don't tell me when you're doing something illegal," Kelsey said.

"Kelsey, you're so darling," the Black man said. "Our little narc."

"I just don't want to be considered an accessory if you get in trouble."

He smiled and patted her head with fond condescension. "If the police make a bust, guess which one of us is getting arrested? I'll give you a hint: it won't be the pretty blonde girl."

"There's a corporate policy for drugs, too," Kelsey said.

"If you're so worried, why don't you call up Mackey right now saying you had no knowledge of anything to do with this, and he'll record you professing your innocence," the hockey guy said.

"Is that a joke?" said the Black man. "I don't get it."

"There's nothing to 'get.' Mackey records his phone calls."

"Are you serious?"

"That's what Kelsey told me. That he records the powerful people he talks to."

"Oh my God. That's so paranoid. It's straight-up Nixon."

"It's not true," Lauren interjected. "He told me that once as a joke. I told you it was a joke, Kelsey."

"It's a joke," Kelsey said. "He doesn't really do it."

At the end of the three-hour dinner, their waiter approached with the bill curled up in a glass. Paul could see the total on the bottom line, astronomical even when divided by ten. (Though his orders amounted to a standard deviation or two below the average, group dinners were the one time these rapacious capitalists embraced socialism.) He had paid for everything so far with Lauren, and this was going to make the biggest dent yet in his already battered bank account. Money that would allow him to live near Mabel was going to some hockey asshole's unmolested and Instagrammed radicchio.

He slipped out to the restroom before the waiter returned, hoping Lauren would pay in his absence. When he came back, the glass was still in the center of the table, holding a bouquet of credit cards.

"They're waiting for your card," Lauren said.

"Do you actually mind getting this one?" he asked.

She didn't say anything. Then she dug into her bag, whipped out a card, and dropped it in the glass.

When they finished saying their goodbyes to the others on the street, Paul asked Lauren if she wanted to get a cab despite the heavy traffic. Maybe she'd agree, for once, to take the subway that was steps away and likely faster.

"I think you should go back to Riverdale," she said.

"What? Why?"

"You really embarrassed me there, making me pay."

He should have just taken the financial hit. He'd already invested so much time and money in this sham; he couldn't afford to lose everything because of one bill.

"I thought you'd maybe want to pay for yourself once in a while. You know, to show you can take care of yourself."

"Is that a fucking joke? I *know* I can take care of myself. I've been doing it since I graduated college. I make two hundred and twenty-five thousand dollars a year. What I don't know is whether *you* can take care of me. And tonight suggested you can't. Or don't want to." Her nostrils inflated with anger. "Do you even pay for your daughter?"

"Of course I do," he said, though early bird specials at the diner were clearly not what Lauren had in mind. "I'm really sorry." He was doing what he had to do, but he hated himself for his weakness in the face of her unconstrained fury—and for her accurate assessment that he wasn't able to "take care" of her, even if he'd wanted to. "It won't happen again, I promise."

She looked at him for a long beat, as if measuring both his word and net worth.

"Get a cab," she said.

Lauren took out her phone and scrolled through Instagram. Paul held up his right arm to hail a taxi before a sharp twinge forced him to switch to his left.

"Paul?"

He turned to the voice.

"Julie," the woman said off his blank stare. "From . . . the James Agee event at the library?"

"Oh, hi," he said. "Sorry, my mind is . . . How're you?"

"Not bad." Julie was alone, wearing her backpack. "Just coming from dinner at a friend's place."

"This is Lauren," Paul said. "Lauren, Julie."

Julie said hello warmly. Lauren glanced up from her phone with a fleeting smile, its hostility triangulated at Paul. Despite the insignificance of his one date with Julie, he felt embarrassed at being seen with Lauren, her high-priced ornamentation and severe beauty and rude manners, the impression she gave of his ostensibly meretricious values an unfavorable contrast with those of a man who went to James Agee panels.

"Been to any good library events?" Julie asked to fill the silence.

"There's one I was actually planning on going to tomorrow, on sixties"—it was on antiwar writing, but he checked himself in front of the probably hawkish Lauren—"writing. How about you?"

"A few. Not the one tomorrow." Then, with a small smile, she said, "But someday." Paul looked at her in confusion. "Like the next chapter of history," she reminded him. " 'Not tomorrow, but someday.' "

He belatedly acknowledged the inside joke with his own smile, and they said their goodbyes as Julie ambled off to the subway station at the corner.

"Who was that woman?" Lauren asked in the taxi.

"I went on one date with her last summer," Paul said. "Didn't feel a spark."

"She's a librarian?"

"What?"

"She was talking about the library a lot."

"Oh. No, she's a teacher. I met her at an event at the library."

"What was she saying at the end?"

"Hmm?"

" 'The next chapter of history'? 'Not tomorrow, but someday'?"

"No idea," he said. "Maybe it had something to do with the event we went to."

Lauren was too pretty compared to Julie, better dressed, more confident, her job valued so much more by the public's frivolous standards, to be threatened by her in the standard ways, but it was possible she sensed that Julie was her intellectual superior. It was an understandable mistake to think she was a librarian, too, given the limited context, though also a reminder that Lauren wouldn't attend an event at a library—not tomorrow, not any day.

She resumed treadmilling through Instagram. How strange it would be, Paul thought, if we pored over friends' physical photo albums late at night without their knowledge. It was the kind of insight Julie would have appreciated.

"What was up with that thing about Colin recording people?" he asked to change the subject, in case the encounter with Julie might somehow exacerbate their earlier row.

"He told me that once when he was drunk at a party. Two minutes later he said it was a joke. I shouldn't have said anything to Kelsey. I love her, but she can be an idiot sometimes."

Paul nodded, relieved that he'd redirected her ire for the moment.

Despite the fight, Lauren was in an amorous mood after a vodka gimlet at home, and they had sex for the second time.

"Fuck me from behind," she said after a few minutes in the missionary position.

Once they'd rearranged their bodies, she had another request.

"Tell me I've been a bad student, professor," she said.

"What?" he asked, and she repeated the command. Paul had never engaged in any role-playing in his history of vanilla sex. He didn't even watch porn. After the divorce, a universe of free videos had proliferated on the internet that hadn't existed when he'd previously been single, but he stopped watching after a few sessions; he couldn't help but think of the female performers as having once been Mabel's age. When he did masturbate, he puritanically restricted himself to summoning up memories of women he'd been with.

"You've been a bad student," he said self-consciously.

"Tell me why I was bad."

"You . . . haven't been paying attention in class."

"It's because I'm so distracted by looking at you."

"Oh," he said. "Well, okay."

"What's my punishment, professor?"

"I'm going to have to fail you, Miss Davidson," he said, getting more comfortable.

"Oh, no. Is there any way I can improve my grade, professor?"

"I can tutor you. In my office. After hours."

"Spank me," she said, "and tell me I'm a stupid bitch."

"No," Paul said.

"Do it."

Benignly playacting was one thing, but this verbal and physical pairing felt more sinister.

"You're . . . stupid," he said reluctantly.

"Say it while you spank me," she repeated. "Come on. Be a fucking man."

It was the second affront of the night to his manhood—the first pecuniary, now sexual—and he could nearly feel the psychic kick to the same area in which an impulse to prove himself was simultaneously ignited. He spanked her lightly.

"You're stupid," he said, still constitutionally unable to add the misogynistic slur.

As she arched her back and bucked her hips, she touched herself, her shoulder blades rippling like trapped creatures, and told him to do it again, harder this time.

"You're stupid," he said, spanking a little more forcefully.

"More," she said. "Harder."

"You're stupid," he said, spanking harder while closing his eyes and transporting them to Colin Mackey's studio, Lauren bowed over the desk, Paul behind her during the "Final Comment" segment, only with his surname splashed across the screen as he faced the camera and millions of viewers. "You're a moron. You're an idiot. You're so fucking stupid."

He kept up the stream of insults, no longer holding back on his spanks, the positive reception of each word and blow spurring him on to deliver the next combination with more power, until she climaxed, and Paul, bubbling over with an erotic energy he'd never before known, followed soon thereafter.

Lauren donned a sleep mask and knocked herself out with a pill, as she had last time. He remained up for a while, thinking back to Julie, trying to picture her making the sexual demands Lauren had. He hoped, again, that she hadn't judged him by his company, and wished there was a way to communicate to her that it wasn't real.

Yet perhaps some element of his relationship with Lauren, despite his ulterior motives, did reveal an unpleasant truth about him beyond his sexual attraction to her. Maybe he'd allowed too much cynicism to seep into his worldview, gradually overtaking his sentiments about not only politics but also individuals. And rather than do the harder work of trying to find the best in others, he'd given up and written nearly everyone off, lumping them all together in one gray, malignant mass, his scope of vision now able to see less beauty than ugliness.

48

Mabel wanted a slumber party at Jane's brownstone with four girls for her twelfth birthday, which fell two Saturdays from then. She was already going to miss the next weekend in Riverdale for an overnight school field trip upstate. If she planned to hold the party at her mother's and stay there Friday night to assist with preparations the next day, that would make three weeks between visits to Paul.

"So what do you want to do, cancel the party?" Jane asked over the phone. "Have it not on her birthday to suit your schedule?"

"We can do it at my place," Paul said.

"At your *mother's*?"

"It's perfectly suitable for watching movies and eating pizza and cake. That's what slumber parties still are, right? They can sleep in the living room, if they bring sleeping bags."

"And how will they all get to Riverdale? You think their parents want to drive them there and back?"

"I'll bring up Mabel on Friday by herself, and then I can pick up the others on Saturday."

"Paul. Please be reasonable."

"I *am* being reasonable. I'm entitled to see my daughter more than once a month."

He could nearly feel Jane's piqued exhalation through the phone.

"All right, you know what?" she said. "Knock yourself out. Have five girls sleep over. Get them there yourself and feed them dinner and breakfast. Don't let me stop you."

"Wait," he said, already regretful but too proud to recant. "Who are they? How do I . . . organize this?"

"I'll text you their moms' numbers and I'll tell them to expect to hear from you." Jane sounded spitefully triumphant. "The rest is on you. I'll let Mabel know. She'll be ecstatic that she's having her birthday party at her grandmother's apartment in the Bronx. Have a ball."

She hung up and blitzed his phone with the contact info of four women.

As he prepared to group-text the mothers, it occurred to Paul that he'd not only never met any of them, but he didn't know any of their daughters, either. He hadn't attended a single event at Mabel's new school. He'd had excuses—living in Riverdale, primarily—but he'd become a satellite of a caretaker the past few months, solitarily orbiting his child's planet, intermittently heaving into view and then just as quickly spinning out of sight. These were crucial, transitional years. He needed to be present for them, to prove that he could be reliable, that he had the stability and gravity of a sun.

49

Paul was an essay planner, not an event planner, but he brought his ample skills for preparation to bear for Mabel's birthday weekend. He fielded dozens of anxious texts from the four mothers about logistics, including, for one girl, a video on how to inject her EpiPen in the improbable event of a bee sting in November; mapped out the most efficient order to pick them up in; drafted an hourly itinerary for Saturday night and Sunday morning; placed advance orders for pizza and cake; and stocked up on snacks and drinks. He'd show Jane—and Mabel—that he could do this as well as she could.

He brought Mabel to Riverdale Friday night, to clear space in the car for the other girls, and gave her her present: a gray cashmere sweater. He'd spent two hours after classes the day before trawling Bloomingdale's, but every item of clothing had made him apprehensive about setting off her body image issues. A roomy, colorless sweater she could hide in for the winter might be a comfort to her.

"It's huge," she said.

"The saleswoman said that that's the style these days," he lied. "And you can grow into it for next year."

Before he left on Saturday to collect the guests, she asked, "Can we put the terrarium in the closet till tomorrow?"

"The plants need the light," he said.

"I know, but some of my friends are scared of bugs, and one day in the closet won't kill them."

"They won't be near it. It's in my room."

"Just in case the door's open or something. Please?"

It wasn't their fear of bugs so much as her shame over *owning* bugs, and for keeping them at her dad's apartment in Riverdale where he lived with his mother.

"Okay, my little dumpling."

"Can you not call me that anymore?" she asked.

"Why not?"

"I'm twelve years old."

Other than "Mabes," he had no terms of endearment for her that had taken. The pet name had become how he thought of her: as a warm, bite-size, doughy pocket of a girl, nearly edible. And though he had long since stopped reflecting on its NICU etymology, every time he called her that it seemed to reinforce subconsciously how he had seen her that first, perilous night, as his little baby girl whose vulnerability had given him a sense of mission beyond himself.

Hopefully this was just another phase he had to ride out, more anxiety over how he might embarrass her in front of her friends.

After giving Mabel permission to watch as much TV as she wanted on her birthday, he made the rounds through Park Slope that afternoon. The first three girls sat in the back, but when the mother of the fourth brought her daughter out to the car, she paused.

"Where's Thea going to sit?" she asked.

"The front," Paul answered.

"She's still eleven," said the woman, whose petite frame made Paul feel oafish. "So that's not really a possibility."

He'd sat in the front all through elementary school, but this sort of anecdote wouldn't appease a contemporary Park Slope mother.

"It's a short drive," he said. "I'll be very careful and go slowly."

"But you'll be on a freeway."

"Okay, I'll move one of the girls up and she can sit in the back."

"Are any of you twelve?" the woman asked through the window. The girls all shook their heads. "That's not going to work, then."

"Well, do you want to drive her?"

"I have to take my thirteen-year-old to his soccer game and my six-year-old to a birthday party."

Of course she'd have three kids (at least), another rich Brooklyn hypocrite who chanted at climate change rallies without recognizing her family's outsize carbon footprint.

He opened his ride-sharing app. "It's sixty-eight dollars for a ride up there," he said.

"She doesn't take taxis by herself yet."

"What if I drove her to the express bus in Manhattan, avoided the freeway, waited till she was on the bus, asked the driver to keep an eye on her, and then waited for her at the stop?"

The woman gave him a look he recalled from his time with Jane, communicating that only a clueless man would come up with such a stupid idea.

"Fine," he said. "I'll drive them up, I'll come back, and I'll pick her up on her own. Should take about two hours."

"Thank you. You know, when you texted the four of us, I assumed you had a car with three rows of seats."

"I don't, because I try not to drive a gas-guzzler that destroys the environment and leads us into wars," Paul said. "Maybe you have one I could borrow."

She shot him an icier stare. A few months ago he would have apologized immediately for what he'd said—or, more likely, he would've just thought it and not said it at all. But he was tired of being amenable with people who didn't deserve it.

He sped off much faster than was warranted, a burst of acceleration to give her something to worry about when he picked up her daughter.

50

After dropping the three girls off and tossing their outerwear in a pile by the door—his mother didn't have a coat rack, and, by the same logic he applied to not making his bed, he considered hanging jackets in the closet a waste of energy—he instructed his mother to supervise them and offer the snacks he'd purchased. He returned to Brooklyn, delayed his order with the pizza place, and headed back to Riverdale with Thea, a quiet, solemn-eyed girl.

"Everything okay back there, Thea?" he asked after neither of them had spoken for twenty minutes.

"Yes. Thank you for driving me."

"Sorry about that little disagreement I had with your mom. We had a miscommunication."

"It's okay," Thea said.

They arrived home over two hours later than the itinerary had ordained, picking up dinner en route. Mabel complained that they'd all been "starving."

"What about the snacks?"

"You got, like, *health* food," she said. Everything he'd bought had some vegetable component or at least connotation, nutritional standards he assumed the girls' parents—and now Mabel—would have demanded. "They were disgusting."

"Well, the pizza's hot," he said.

The other girls swarmed the two boxes, but Thea peered at them from a distance. "Is one of them gluten-free?" she asked.

"I'm pretty sure neither is," Paul said.

"Oh. Then I can't have it."

"Can you maybe eat just a little? Or scrape the cheese off and eat that?"

She shook her head. It was likely her overprotective mother's adoption of a fad Park Slope diet, but he didn't want to incur further wrath from that woman by violating it. Paul called the pizzeria, which didn't have a gluten-free alternative, and two other places in the area didn't pick up.

Before he dealt with a solution, he told the girls to choose a movie to watch. They unanimously selected a new release, and the only option was to buy it, which cost twenty dollars. He laboriously punched in his credit card information.

"This chair's so gross and old," Mabel said, stroking the deteriorating fabric of the green velvet armchair next to which she was sitting. "It's molting."

Her guests squealed. "Chairs don't melt!" one exclaimed.

"I said *molting*," Mabel maintained with dignified calm. "Like when a bird sheds its feathers."

Paul was upset by her willingness to insult her grandmother's furniture for the benefit of her friends, but proud that she alone knew what molting was and hadn't caved to the mockery of the group. Maybe she wouldn't turn out to be her mother's daughter when it came to resisting peer pressure.

"What about Chinese?" he asked Thea from the kitchen, rifling through the drawer of takeout menus. All his mother ever ordered in was Chinese food.

"That usually has gluten unless it's a really nice place where they promise they won't use it," Thea said.

None of these places was really nice.

He foraged through the refrigerator. The only thing he deemed safe and palatable to a young girl was an unopened box of greens.

"How about salad?" he offered.

Thea looked forlornly at the girls devouring the pizza.

"I guess," she said.

Paul dumped the greens into a bowl, splashed on balsamic dressing from a bottle, and served it to her. He was about to disappear into his room when the TV screen went black.

"Dad!" Mabel cried.

"Relax," he told her. "It'll restart in a minute."

A minute later it hadn't. He unplugged and plugged the streaming device back in. Nothing changed. The Wi-Fi was out on his phone, too. He went through the same routine with the router and the modem stationed in his room but couldn't restore the connection.

"I'll call the internet company," he assured a glowering Mabel. "I'm sure they'll fix it right away."

After fifteen minutes of automated menus, hold music, and three interdepartmental transfers in which he had to reiterate his mother's account information and the nature of the problem, he reached technical support, which asked him to go through the restarting paces again. When that didn't work, the tech support guy told him he would reset his connection remotely.

Mabel yelled into his room for an update.

"I'm trying to fix it," he called.

The reset also failed.

"So the problem is you're not getting an internet signal," said the man on the phone.

"Oh, really?" Paul said. "There's no internet? I hadn't realized. That's good to know."

"If the situation doesn't resolve on its own, a technician will have to come in and examine your connection."

"That's it? You're hoping it magically resolves on its own?"

"Sir, I've done everything I can do remotely."

"Can we get someone over tonight?"

"No, sir, that won't be possible. If you like, I can expedite this and get a technician tomorrow between one and six P.M."

"So I have to be ready for them anytime in that five-hour window. Perfect. Thank you. That sounds absolutely ideal."

"Sir, are you confirming that you'll be available in that window?"

"I don't have any choice, do I?" Paul said. "You've made it so we're addicted to this brain-addling technology, and then when it doesn't work, we have no idea how to fix it ourselves, so we need you to come in, but not like a normal appointment where somebody says, 'I'll be there at this time'—no, it's 'I'll be there at some vague point during the day and, oh yeah, if you're in the bathroom and don't answer the door in time, I'm leaving and it'll take three days to get another appointment.' "

The man didn't speak. Paul had contempt for people who took their frustration out on customer service representatives.

"I'm sorry," he said. "It's been a long day. Please schedule the appointment. Someone will be here."

He returned to the girls and explained that the internet would likely be out the rest of the night.

"Let's watch the rest on your iPad," one of the girls said.

"It's not allowed here," Mabel said bitterly, looking at Paul out of the corner of her eye.

"I have a big movie collection," Paul said. "Tons of stuff for kids."

He retrieved his plastic crate of DVDs from his bedroom closet and set it on the floor. The girls approached as if it were booby-trapped.

"What is this?" one asked, holding up a DVD case.

"*For Whom the Bell Tolls*," Paul said. "It's a great movie, and novel, about—" He anticipated a lecture from Jane about his scaring the children with a plot summary of fascism and Robert Jordan's sacrificially mowing down the enemy with a gun in his dying breaths. "Spain. But I don't think you girls would like it."

"No." She tapped the case. "What is this thing?"

"The DVD? You've never seen one?"

She rotated and examined it strangely.

"I suppose you're more into Betamax," he said. None of the girls registered it as a joke.

"I'll find something you'll like," he said, rooting through the box. The conventional children's offerings were slim, and he didn't have much of anything made in the past few decades except art house and foreign films. "Something tells me you're not into cowboys and Indians," he said as he picked up *The Searchers*.

The girls looked at one another.

"Dad!" Mabel scolded him. "No one uses that word!"

"Sorry, you're right. Cowboys and Native Americans."

"*Indigenous peoples*," she said.

He recalled his grandmother, in his teenage years, speaking of "Orientals," and imagined he'd looked at her in the same horrified way Mabel was glaring at him now.

"Any of you ever seen *A Hard Day's Night*?" he asked; the film was as apolitical and preadolescent-girl-friendly a choice as his collection permitted. "Mabes, I've shown it to you, haven't I?"

She shook her head.

"You guys like the Beatles, right?" he asked.

There was a silence after his question reminiscent of his classroom.

"I think my dad likes them," a girl finally said.

"Everyone likes them," Paul said. "They're the best band of all time. Well, not *the best* the best—their early stuff is bubblegum, and their politics are hippie mantras, and I generally prefer the Stones' sensibility, plus the Clash mattered a lot more to me when I was younger—or, I guess I should say, they're 'the only band that matters,' period—but in terms of innovation and prolificness and sheer virtuosity, no one else comes close. Except Dylan, for lyrics. Though he's actually very underrated for his melodies."

The girls were regarding him as subway passengers would a person jabbering to himself.

Paul missed having friends.

"You'll like them," he said. "Start watching, I'll get the birthday cake."

He took the ice-cream cake he'd bought that day out of the freezer. As he sliced it with his mother's serrated knife ("serenaded knife" bounced into his head in Marvin's voice every time he used it), Mabel came in.

"Dad? Thea says she's not feeling good."

He put down the knife. In the living room, Thea was in a fetal position on the couch.

"Thea? What's wrong?"

"Stomachache," she said.

"You think it was the salad?"

She nodded stoically. He picked the greens container out of the recycling bin. It was good for another week. The bottle of salad dressing also had a distant expiration date.

"It was just a spring mix," he said. "Does that normally get you sick?"

Thea grunted in gastric pain. "Is the salad dressing gluten-free?"

"Isn't it naturally? It was just balsamic dressing. There's no bread in it or anything."

"Did you make it yourself or"—another grim moan—"is it from a bottle?"

"It's from a bottle."

"A lot of bottle stuff has gluten. Does it say gluten-free on the label? Usually it's in a circle."

"It doesn't," he said after searching desperately for it. "Why didn't you . . . say something?"

"Everyone I know makes their own dressing," she said through a wince.

"I'm really sorry, Thea," he said. "It's not your job to warn me. I normally make my own dressing. I was in a rush. How serious is it? Do you need to go to the emergency room?"

"No, it's not that bad," she said. "Do you have liquid Pepto-Bismol?"

His mother's medicine cabinet had antidiarrheal caplets but not the liquid formula.

"Only the liquid kind helps," she said.

"Do you want me to call your mom?" Paul didn't look forward to this conversation. "Or does she maybe go to sleep early and I shouldn't disturb her?"

It was eight thirty.

"It's really not that bad—I don't want to bother her with this." Then, clutching her stomach, Thea bolted to the bathroom outside Paul's room.

He started to text Thea's mother. But a few messages back in their archive, after he'd mentioned he would serve pizza, she had informed him that Thea had celiac disease and was generally aware of what she couldn't eat, but he should check with her about any other foods he was unsure of. In his haste to fend off the onslaught of other mothers' questions and concerns, Paul had given the text a thumbs-up without reading it.

All the neighborhood pharmacies would be closed now. There was a bodega by the subway that probably sold Pepto-Bismol. He knocked on his mother's door and asked her to watch over the girls again, drove to the bodega, double-parked, bought a dusty pink bottle, and sped back. He had Mabel deliver the medicine to Thea, still parked on the toilet.

He cleared the dishes they'd used for the pizza. The cake was still out on the counter, the brown box dark and soggy. Inside, all the ice cream had melted into a gooey vanilla and chocolate soup. He cursed quietly.

There were still some semi-intact spongy layers drowning in the ice cream. He forked these out, making even more of a mess, and served them in bowls to the other girls.

"What *is* this?" Mabel asked, looking repulsed by the crumbly bits of cake coated in ice cream like some kind of dessert chowder.

"It's a special Italian cake," Paul said. "It has an ice-cream glaze."

"Where's the candles?" one of the girls asked.

He hadn't even thought of candles. His mother wouldn't have any. Where did you even get them—the supermarket, a drugstore? He'd never bought birthday candles in his life. It was the sort of thing Jane had always dealt with, even for her own birthdays.

"The Italians don't do that," he said. "A candle couldn't stand up in the soup. The glaze, I mean."

"Wait, you're *Italian*?" a girl asked Mabel.

"No," she said.

"The cake is," Paul said. "Just think of your wish, and pretend to blow out a candle."

Mabel looked down at her bowl. "It's okay. I don't need to."

"Well," Paul said, "then just dig in."

She took an apprehensive slurp from her spoon.

"How is it?" he asked.

"It's fine," she said.

He sat with the girls as they ate and watched the movie. By their reactions he suspected the cake wouldn't have been that good even if it hadn't melted.

"Why aren't there any colors?" one of the girls asked.

"Older films are in black and white," Paul said. "And some still are. It's considered more artistic."

"Do you have another movie?" Mabel asked him.

"You don't like this?"

"It's kind of boring."

"Okay, fine, *you* choose something."

With his foot, he pushed the crate of DVDs toward her. She gave them a cursory review.

"Old movies suck," she said.

"Excuse me?"

"Old movies suck," Mabel repeated more loudly. "No one likes them. Admit it."

The other girls giggled, hands over their mouths. Mabel looked proudly insolent.

This wasn't his sweet, curious, empathetic daughter, he told himself. She was acting out because it was her birthday and her friends were there and a few things had gone haywire.

"Mabel," he said. "You have guests, so I won't send you to your room for a time-out. But I do expect an apology."

"I don't *have* a room here," she said. "You don't either, really. It's Grandma's house."

Paul restrained himself from responding.

"Shit—has anyone checked on Thea?" he asked.

"He said the S-word!" a girl said.

Mabel marched to the bathroom.

"She said she's probably going to be there a while," she reported with a smirk that reminded him of Colin Mackey.

"Okay," Paul said. "We still get regular network TV. You can watch anything on that. Everyone should use the bathroom in Mabel's grandmother's room now, and you can either go there again or hold it while Thea's in the other one. I'll stay up till she's feeling better."

"We haven't even set up our beds," Mabel said.

"All your sleeping bags are out."

"We need *pillows*."

He'd forgotten about pillows and hadn't asked the mothers to bring any. In the linen closet was a nearly deflated one made during the Cold War, half its weight constituted by dust mites. He grabbed it, the one from his own bed, and the two throw pillows for the couch and dropped them all on the carpet.

"This is only four," said Mabel. "There are five of us."

"I'm not going to ask your eighty-six-year-old grandmother to give up her pillow," he said. "You can go without one, Mabel. I'll give you some clothes you can lay your head on."

He dug out a few sweaters from his drawer for her. Then he knocked gently on the bathroom door.

"Thea? You okay in there?"

The toilet flushed in a reflex of shame. "I need a little more time," she called.

"I'm going to stay right outside here, okay? I won't go to sleep until you're out."

The faucet whined and ran.

"You're coming out?" he asked.

"Not yet." Without a fan in the bathroom, she'd evidently reached over to the sink to camouflage whatever sounds she was making.

"You don't have to be embarrassed about anything," he said. "But do you want me to wait farther away?"

"Maybe like a few feet."

He checked on the girls. They were watching a police procedural he would have under ordinary circumstances censored.

The arrangement of four girls watching network television at a slumber party brought back a shadow of a banal boyhood memory, a group sleepover at a friend's house where, deep into the night, they'd played Dungeons & Dragons, all the rage that year in his grade, fueled by soda and potato chips, their fates dictated by a twenty-sided die and a redheaded dungeon master named Jordan Cartwright given to fetishistic descriptions of wood nymphs.

One of the girls brought out her phone, and they all posed for a selfie as two onscreen detectives surveyed a grisly murder scene. The phone produced a series of shutter sounds. Another skeuomorph whose previous iteration they probably didn't even know.

It wasn't just what he'd said to Russ at his dinner party, about the innocence of childhood ending. The innocence of the country had been extinguished, even compared to that post-Vietnam, post-Watergate night of D&D. Disruptors of all stripes—political, technological, economic, cultural—had achieved their aims, disrupted life as it was, a life that was certainly unfair and imperfect but that allowed, at least for some people, some of the time, a measure of genuine contentment. Their efforts had established a definitive Before and After, and these girls—his girl—had been saddled with the After, never having even glimpsed the Before. And those who were older had become so habituated to things as they were now, frogs slowly boiling in chemical-contaminated water, that they'd forgotten how much better they had once been. How much more authentic their existence used to be.

People in every generation throughout history, especially concerned parents, had surely had these thoughts. But it was different now. Too many genies had been disrupted out of too many bottles. The old way of life was irrecoverable.

Paul was welling up. He blinked away the tears before they could form.

"Don't put the volume on too loud. Your grandmother's going to sleep," he said.

"How's Thea?" Mabel asked.

"She'll be a little while longer."

"I'll wait with you."

"You should stay with your friends."

"No," she insisted. "I want to be there for her. I'll lay down outside."

His irritation with his daughter subsided. She would rather wait outside a bathroom with her sick friend than enjoy her slumber party. They'd done something right in raising her.

"That's very kind of you," he said. "And it's 'lie down,' by the way."

"What?"

"The present tense for 'lie down' is 'lie,' not 'lay.' When it's a transitive verb that takes—never mind. Get your stuff."

Mabel brought her sleeping bag and makeshift pillow to the hall outside the bathroom, and Paul read on the carpet just inside his room as the two girls talked through the closed door, the spigot flowing in intervals. After a while, Mabel fell asleep.

"Thea?" Paul said at the door. "Mabel's asleep."

"Um," said Thea, "I ran out of toilet paper."

He retrieved the last roll from the linen closet. All the other girls were asleep, as was his mother.

"Everyone's asleep," he said at the bathroom door. "If I leave the toilet paper just inside the door, would you be able to get it?"

"Not really," she said.

If he rolled it to her, it might go off the mark, too. "Is it all right if I come in with my eyes closed and hand it to you?"

"Can you also hold your nose closed?"

"Of course. I'm coming in, all right?"

With his eyes shut and nose pinched, he walked in a few steps with the toilet paper held out as in a game of Pin the Tail on the Donkey. He thought the request had indicated that she was nearly done, but a few minutes later, more grunts indicated that the job was unfinished.

"God, I just feel terrible about this, Thea," he said.

"It's okay," she said. "I'm supposed to ask about things like dressing."

"No, I should've known. And you're a real trooper. I bet your parents are very proud of you."

She was silent for long enough that Paul asked again if everything was all right.

"How old was Mabel when you and her mom got divorced?"

"She was three." He waited. "Is there any reason you ask?"

"No," she said.

Now he felt bad about what he'd said to her mother.

"It was hard at first, but in the end it was for the best for everyone, and now her mom and I are friends again," he said.

Thea didn't speak again until the toilet flushed. "I think I'm done," she said.

Paul carried Mabel in her sleeping bag back to the dark living room.

"You feel better?" he asked Thea once she was in her sleeping bag.

"Yeah," she said. "Sorry I made you stay up so late."

"No, I'm sorry, Thea," he said. "It's not your fault at all."

51

In the morning he bought bagels and cream cheese for the girls before they woke up and fixed scrambled eggs for Thea, painstakingly safeguarding her plate and fork from any rogue gluten. They all picked at their breakfast.

"The bagels in the Bronx are weird," one of the girls complained.

"I like everything bagels," said another. "Or at least sesame seeds."

"Well, you were all still asleep and I didn't know what you wanted, or if anyone was allergic to anything, so I got plain," Paul said.

He ferried them home to Brooklyn, again in two separate rides, dropping Thea off first. He apologized to her mother at the door after the girl went inside.

"Didn't you see my text about how you should run anything new by me first?" she asked.

"I'm so sorry. I didn't realize dressing had gluten."

"Jesus Christ," she said. "You're lucky she didn't have to go to the ER. How could you not have looked at the label?"

He was about to tell her that maybe he wouldn't have been as distracted had he not had to make two separate round-trips to Brooklyn the previous day. Then, as the woman glared at him, he remembered what Thea had asked him from the bathroom.

"Again, I can't apologize enough," he said.

On the second trip he took the remaining girl to her apartment and saved Mabel for last. They had hardly spoken.

"Mabes, I'm really sorry things didn't go quite as planned," he said.

"It's fine," she said.

"No, it's not. I tried my best to throw you a good party, but I shouldn't have had it at Grandma's. You should've had it at home. Your home. I guess I'm not great at this kind of thing."

She didn't respond.

"It's been a hard few months," he said. "It'll get better. I'll be back in Brooklyn soon."

"Mm-hmm," she said.

He glanced at her in the rearview mirror, perversely hoping she was crying or at least fighting back tears. But she just looked indifferent.

There was a specific day in Paul's youth when he'd seen his parents for the first time with clarity, a shedding of a child's myopia. He'd been twelve and had a friend over to the house who asked what the stacked cans of powdered milk in the pantry were.

"No one drinks milk from a powder," said the boy with a mocking laugh when Paul explained what they were. "Your family's weird."

Paul's mother had always bought powdered milk, for savings and longevity, telling him it was just as good as regular milk, and he'd never given it any thought, even though every other house he went to had cow's milk. After that episode, though, he viewed his parents as not merely frugal or archaic compared to his friends' parents, which he'd roughly been aware of, but as something far worse: weird.

Mabel, too, was seeing him mercilessly, as he was on paper: a forty-six-year-old underemployed writer who lived with his mother and didn't shave every day, dress formally, and go to work like other dads. A crazy-haired wearer of T-shirts with holes who hid in his room to write a book about how modern life was terrible. A weirdo. And she was, as any girl on the cusp of puberty would be, recoiling.

"Hel*lo*?" Mabel said. "Dad, you've got a green light."

They were stalled at a green light, cars behind them honking.

"Sorry," he said as he drove.

"You're always checked out when you're driving. It's dangerous."

"I was at a red light, and I was *thinking*," he said. "Which is a vanishing art form."

They arrived at Jane's brownstone. He usually double-parked right outside so he could walk her up to the door, ensure a peaceful transfer of power, and foster a semblance of co-parenting harmony.

"I'll just wait here till you get in," he said.
"Okay," she said.
"Love you, Mabes."
"Love you," she said, almost one word, as she jumped out of the car.

52

Paul's mother told him that she and Marvin were going on a cruise through the Caribbean and wouldn't return until December.

He was embarrassed by his mother's taste—a retirement cruise past poverty-stricken countries, it couldn't be tackier—but grateful to have the apartment to himself, and without Colin Mackey's bloviations.

53

Paul discovered that the news was no longer merely outraging him, as it had before; when a fresh atrocity broke out, he now licked his verbal chops at the opportunity to weigh in with a clever put-down or persuasive analysis on RealNews. But no matter how doggedly he posted, he was unable to garner much in the way of likes, an outcome he told himself was meaningless yet irked him nonetheless. A stalwart battalion of commenters, likely unemployed and with no personal obligations, remarked multiple times on every article, scooping up far more acclamation through brute force and prior reputation than he ever could—the rich getting richer.

The problem was that he was trying to compete with them at their own game, sending out pithy jabs and one-line diagnoses. Anyone could do that; most of these people were poor writers and facile thinkers, and even they could manage a cutting sentence here and there. He had something different in his arsenal: the ability to write long and deep. That was what was missing in this age of mayfly attention spans. People still preferred carefully prepared, savory meals, even if they craved sugar highs—this was, at least, one of the arguments of *The Luddite Manifesto.*

RealNews capped comments at four thousand characters, about four pages of regular text, but it was unnecessary; no one ever came close to reaching the limit. His first screed at maximum length, written on his laptop, concerned the president's most recent adventure in self-dealing. It was met with a humbling zero likes and a few "tl;dr" dismissals and antiquated "They have something called decaf now" jokes. But Paul was undaunted, and the next morning he woke up early before school and penned another, this time about how Colin Mackey had brainwashed his mother. The few users who saw but didn't take the time to read it delivered a second round of insults.

Later that morning, as he stood at the urinal in a men's room at school, Paul's phone buzzed with a notification: Your comment has been recommended by the editors of RealNews.

On the site, his comment, formerly buried, was now the first thing people saw under the article on which he'd posted. Just a minute after the recommendation, it already had eighteen likes. In his excitement, he nearly dropped his phone into the urinal.

Paul checked on it through the day as his essayistic comment accrued more and more approvals—fifty, two hundred, six hundred. The pace was so vertiginous that his phone overheated with notifications, and he had to disable them. By that evening it had pride of place as the site's most endorsed comment of the day, that designation itself leading to more approvals, with a satisfying 6.4K next to it, its numerical popularity so vast it required a letter of abbreviation.

I always thought this site was filled with idiots making puerile jokes, one user had remarked on his post. So refreshing to read something substantial and beautifully written. Thanks, @TheLuddite.

The next morning he wrote a third long entry.

54

On his phone, Paul read about the president's newest ethics scandal over coffee and omelets in Lauren's apartment. (She ordered in breakfast every day, an indulgence he'd never known anyone to partake in once, let alone daily; she covered the bill, at least.) Her phone rang, for the first time in his presence a normal tone, not the Madonna song, and she picked up immediately.

"Hey," she said, turning away a little from Paul. "Yeah, I'm reading about it now. I agree, too big to ignore. I'm thinking steer into the skid. Find a time a Democrat did something in the ballpark, say this is the way it's always been done and no one cared till he did it. I can get Tom to start looking for anything useful." She listened for a while to a man's voice that Paul couldn't distinguish.

"That the executive producer?" he asked when she hung up.

"Colin." She resumed tapping at headlines on her iPad.

"You were figuring out how to handle this thing on the show?" Paul pointed to the headline on her iPad. She murmured her assent. "So you're trying to find a liberal equivalent, and point out that both sides—"

"I'm gonna have to deal with this all day after you leave, so if you don't mind, I'd rather not discuss it now," Lauren said.

He told her it was no problem, and didn't speak again until they were done with breakfast.

"You feel like getting together Thursday night?" he asked before he left. Thus far they'd seen each other only on Fridays and Saturdays. "I'm teaching that day but could come over after."

"You know what my weeknights are like," she said. "I doubt you want to eat dinner at ten thirty."

It was apparent by now that Lauren wasn't going to invite him onto the show. Starting a relationship with her had only further dissuaded her—she wouldn't want to mix her private and work lives. Booking guests probably wasn't even in her purview. His only shot was finagling an impromptu encounter with whoever was in charge of that at her workplace, slipping into the conversation his angst over being a conservative professor in New York, and snagging a guest spot himself.

"I could come during the show, hang out at your office, and we could go from there to someplace that's still open," he said with his best pantomime of casual disinterest. "I'd love to see a taping, anyway. Or whatever it's called when it's a live show."

"It's a closed set. They don't let outsiders watch."

"Well, just your office, then. I'm curious to see where you work."

"I'd have to be available to let a visitor in, and I'm in the control room during the show and I'm slammed for hours before it starts."

She didn't want him there. He'd allowed his contempt for Mackey to peek through in the moments she'd brought him up; he never should have had that discussion with her about him and the president. This was yet another sign he should end things now. It was bankrupting him, economically and morally, and if he even did somehow maneuver himself onto the show, he'd only panic in the bright lights and stammer a few warmed-over criticisms of the network before they cut him off. Or, if he did control himself, he was far too restrained and professorial to secure the attention of the network's audience. The only people they respected were raucous and shameless—and cutthroat, to quote the hockey analyst. Paul wasn't cutthroat. The whole thing had been a quixotic pursuit from the start, a fairy tale to distract himself from the entropy of his life.

But no—he had to try. Someone like Russ, if he'd ever had the imagination and gumption to attempt a feat like this in the first place, would be giving up now.

"Couldn't someone else let me in? What about Kelsey?"

Lauren bit her bottom lip, mulling the request.

"I guess," she said. "You could watch the show on the office feed, but you'd have to be at my desk. They're very stringent about security."

"Makes sense," said Paul. "I'm sure they deal with a lot of nut jobs."

55

After a weekend away on a family trip with Jane and Steve, Mabel was with Paul for the first time since the disastrous birthday party. Her visit coincided with a deadline from his editor for the first few chapters of *The Luddite Manifesto*, which he'd neglected since his initial Adderall spree.

"I'm really sorry, my little—Mabes," he told her as they drove to Riverdale. "I'll be working right in my room, and you can watch whatever you want on TV."

"Okay!" she said, not bothering to hide her relief and excitement.

She spent all day in front of the screen, sampling the channels like a glutton at an all-you-can-eat buffet, chipping away at her mind's ability to sustain attention as her father built up a treatise on the same topic. He felt guiltier as the day wore on, no more present than the workaholic businessman who saw his child for a few hours a week.

"Would you like to go horseback riding tomorrow?" he asked during a break between shows. She'd never ridden a horse before, but he'd recently seen an online ad for the stables in Van Cortlandt Park. He wondered which of his internet searches had tipped them off to his having a preteen daughter, the ripest age and gender for the activity.

"Sure," she answered without looking away from the TV.

He booked a lesson for Sunday morning. The stables mandated a half-hour private evaluation for all new riders, bringing the price, in addition to an hourlong group lesson, to one hundred and twenty dollars. He should've confirmed the cost before asking Mabel, especially given her half-hearted attitude.

Sunday unveiled a perfect autumn morning, sunny and crisp, the oaks in Van Cortlandt Park orange flames licking the cyan sky. Paul took his laptop and watched outside a fenced-in area as an instructor helped Mabel mount a tawny horse, whose bridle she clutched tensely. Paul had taught her how to ride a bike but otherwise hadn't given her much meaningful instruction for navigating the physical world. Steve took them camping each summer.

Once Paul was satisfied that she was safe and not too anxious, he sat on the grass, wincing as he lowered himself to the ground. The tenderness in his shoulder had returned after he'd finished his course of diclofenac, but when he'd called the sports medicine practice and asked them to refill the prescription, he was told he'd have to make another appointment for the doctor to examine him. He couldn't afford it, even sans X-rays, and decided he'd see if it improved on its own.

He massaged his first chapter, having surreptitiously taken an Adderall before they left the apartment so that he'd be peaking now. By the time he looked up from his laptop, Mabel was already in the group lesson in the distance, one of five girls and a boy on horseback gathered around the instructor like history's least fearsome cavalry. The adult led them in a procession in Paul's direction.

Like a school of fish, the horses turned to follow the instructor, and Paul caught a glimpse of Mabel's smile beneath her too-big purple helmet. She'd smiled in his presence over the last few months, of course, had laughed some, too, but he hadn't witnessed this kind of unshackled joy in a while. As a preverbal toddler spotting dogs on the street, she'd excitedly point with a gasping rale that strangers sometimes mistook for an asthma attack.

"So you had fun?" he asked in the car afterward.

"Uh-huh," she said.

"It'll probably be too cold to go riding again this winter, but we can try it again in the spring." He'd have more savings by then, or he could take extra fares, a biweekly indulgence to make her time in Riverdale less dreary.

"Okay."

They didn't talk much the rest of the drive. There was no parking available on Jane's street, and, with a police car behind them, Paul stayed in the car rather than double-park.

"Love you, Mabes," he said automatically as she got out of the car.

"Bye," she said.

Paul waited as she clambered up the steps to the brownstone and rang the bell. Steve opened the door and shielded his eyes with a hand on his forehead, scanning left and right like a sailor as he pretended not to notice her below his line of sight.

Mabel looked up at him and, in profile, Paul could see her giggling. Steve kissed her scalp and scooted her in as he closed one of his sturdy oak double doors.

56

Superb work thus far!" his somewhat buttoned-down book editor wrote back regarding his first three chapters, along with a few other compliments. "I eagerly await the rest."

After shriveling for years, his confidence in his writing ballooned. His long entries on RealNews were now routinely recommended by the editors and considered required reading for all the regulars. When he hadn't yet weighed in on a controversial subject, various commenters beseeched him to. On a thread in a discussion group, some users were speculating on the identity of TheLuddite, accurately guessing, given the erudition of his posts, that he was either a professional writer or an academic.

He'd never enjoyed such a large audience in his life—probably more than forty thousand readers.

57

Between his third and fourth Thursday classes was the monthly department meeting that he often skipped. But this one would include the vote on extending health insurance to the adjunct instructors who taught three or more classes per semester. He sat around a table with a few dozen full-time professors and adjuncts in a dingy seminar room, drinking boxed coffee and passing donuts that nearly everyone declined; to eat them would reveal weakness of willpower, and, furthermore, the treats were too déclassé to consume in present company.

"Before we put the insurance subsidy to a vote, is there an adjunct who'd like to make a case for it?" Nathaniel asked.

None of the other adjuncts, all significantly younger than Paul, piped up. He didn't want to beg for help, either, but someone had to put a human face to their request.

"This is my ninth year here," he said. "Due to budget cuts, my title was downgraded from senior lecturer to adjunct instructor." He detailed his drop in income, told them about his moonlighting as a driver, and stated what paying for insurance on his own would cost. Airing his financial dirty laundry in public was embarrassing for him and uncomfortable for everyone else. None of the full-time professors made eye contact with him when he finished.

"Though I don't personally have a vote in the matter," Nathaniel said, "the administration has asked me to remind everyone that subsidizing the adjuncts in our department will raise your premiums by about sixty-two dollars."

"That's for the full year or quarterly?" asked a gray-bearded professor.

"Monthly," Nathaniel said. "All the details are in the attachment in the last email I sent out."

Judging from the gray-bearded professor's face and the surprised reactions of others in the room as they mentally tallied the annual cost, few of them had bothered to open the attachment.

Paul counted the number of full-timers in the room. Not all of them had shown up, probably because the absentees also hadn't realized what the full outlay of the subsidy would be. They still outnumbered the adjuncts by five, but as everyone present would submit their votes by private ballot after the meeting, he was certain enough of them would choose altruistically.

Nathaniel concluded by reminding everyone of the new school-wide policy when teaching works containing "problematic" words. Trigger warnings should, of course, be issued before assigning these texts, as they had been for years. But now any student who requested not to read them or be present for the class would be granted permission, no questions asked.

"We also urge you to consider carefully the value of assigning such a work in the first place," Nathaniel said, reading from his marching orders. "If you need to, put yourself in the position of a marginalized student who might be disturbed by it."

Paul had sat quietly on the sidelines of this ongoing debate in recent years, privately rolling his eyes over demands for "safe spaces," students' fragility concerning certain words, and the enforced adoption of new identificatory terms (the first time he saw it, he'd assumed "folx" as a substitute for "folks" was a joke) while also acknowledging that he had little idea how others who didn't look like him might truly feel when inside spaces they considered unsafe, hearing or reading these fraught words, or being unsatisfactorily labeled. But asking teachers to self-censor as a way of heading off controversy—perhaps even the cynical Colin Mackey had a point after all. That was the problem, though: if Paul spoke up and defended principles that were supposed to be unassailable in America, and certainly in a liberal arts institution, he'd be tagged as another straight white male aggrieved that the playing field, radically lopsided in his favor for all of history, was now leveling out.

More to the point, he couldn't risk alienating any colleagues—especially the younger ones most vociferous in these debates—before they voted on his health insurance.

58

After the faculty meeting, Paul limped off to his last class of the week. The latest set of internet essays, choked with snark and idioms he could only partially decode from context ("I'm dead"? "It me"? Had his generation sounded this asinine to its elders?), had again failed to arouse any more of a reaction from his students than the literary texts. All this condescending for nothing.

Yet another question canned by the department yielded silence from his moribund charges, the dead-eyed boys in sports paraphernalia, the girls swaddled in logoed sweatpants like plane passengers lounging gate-side. To wear attire with such brazen corporate insignia in his college days would have been unthinkable.

No wonder they were such lemmings. The school didn't want to assign them anything that might "disturb" them—even though the very point of higher education was to disturb their minds, to force them to reevaluate the notions they'd unquestioningly carried for eighteen years.

"Did you guys even read the assignment?" he asked. No one responded, but he had their attention. "Or are you just hoping to skate by with a B plus so you can graduate and make money selling tracking ads on the internet?"

"Both," Jason said to a smattering of laughter from the boys near him.

Paul shotgunned accusatory glances around the room, a courtroom lawyer shaming the townsfolk in the gallery for their presumed biases. "Seriously. Are you able to read for half an hour straight? Or just think for a minute without stimuli? Have you ever willingly let yourself be bored? Or have your brains been completely damaged by your phones, and the only thing that stirs them anymore is a notification?"

They were staring at him with vacant, bovine expressions.

"Your government is annihilating your future—not just some stranger's in the Middle East, but *yours*—and you still don't care, because you can stream all the TV and music you want, get all the food you want delivered, message your friends through a phone screen, and never have to think about anything outside of your immediate gratification."

He paused for dramatic effect.

"*This* is what Hegel's dialectics has led us to?" he asked. "Unlimited TV and takeout in your apartment, but at the price of a dystopian hellscape right out your window?"

"I thought Kegels were what women did to keep in shape down there," Jason said to muffled laughter from his nucleus of cronies.

"*Hegel*'s dialectics, Jason, is the idea that history proceeds first as a thesis, which leads to an antithesis that negates it, which is resolved in a synthesis, which becomes the new thesis, and so on, toward progress. Although when I look around at your generation, it doesn't look much like progress." He tossed in an epigram he'd recently written in *The Luddite Manifesto*: "And it's certainly not revolution, either. Martin Luther posted his ninety-five theses on the door of a church to protest corruption and kicked off the Reformation. You guys post pictures of your dinners and celebrities to get likes."

Another silence, similar to the one he'd caused in the faculty lounge. He'd chastised them enough and was about to issue a brief apology, as was becoming his custom, and move on.

"That's a pretty reductive argument," Elena said from the back of the room. Everyone turned to her, impressed by the conviction of her rebuttal.

"Look at all the marginalized groups who can organize and get their message amplified now," she went on. "Videos of police brutality people take on their phones and spread around on social media. Or victims of sexual assault and harassment no one listened to in the past. People in authoritarian countries who can show the world what it looks like. I'd call all of that revolutionary. Saying these tools simply lead to apathy and stupidity sounds like something only a person who's always had a voice and has never been in real danger would say."

As he listened, Paul's eyes were magnetically drawn to the metallic Y the zipper formed in her ever-present hoodie.

"Those are very good points," he conceded. "I was playacting the role of a curmudgeonly crank opposed to the ideological underpinnings of this essay. A critical thinking skill is outlining and subjecting to scrutiny the ideas of someone you may disagree with. For an exercise, I want you all to spend five minutes writing, as a similar character, a critique of this essay, then five minutes countering it, without repeating any of my or Elena's arguments."

Pens and paper came out and dutifully scratched away. They seemed to buy his cover story. Or perhaps they just didn't care enough and were used to obeying commands.

"Wait, the dude posted ninety-five *feces* on the door of a church?" Jason asked. "Isn't that unsanitary?"

Paul ignored the comment as Jason's coterie laughed again.

59

Per Lauren's instructions, Paul arrived at network headquarters fifteen minutes before the show started. The lobby was cold, in temperature and in gray-and-black ascetic design. At the front desk, he gave his name and Kelsey's to a uniformed man. After calling her, the man directed Paul to a set of turnstiles, which he passed through to reach a metal detector with another security guard. He emptied his pockets and removed his belt, but the machine still sounded. The guard waved a wand over Paul's body. It beeped by his waist; the interior metal clasp for additionally securing the pants beyond the button seemed to be setting it off. He'd bought a new outfit for the occasion, a "sports coat and slacks," as his mother had always called them. (She also classified all sneakers as "tennis shoes.")

"It's just the clasp," Paul said.

"Got to do a pat-down," the guard said.

"Just for a clasp?"

"That's the policy."

Judging by his squat, uncaring face under a buzz cut, the man would've made a good Nazi. You had to have that mentality to work at a just-following-orders place like this—from senior producer on down.

Paul submitted himself to the minor mortification of being publicly groped before entering an office.

The guard sent him on to a row of elevators. Like an amateur thief breaking into his first bank vault, Paul felt more nervous the closer he drew to the inner sanctum. Everyone he encountered from here on in would be a morally compromised person to some degree, whether it was a Colin Mackey, actively sowing destruction, or a Lauren, indifferently facilitating it.

The elevator, which had a screen playing Mackey's show just as it was beginning, shot him upward to the thirty-third floor with flattening g-force.

"So great to see you again!" Kelsey said when the door opened, though they'd hardly spoken the night of the group dinner. "Nice haircut." He'd paid for his first professional trim in six months and had instructed the barber to make it very short.

"Thanks!" he volleyed. "Great to see you, too!"

The politesse—the *civility*—of the professional class was partly responsible for the rise of this president, the inauthentic transmission of greetings, intimacy, sympathy, gratitude, and remorse, their written communications and speech riddled with disingenuous exclamation points. The network's blue-collar viewers believed, with good reason, that the highest echelons of life were all a Kabuki theater of finishing-school postures and hollow sentiments and ten-dollar words that danced around the truth, from government leaders professing to feel their pain to air kisses at cocktail parties, so why not just elect a crass fraud who was nearly honest about his dishonesty, who took a monosyllabic machete to the letterpress stationery of upper crust niceties?

Paul apologized for his lateness, explaining his problems getting through the metal detector.

"No worries," she said. "They're bonkers about security here."

The elevator opened to a vestibule between two glass doors. Kelsey swiped an ID card over a reader affixed to one. "This is the main office," she said. "That door leads to the studio wing and the production control room, where Lauren works during the show."

"Where the magic happens," Paul said, trying to sound a little jaunty and excited.

She ushered him past wall-mounted TVs on closed captioning and through a maze of cream-colored cubicles and windowless conference rooms. A few dozen employees sat at their desks or stood chatting with the relaxed body language of session musicians. The squarely groomed men could have been uprooted from any Fortune 500 office. A disproportionate number of the women resembled Kelsey: gym svelte, golden helmets of hair, flagrant lipstick and makeup, flight-attendant-like manners. A bayonet of inadequacy gutted Paul every time he entered a corporate office, no matter how monotonous or despicable he found the environment or nature of the work. It reminded him that he'd shied away from the savage capitalist jungle for the padded confines of academia and writing, where competition was, at most, repressed, and mild-mannered introverts siloed themselves in library carrels from lifelong fear of confrontation. Even if he'd wanted to, he knew he couldn't hack it in a place like this; natural selection would quickly spit him out onto the sidewalk. A friend from college, who had wound up becoming an attending physician at Memorial Sloan Kettering, had once remarked that when most people walked into a roomful of strangers, they asked themselves whom they could befriend, but that he asked himself how he could run the place. Paul's instincts had evolved over the years from asking himself whom he could befriend to hoping to find one person with whom he might have a meaningful connection to strategizing how soon and inconspicuously he could leave.

A few pictures of Lauren's niece and nephew were stationed around her otherwise Spartan desk. Nothing adorned the nubby walls: no calendar or cartoons, not even a Post-it. The attrition of printed décor in the workplace, he noted to himself for inclusion in his book, a previously easy way to signal one's artistic or wacky or sentimental personality, was yet another casualty of the digitally streamlined postmodern identity. It looked like a cheerless place to spend the extended hours she caviled about.

"I have to do some work while the show's going on," Kelsey said as she sat in the opposite cubicle, "but you can hang out till Lauren comes back. And grab some food—they put out a good spread for the late shift."

Paul wandered into the kitchen she'd pointed to, where a catered dinner steamed in trays. He could fill up now and order just a beer at the restaurant to economize. He piled lasagna, chicken breast, and salad onto his plate and took a plastic fork and knife.

When he hung his sports coat on Lauren's chair to keep it clean, he discovered he hadn't removed the price tag. The plastic knife was too dull to cut it off, so he asked Kelsey if she had scissors. She handed him a pair of safety scissors with blunted ends.

"Sorry," she said. "It's ridiculous, but they don't allow real scissors—or anything sharp—in here unless you file a request the day before. A janitor got in a fight with a deliveryman or something a few years ago and stabbed him, and there was a big lawsuit."

Did Kelsey have the capacity to register the rank hypocrisy of a network that endorsed the open carry militarization of civilians but banned scissors from its own premises? How many abortions had the employees procured or funded despite the pro-life company line? How much coke had they snorted in the toilet stalls as the on-air personalities clamored for a draconian police state and drug laws?

"No problem," Paul said as he snipped the tag. "It reminds me of the scissors my daughter learned with."

"Aw," she said. "Do you have a picture of her?"

He hadn't taken any pictures of Mabel with his phone. For years he'd used a camera with real film, snapping photos sparingly, not wanting his experiences with her to be mediated and interrupted by a lens. Now parents took more pictures of their kids from a single vacation than Paul's had during his entire childhood (and there was certainly nothing of him on video). Beyond whatever damage it inflicted on their ability to "be present," it had to have an injurious effect on their memories themselves, too, supplanting the textured ones in the hippocampus with the unchanging images from the camera's cold eye that pretended to objectivity. Even the sharper picture resolution now felt like a rebuke to the fragile human beauty of grainy recollection. That was how, owing to their primitive methods of visual documentation, Paul nostalgically remembered the seventies and eighties: as a softer, fuzzier, warmer time.

"Just got a new phone and I haven't transferred my pictures yet," he told Kelsey.

She looked genuinely disappointed as she returned to her computer.

"So Lauren said you work with social media here?" Paul asked.

"Sort of," she said.

"Do you write the tweets or something?"

"Not quite. It's more like data science."

"Really?" He knew he sounded too flabbergasted that someone who resembled a college football cheerleader would be toiling in a field with hard numbers. "What does that entail?"

"Oh, it's kind of boring to most people."

"No, I'm interested—really. What are you doing right now, if you don't mind my asking?"

"Well," said Kelsey, "I've been working for a few months on a data analytics program in Python that scrapes features related to sentiment and content from TV broadcasts. It analyzes language and tone from the broadcast and categorizes how they influence the emotional state of the viewer. Then I use that to predict how viewership increases or decreases during and after the broadcast, its probability of going viral, and the likelihood that viewers will increase or decrease their watch time in subsequent days."

"Where did you . . . learn how to do that?"

"Mostly in college."

"Where was that?"

"Around Boston," she said, the evasive geography a giveaway to her elite education. Then she hastily added, "But I'm honestly pretty low on the totem pole here."

Paul silently tucked in to his meal, chastened over his disproved prejudices.

No TVs were visible from his seat; he could only imagine the venom Mackey was expectorating from nearby. *Colin Mackey* was in the same building, the *same floor*, doing his show *right now*, live on the air. Revolting as he found him, it was thrilling—more so, perversely (as it seemed to be with Lauren in bed), than if he were someone Paul admired.

"Do all the producers work in this area, too?" he asked Kelsey as she typed. "Keith, I think Lauren said the executive producer's name was?"

"Keith's office is near Colin's on the other side of the building," she said.

If he asked who booked the show, she might tell Lauren. He'd seen Keith's picture online and would keep alert in case he entered the room.

Lauren didn't emerge until twenty minutes after the show ended, drawn and looking in a foul mood. Several times she'd compared the stress of producing a live news program to working in triage, a medical analogy surely fueled by her sense of familial shortcoming. She told Paul to give her a few minutes as she dealt with some "work shit" on her computer. He stood, taking in his surroundings like a skittish gazelle at a watering hole.

No sign of Keith. The office had thinned out since he'd arrived, with just one live show to go and a younger crowd than before, the only ones willing to take a job that locked them in an office until midnight.

He was despairing over yet another wasted night when through the glass doors walked Colin Mackey, trailed by an unsmiling younger man whose athletic physique looked incongruous with his dark suit.

No one paid Mackey much mind as he strode through the near aisle; they must have been used to seeing him, despite the distance of his office. But, as with any celebrity, it was a shock to Paul to see him embodied after all this time as a two-dimensional talking head.

Mackey passed by, just ten feet away, heading toward a cubicled woman at the far end of the room. The two of them conferred as the hanger-on waited nearby. Paul at first thought he might be Keith, but he was far too young and muscular to fit Lauren's description. Of course—Mackey's bodyguard. A strange job; through a financial relationship, he had to pledge—in theory, at least—the same sacrificial loyalty Paul had to Mabel after her birth and value the life of another man over his own. At least soldiers unwittingly protecting the interests of the rich and powerful could deceive themselves into thinking it was for their country.

"Do you think I could meet Colin?" he quietly asked.

"Hold on a minute," Lauren said, her eyes fixed on an email.

That wasn't a yes or a no. Mackey finished his conversation and turned back. Lauren was pecking away at her keyboard.

"He's coming," Paul said.

"Just hold *on*," Lauren said. Her voice reminded him of Jane's at the end of their marriage, when every sentence was delivered with the irritability of an overextended mother.

Mackey approached, the bodyguard at his heels like an obedient pit bull. He would never get another chance like this. But he felt paralyzed, constricted, as if a belt were cinched around his chest.

This was the big swing he'd been hoping to take.

"I'm sorry," he said after he stepped backward into the aisle, pretending not to have noticed that he was blocking Mackey.

"Quite all right," Mackey said. Unsettling to hear the voice in person, too—a velvety basso profundo, commanding and soothing at once. He must have been good on the radio.

"Colin, this is my friend Paul," Lauren said from her chair.

"Hello, friend Paul," he said, extending his hand. He was hail-fellow-well-met handsome up close, with implausibly white and straight teeth and an age-defying quantity and luster of hair. Mackey was only about a decade older, and they were roughly the same height—though the former wrestler's frame now carried significantly more golf-club padding—but Paul felt like a child meeting a parent's friend at a formal event. "How you doing tonight?"

"Good," Paul responded.

He knew what he should do: flatter him, segue into his own job, inveigh against the liberal academy. But, petrified in the headlights of Mackey's fame, he clammed up.

"Nice meeting you," said Mackey, likely accustomed to strangers being dumbstruck in his presence. "See ya, Laur. Thanks for tonight."

He swept out with the bodyguard in his wake.

Paul had blown it, said little to make himself stick in Mackey's mind, certainly nothing to warrant an invitation onto the show. And even worse: Mackey had been polite, friendly, even *charming*. Perhaps Lauren was right that his show was mostly just an act—one with supremely dangerous consequences, but an act nonetheless—and Mackey was a decent person beneath his public persona. Regardless, Paul had found himself pulled toward the magnet of his charisma, just like Mackey's gullible audience. Something deep in his psyche had implicitly recognized Mackey as a kingly force, bending the world to his will—a "great" man, a shaper of history—while he was a man of inaction: a pawn, bent, shaped.

Paul went on autopilot through their dinner date. All he had to do was set Lauren off on a personal subject—her college days, her parents' favoritism of her brother, the endless cascade of work complaints—and *uh-huh* and *oh-wow* along. She had a tendency to repeat the same grievance three or four times in a row without adjusting the language. Her perseveration reminded him of the president, and while cognitive erosion, stunted vocabulary, and belief in the propagandistic value of reiteration were the probable causes with him, it seemed as though it came from the same place of insecurity: despite their positions of power, they felt they weren't being heard.

Most of her vocational grudges centered on the executive producer. Keith took credit for all her good ideas while shifting the blame for every failure to her; though he spent more time at swanky events and Scotch-soaked dinners than in the office, she was positive she made a fraction of his salary; he was the epitome of every entitled, chauvinistic, old-boys boss she'd ever worked under.

Had she been employed at a nonprofit, Paul would have been highly sympathetic. But her job aside, he had a hard time mustering much pity; what an unforeseen coincidence that the only time Lauren, a high-ranking woman in corporate America, had ever cared about systemic inequality was when it came to the plight of high-ranking women in corporate America.

"I'm so sorry you have to deal with a guy like that," he told her. "It sounds completely unfair."

In her apartment, after their routine of a cocktail and spanking-assisted sex, Lauren fell asleep, but he stewed over his failed interaction with Mackey. After some time he went to the bathroom, where he sat on the toilet and replayed part of that night's show on his phone.

He was expecting it to be a more conciliatory, open-minded program, in keeping with Mackey's real-life demeanor, but if anything it was more hateful and fascistic than usual.

It was utterly villainous. The network was villainous for broadcasting it. The woman in the other room, with whom he'd just had sex, was villainous in her blithe shrugging at the evil she was helping spread, the suffering it was causing.

But most of all, Mackey was villainous, and that he could be friendly in person only showed that, unlike the innately cruel president, he knew the value of common decency. He just didn't care.

60

Lauren scrolled through the morning headlines on her iPad. He'd learned never to bring up anything in the news for discussion, not from the risk of exposing his beliefs or fatiguing her by talking shop outside the office, but because her intellectual interest in the world resided chiefly in whittling complex issues down to a two-minute segment. He might have been less judgmental if she were as obtuse as the content of her show. But she wasn't—despite her kink for Paul to demean her intelligence in bed—and she'd applied her sharp mind toward manipulating the dullards, just as Mackey had done to the nth degree.

Nathaniel sent an email to the department covering a number of topics, most of them irrelevant to Paul. At the bottom, he wrote, Lastly, the measure to extend health insurance to the adjunct instructors was rejected by majority vote.

Paul thought he'd misread it at first. All the adjuncts had obviously voted for the insurance; they'd simply needed three defectors from the tenured faculty willing to pay an extra sixty bucks a month to give their tenuously employed co-workers affordable health insurance.

"The contrast between what my colleagues preach in their classes and how they actually conduct themselves is remarkable," he said, and for the first time there was sincere peevishness behind the complaint. He skipped over the insurance vote and apoplectically relayed the school's new guidance concerning reading material.

Lauren grunted as she read.

"A lot of editors have asked me to write an essay about this stuff. I've been worried about blowback at school, but I think I've finally had enough."

She again didn't respond.

"You don't think—forget it."

Lauren finally looked up. "What?"

"I was going to ask if you think Colin would ever want to interview me on the show, so I could get people to see this other side to the story the mainstream media never covers"—he had to couch it in newsy terms, make it seem like their team was the silenced one—"but I don't want to put you in that position. Never mind."

She resumed reading. He'd screwed up by giving her an out. A great man, a shaper of history, wouldn't end his request, even as part of a hustle, with "never mind."

"It's probably Keith who arranges guests on the show, anyway," he said. "Sorry I brought it up."

"Emily—the booker—takes my pitches," Lauren said defensively. "I've gotten plenty of people on."

"Oh." He made himself look as though he'd never expected this. "Well, only if you think it's a good idea."

She drank from her coffee mug. Her facial expressions were obscured, but he could nearly see her eyes weighing the ratings value of Paul as a guest against the unprofessionalism of booking her boyfriend on the show.

"I'll mention it to her," she said.

"Thanks." He bit into his toast to hide his smile. "Do you want me to send links to stuff I've written?"

One of the benefits of his miserly production in recent years was that when he'd audited his online body of work, nothing that came up was overtly political. To cover his tracks further, he'd created a bare-bones website for himself that listed "Selected Publications" and linked only to essays in small outlets no one at the network would even have heard of, let alone accuse of liberal bias. By all appearances, he was someone that Colin Mackey could approve of featuring on his program to tell his woeful story as an oppressed conservative professor in New York City.

"You don't want to look too thirsty," Lauren said.

"What do you mean by 'thirsty'?"

"You know—desperate, eager. You've never heard that before?"

Paul shook his head.

Lauren laughed. " 'What do you mean by 'thirsty'?' " she mimicked in a stilted baritone. "You're like software that hasn't been updated in decades."

61

Paul had planned to spend a few hours on Saturday with Mabel in Prospect Park, reading under a tree to sip the last honeyed drops of November sunshine, before he brought her back to Riverdale.

"Got all your homework?" Steve asked as he saw her out the door.

She reached around to pat her backpack. "Yep."

"Including your math workbook?"

"Yes."

"You sure? It's definitely *not* still on the kitchen table?"

"Oops. Sah-wee."

Steve tousled her hair as she scampered past him and watched her go with a smitten grin.

"Any excuse to conveniently forget her math book," he said knowingly to Paul.

"Right," Paul said, though he thought Mabel liked math.

The morning had turned from sunny to cloudy during Paul's drive, and when they reached the park it began to rain. Paul hadn't checked the forecast, which now predicted showers all day. He didn't want to take her back to Riverdale immediately—there was even less to do in inclement weather there—but there were no good kids' movies to see, and they'd gone to all the Brooklyn museums she liked too recently for a repeat visit. They found cover in a bodega as he pondered where to go.

"I know!" he said. "You've never been to the Tenement Museum."

"What's the Ten Mint Museum?"

"Ten*ement*. Apartment buildings. It shows how immigrants lived on the Lower East Side at the turn of the century. The twentieth century."

She didn't seem excited.

"It's where some of your ancestors lived," he said. "On my side—my father's father when he was little, before his family moved to New Jersey. You'll like it, I promise."

"Can I get a Coke for the ride?" she asked.

He and Jane had upheld a limited-exceptions soda ban for years. But it might make her more enthusiastic about the trip—and this could also be the way to earn back her affection, one high-fructose corn syrup bribe at a time. A lot of fathers did much worse to curry favor with their kids.

"Get a can, not glass," he told her. "It's better for the environment."

"Mom doesn't want me drinking from cans because of BPA."

"That's ironic, given that she—"

He stopped before commenting on Jane's injecting herself with a toxin that causes botulism, a disease often found in canned food.

"That she what?" Mabel asked.

"I thought she was the one who told me cans were better, but I guess I was wrong."

Finding parking on the Lower East Side took twenty minutes in the gathering downpour and forced them five blocks from the museum. There were no umbrellas in the car, so they made a dash, ducking under awnings like two frogs leaping from lily pad to lily pad. Last year they'd done this one afternoon, when he'd picked her up from school and chaperoned her to Jane's during a storm, and Paul had shielded her with his arms. It had barely protected her, but they'd laughed the whole way.

By the time they reached the museum, Mabel was miserable, her head soaked and sneakers waterlogged.

"It's atmospheric," he said with false merriment. "This is how they would have lived a century ago—wet and cold."

Tickets for an exhibition that told the stories of two representative late nineteenth-century immigrant families set him back nearly fifty dollars. A guide led their group through a few cramped rooms outfitted with furniture, trunks, and bric-a-brac authentic to the era.

"Isn't it cool, seeing household items from over a hundred years ago?"

Paul asked, in camp counselor mode. "Can you imagine living like this—no dishwasher, no laundry machine, not even any electricity? Nothing like the Sharper Image, right?"

"You didn't have a dishwasher or laundry machine in your apartment," Mabel said.

In the kitchen, the guide informed them that rats, a scourge in the tenements, sometimes chewed on babies in their cribs.

"Yikes," Paul said to Mabel.

"This place is dirty," she said under her breath.

"It's clean now. She's explaining what it used to be like."

"Do they show a movie at the end of this?"

"It's not that kind of place. But you don't need it. We're *in* the exhibition itself. You can't get this experience from a movie."

"What's that thing?" she asked.

"It's a chamber pot. It's how they went to the bathroom, instead of using a toilet."

"How does it flush?"

"It doesn't. They had to carry them out to an outhouse."

Mabel grimaced. "Why would you take me to an apartment where they pooped in pots? It's gross."

Paul steered her by the shoulders back to the previous room, out of earshot of the group.

"I took you here to show you what life used to be like for some New Yorkers," he said. "Including people you're related to."

"Mom's relatives didn't live like this," she said. "They were rich."

Paul had a desire to shake her.

"You know what? A lot of people around the world *still* live like this, or worse. They don't have running water or electricity. And they don't live in garden duplexes. So maybe if you stop making snot-nosed comments, you'll learn something about how life can be hard for people who aren't spoiled brats."

He'd never once name-called her like this. Mabel's face blanched and her eyes appeared seized with the flinching fear of an angry father; then, after a moment, they dimmed, as if she had mentally traveled far from Paul and the tenement museum.

"Let's join the others," he said.

She and Paul were silent the remainder of the tour, keeping a few feet from each other.

It was still drizzling when they left. They didn't say anything as they walked to the car.

"I apologize for how I spoke to you, Mabes," Paul finally said as he drove up the West Side Highway. "That wasn't nice of me. I can see how the place might have felt weird to you. And I don't think you're spoiled."

"It's fine," she said, her constant rejoinder lately. He would have rather she fought back. A Rubicon had been crossed. His once affectionate daughter, who used to bathe in her father's unerring adoration, who'd received his tickles and zerberts with delight, now batted away his gestures of love as if they were mosquitoes.

They parked in the garage of his mother's building.

"Probably a lot of worms out from the rain. Want to get some?" he asked as a peace offering.

"Okay," she said.

She followed him to the front lawn of the complex, where they found a couple and housed them in his Altoids tin. In the apartment he let Mabel drop them into the terrarium.

"Welcome to South Slope," he said.

"We're not in South Slope."

"It's just a saying. But we'll—I'll be back there soon."

"When?"

"Soon," he said vaguely.

She watched television as he graded writing exercises. After a dinner of takeout Chinese he allowed her to return to her post. By eight o'clock he was exhausted. He hadn't been on RealNews since that morning and, itching to see the latest developments, treated himself to a peek. Reading an article about the president's most recent Twitter salvo—absurd, still, that a single man, with a relatively cheap handheld device he controlled from the toilet seat in his bathroom lair, could make the world go topsy-turvy within minutes—he couldn't hold back from commenting at length about a raft of Occupational Safety and Health Administration bills the administration wanted to pass to weaken workers' safety protections. In the last line he wrote, His intentionally inane internet droppings, meanwhile, are on the front page of even this site, which normally ignores the distractions. The comment immediately floated to the top and received a slew of likes, the numbers climbing every time he refreshed the page.

The TV was blaring in the living room. It had been a difficult day; she could watch a little longer.

He sank back into the gratifying universe of RealNews. By the time he looked up, it was ten thirty and Mabel had fallen asleep on the couch.

He was disgusted with himself. He scooped her up and cradled her away to his bedroom, careful not to rouse her with any turbulence, a pilot on a red-eye. As he prepared to lower her onto the bed, she stirred. He paused to let her drift back to sleep.

"Daddy?" she asked dreamily, half-conscious, eyes lidded. He couldn't remember the last time she'd called him that. Years, maybe.

"Shh, baby," he whispered, kissing her forehead and depositing her onto the unmade bed, covering her with the blanket. "Go to sleep."

He punished himself by turning off his phone. But when he tried reading Nabokov's *Speak, Memory* in his mother's empty bed, he found it hard to concentrate on the ornate sentences. Sleep wouldn't come easily, either, though he felt drained. He eventually succumbed and hit the power button.

The screen's light dawned in a tranquil indigo, a comforting assurance of endless diversion and company.

62

After sending Mabel home, he spent the next two days on Adderall grading his students' second papers. (He'd called the psychiatrist, told him he'd been having narcoleptic episodes, and received a stronger prescription.) This time they'd had to write critical essays, and evidently no one had ever taught these kids how to do so. He had long been the kind of teacher who red-inked each sentence, showing his students what dangling modifiers were, how to link paragraphs, why "involved" was an empty word. But they hadn't learned anything from the last set of essays he'd given that treatment to; if anything, they'd regressed. What was the point? He was a lone dam against a tidal wave of pass-the-buck education. All it did was frustrate him.

But he still couldn't stop himself from issuing the odd, scolding correction. If he didn't fix it, who would?

He chipped away at the pile, handing out B pluses for work that was at least coherent, C minuses for the business majors who couldn't be bothered to proofread. He gave Jason a B / B plus; the writing wasn't that bad, but he'd fudged the margins and line spacing to reach the minimum page count. He was saving Elena's essay for last as a reward.

On Monday night he reached her paper, which was remarkably thick, perhaps fifty unnumbered paper-clipped pages, well above the required eight to ten. After the cover page (YOU SAY YOU WANT A REVOLUTION: THE INTERNET REFORMATION OF YOUTH CULTURE), he was greeted by a picture of Meryl Streep cupping her mouth with her hands at an awards ceremony. A sentence in white capital letters overlaid it: 1. THESIS: YOU PROCLAIM THAT HUMAN BRAINS NO LONGER FUNCTION.

Below it was another picture, of Denzel Washington placing his hand over his chest in apparent relief. Superimposed was the text 2. ANTITHESIS: BUT MAYBE THEY'RE ELASTIC AND WIRED DIFFERENTLY NOW TO ACCOMMODATE AN EVOLVING WORLD.

Paul knew enough about internet culture to know these were . . . memes? GIFs? He wasn't completely sure what the distinction was, and the form was jarring to see in print. Nonetheless, a creative way to open an essay on the subject in lieu of a conventional epigraph.

But when he turned the page, he encountered two more photos of celebrities: Leonardo DiCaprio, raising a glass (3. YOU, AN INTELLECTUAL: NO ONE READS ANYMORE), and an actor whose name he couldn't place looking as if he were crying (4. ME, A STUDENT: YOU HAVE A LOW AND NOT VERY NUANCED OPINION OF TODAY'S YOUTH, WHO GENERALLY READ A LOT, THOUGH NOT NECESSARILY TRADITIONAL MEDIA OR DEAD RACISTS AND SEXISTS).

The rest was the same, two images to a page of celebrities mostly addressing a nameless, crotchety, Professor Webbian "you" and arguing that internet culture had the potential to be just as revolutionary as the one "you" had previously inherited.

The final page featured a contemplative photo of Martin Luther King Jr. facing a portrait of Martin Luther, with the concluding statement 95. HEGELIAN SYNTHESIS TO BE POSTED: WHEN YOU REALIZE MAYBE YOU SHOULDN'T BE SO REACTIONARY NEXT TIME YOU WANT TO CRITICIZE SOMETHING YOU DON'T FULLY UNDERSTAND, LEADING TO PERSONAL REVOLUTION AND REFORMATION.

Paul wrote, "A series of stitched-together memes is not what I expected from this essay. Moreover, what text is there directly addresses the reader in a taunting, juvenile tone. The world is intent on bringing original thinkers like you down to its level. They want to make you one of them—to think like them and speak like them. A stunt like this may seem like a clever act of rebellion to you, but to me, it's just surrendering to those poisonous influences."

He gave her a D.

63

Nathaniel called him a few days later. Elena had complained about her grade on the last paper, and Nathaniel needed to hear Paul's side of the story.

Paul had dealt with plenty of disgruntled students over the years, and the department had always backed him up. He was surprised and disappointed that Elena would resort to such pathetic grade-grubbing.

He noted all the ways in which her submission fell short as an academic essay. "I'm not even sure that if you added up all the words it would've met the page requirement," he told Nathaniel.

"Nothing else you want to add? Any other interactions with her worth noting?"

"Yeah, I did extra work with her on her first essay and helped get it accepted by the lit mag. No good deed. I'm sure she didn't mention *that* to you."

"She did, actually," Nathaniel said. "Where'd you help her, again?"

"It was . . . the student union."

Paul could hear Nathaniel typing in the background.

"Okay," Nathaniel said. "While this is under review, what do you think about taking a week's leave? You'll be paid for the time off, of course."

"*What?* A week's leave for an academic dispute over a single essay?"

"So you can avoid having to see her while we work on transferring her to another class for the end of the semester."

"You're not serious. A student complains about a bad grade, she gets to switch classes, *and* the teacher has to leave for a week? I know tuition's gone up, but are you really kowtowing to the customer *that* much these days?"

"We think it's the best way to proceed with . . . this sort of teacher-student dispute," Nathaniel said. "Think of it as a little sabbatical to work on your book."

64

Maybe Nathaniel's disingenuous suggestion was a silver lining. He'd been avoiding *The Luddite Manifesto*, intentionally or not, and if he treated the paid leave as a sabbatical of sorts, he'd be more motivated to make headway. He had eighty pages of prose so far and his outline for the rest. If he forsook driving and committed himself to fourteen-hour workdays, producing new material while collaging his better posts from RealNews, he could crank out about a dozen pages per day. After a week, that would be enough for a draft.

It would be unlike anything he'd ever done, but he could increase his dose of Adderall past the prescription to energize the sprint. As it was a controlled substance, he wouldn't be allowed to refill it until the monthly cycle turned over—but he wouldn't need it once he finished the book.

65

The Adderall surplus electrified his neurons, boosting his stamina beyond the wall he used to ram against after eight hours of writing, and when he ran out of juice he'd take another twenty-milligram dose and keep chugging along. By the second day he had happily deviated from his outline and discarded his original eighty pages—they were too measured, so concerned with understatement that they fell into a spineless centrism, in oatmeal prose that wouldn't upset any delicate constitutions—and restarted the book from scratch.

He restricted himself to fifteen minutes on RealNews and one comment daily, with an excerpt drawn from what he'd written for *The Luddite Manifesto* that session. It was a good way to gauge its appeal with a troop of amateur editors giving crowdsourced feedback in real time.

He hadn't been this content while writing for years, since the days Jane had glimpsed him in the flow state and fallen in love with him.

66

Paul told Lauren he was on deadline for his book but broke away for a Friday night dinner, hoping to suss out his status for an appearance on *Mackey Live*.

He mentioned that he'd been placed on temporary leave after the school had buckled to a student's picayune gripe, hoping this might finally impel her to place a direct call to Mackey.

"Just because of a bad grade?" she asked.

"That's it," he said. "College students have become coddled tyrants. And the school is terrified of them."

She didn't say anything else about it beyond expressing sympathy for his predicament. As she carped about a belligerent colleague, he wondered why she was still interested in seeing him, beyond her veneration of his job (and its beneficial impact on their sex life). It had been nearly a decade since her last significant relationship, with a lawyer who traumatically broke off their engagement six weeks before the wedding date. Despite the many suitors who filed through her revolving door, there could only be one real explanation: she was lonely, and Paul—when on his best behavior—was unobjectionable enough to keep around for company.

"By the way," he asked in the cab home from dinner, "did what's-her-name—Emily?—say anything about the sample from my book?"

Lauren had asked him to send a short excerpt for review. Once he'd started writing the fake chapter of *The Technophile's Manifesto*, he found ventriloquizing a conservative crank easy. He'd begun with his customary careful attention to the sentences before remembering that they wanted the opposite: clichés and sloganeering, language that admitted no ambivalence, just vitriol.

"She liked it," Lauren said. "They're talking about it."

He kept mum. He was close; hunger was good, but he couldn't let his "thirstiness" ruin his work.

In her apartment he took a postcoital trip to the bathroom and passed the full-length mirror outside her bedroom. At first he thought it was another person, someone years older. He scrutinized his reflection above the sink. For a long time he'd been a touch vain about looking younger than his age; in the first halves of his thirties and forties, people had often assumed he belonged in the previous decade. Now his face, with its collagen loss and sun damage and silvering temples, showed all his forty-six years, if not more. In profile, his neck was cocked at an unflattering diagonal, like the uppermost curve of a flamingo's—all that time tilted down at a phone. He'd probably need reading glasses soon. Lower down, his jogging, in addition to his generally healthy diet, had staved off the sag and bloat of midlife. But the metabolism-speeding Adderall had made him look emaciated rather than trim, and his spine was more hunched than he remembered it, the cost of sitting in the driver's seat so much.

He peed out a weak half parabola and lingered at the toilet to void his bladder completely. This nuisance of trickling had barely afflicted him before the last few years, and now he had to perch for half a minute over the bowl, waiting for the garden hose to dribble out after the faucet had been turned off, lest he humiliatingly wet his boxers.

If he were still married to Jane, he could tell her about this pesky problem, and they'd laugh about it together. One of the consolations of even a subpar marriage, that you had someone with whom to share your shame or displeasure over bodily foulness and malfunction, a person you could trust to enter the bathroom after you'd desecrated it. He still hadn't had a bowel movement in proximity to Lauren.

Because he was on leave, he was temporarily banned from the gym at school, though he hated going anyway, all that motion without any displacement, the robotic purposelessness of raising and lowering iron, a sweaty room of self-torturing humans like lab rats on running wheels. He toyed with investigating some sort of app-assisted exercise program. No, he'd do it the old-fashioned way, with his body and gravity. He'd add sprints to his Van Cortlandt Park jogs, and tomorrow he'd install a chin-up bar in his bedroom and commence daily push-ups; his shoulder could tolerate it.

It wasn't narcissism. This was how people—men his age, especially—lost control of their lives, let themselves be buffeted by misfortune until they no longer had any fight left.

Despite his precautions, he ended up blotting his underwear.

Lauren was already asleep. Incredible that she hadn't been repelled by his state of decay. The double standards only widened with the years as the pool of acceptable men evaporated into a dingy puddle.

He slid under the sheets and pulled out his phone, planning to indulge in RealNews for a few minutes.

At three A.M., having thumbed in four long comments, his eyes parched and stinging, he forced himself to put away the phone. He used to be content to spend a night alone with a book, reading till daybreak. Some of his greatest intellectual experiences had come from that habit; in college he'd gone to bed one person before starting *In Cold Blood* and woken up another, newly alert to the world's mechanics and language. Now he required some contemporaneous tether to the outside, a feeling of being plugged in to information that was dynamically changing by the second, not a book that had been typeset decades ago.

Maybe if he were in a meaningful relationship he wouldn't hunger for this remote connection. But the prospect of that was so distant, so alien now, as to render it a sepia-toned photograph of a historic era.

67

Seven days after he was put on leave, on the seventeenth hour of an Adderall binge, Paul completed a draft of *The Luddite Manifesto*. He normally set aside any project, regardless of its length, for a minimum of forty-eight hours before rereading and revising. But some of the manuscript's power derived from its urgency, its authorship by a man writing to ward off global and personal crises.

Also, he was clean out of pills. He sent it to his editor.

68

As he waited for Nathaniel and the administration to resolve the grade dispute and for his book editor to reply with notes, Paul made up for lost time driving and commenting. He considered inquiring to the editors of RealNews about joining as a paid contributor; through his credibility there, newspaper background, and academic status he was certain he'd be received warmly. The pay would be meager, probably fifty bucks a post, but it would justify his labor and maybe enhance his profile when *The Luddite Manifesto* was published.

Yet once he accepted money for his work, he'd be thinking about clicks and "eyeballs," not just the merit of the writing. Co-opted, another journalistic prisoner to capitalism's imperatives. Better to stay with the rabble and say whatever he liked without fear or favor. The one thing the world couldn't take from him was his freedom of expression—bounded in a nutshell and still a king of infinite cyberspace.

69

After two days without Adderall he was irritable, fatigued, ravenous. A good thing he wasn't teaching yet; he couldn't read more than a page without scurrying into a mental escape hatch.

70

During his semester abroad in Riverdale, Paul had kept up his membership at the Park Slope Food Coop to retain shopping privileges for its organic produce. He was pulling his monthly shift on the registers when Russ appeared at the front of the line, steering a full cart. Paul pretended not to notice him and processed his customer slowly, hoping the neighboring cashier would be free first. He wasn't able to delay enough, though, and Russ was forced to stack his goods on Paul's conveyor belt.

"Don't know if you heard about my situation," Paul said after they greeted each other. He ran down the basic facts as he scanned the items.

"That's absurd," Russ said. "I can't tell if the students are getting more entitled each year or if I'm just rapidly turning into my dad."

Russ could be funny sometimes.

"When's your next shift here?" Paul asked. "Maybe we could sync up and get a drink after."

"This month is, sadly, the end of the Coop for us. Our new place is far enough away that it doesn't make sense to keep coming."

"Oh," said Paul. He waited for a suggestion of another time to meet, but Russ continued arranging his groceries on the belt.

The price tag was missing on a tub of hummus. "It's $5.39," Paul said, punching in the numbers. He bought that brand—for mixing with his sardines—every time he visited the Coop.

"I think it's actually $4.39," Russ said.

"It's definitely $5.39. I buy it all the time."

"Pretty sure it's $4.39. I can run back and get another to show you, if you really want."

Paul sighed and reentered the numbers. "Okay, $4.39 it is. Use the extra dollar on some cute protest signs."

Russ didn't say anything. After he paid and said goodbye, he carried his groceries away, then stopped.

"What're you doing, Paul?" he asked.

"What do you mean?"

"What are *you* doing to change anything? You sit back high and mighty, judging the rest of us—and, okay, maybe we're not perfect, but at least we're doing something. Larissa and I go to protests, even if you think they don't accomplish anything. We donate to progressive candidates we believe in, though I'm sure you think money in politics is the biggest problem of all so we shouldn't bother. What else? Oh, we go once a month to a Park Slope parents' group that trades notes on the schools and organizes petitions for our representatives. I invited you once, years ago, and you said you were too busy but you'd get in touch the next time, which you never did. Larissa helps underprivileged kids every fall with their college essays, but you didn't know that, because she doesn't brag about it. Or you'd probably say that perpetuates the unfair meritocracy by sending off the talented tenth to college to be corporate tools, something like that. We're just milquetoast moderates for incremental change, right? But at least we're *trying*. You, on the other hand"—Russ looked disgusted with him—"all you do is criticize."

Paul was unhorsed by the outburst. It took him a moment to offer a comeback.

"Well, thanks so much for voting to give me health insurance," he said. "I really appreciate you incrementally changing things for the better there."

"For your information, we both *did* vote to give you insurance," Russ said. "Despite your thinly veiled hostility toward us, we still care about your well-being."

He shook his head in disdain and left. After the sting subsided, Paul collected himself. Russ and Larissa, in spite of their occasional acts of noblesse oblige, were still entrenched elitists. What Russ had said about themselves was true: they wanted change, but only enough to feel good about themselves without endangering their status. Conformist to power but mildly critical of it. They disbursed some money they could easily spare, gave away a few hours to the college admissions racket while they probably hired a babysitter to look after their kids, attended lightweight Park Slope meetings that were pretexts for wine drinking and gossip. Those weren't sacrifices. Real sacrifices incurred real costs. He wanted to pound this into their heads almost as much as he wanted to change his mother's mind.

But he couldn't shake Russ's line of attack, which Paul had been more and more aware of as his prominence on RealNews grew. He'd been sheltering behind a screen, convincing himself that what he wrote wasn't simply bouncing around an echo chamber or falling on willfully deaf ears. His fury over the unconcern of others was authentic, but ultimately a projection of his self-loathing over his own inaction. He hadn't given succor to an abject person, nor, in a meaningful battle in a physical space, opposed anyone malevolent. Though he certainly had no townhouse to sacrifice, he hadn't voluntarily given up anything of real value, either.

He checked the price of the hummus after his shift. Five glorious dollars and thirty-nine cents. He wasn't so petty as to text a picture of it, but he smirked at the thought of Russ's seeing the price tag next time—before he realized that Russ might not even come back to the Coop again and would never know he'd been in the wrong.

71

His mother returned from her Caribbean cruise. She'd had a "wonderful" time, and the food on the boat had been "delicious—the best steak I've had in my life."

"Oh, good, I'm glad you had access to red meat aboard a ship," Paul said. "I'm sure that was the most environmentally sustainable option."

"What?"

"What'd you do on land?"

"Shopping, mostly. We only had a few hours in each port."

It was pointless to lecture her that she could have stayed on a boat docked in Florida if that was all she did. He asked if she wanted anything for her birthday the next week.

"Marvin is taking me out for a nice dinner on Saturday. Why don't you come along?"

"How about I just do something separately with you?"

He thought she'd consent to this simple request, but she said, "He's an important part of my life. I think it's fair to ask that you see him again. As a birthday gift."

"All right," he said, nearly suppressing the inner voice that told him, from years of Jane's chiding, to use the word *present*; *gift* was middle-class frippery.

72

He was summoned by Nathaniel to campus to "discuss the issue at hand," with no details beyond the time they would meet in his office. In anticipation of appearing before a small panel of colleagues, Paul dressed in his sports coat and slacks, with printouts of his previous comments for Elena over the semester in hand to prove how much academic attention he had devoted to her.

New copies of the student literary magazine lay fanned out on a table by the entrance to the English department. He'd been curious before to see whether Elena had mentioned him in her bio, as it would have been put into production well before their dispute. Now it could be public evidence of his role as a helpful teacher to whom she'd previously expressed gratitude.

Among the self-congratulatory bios rife with quirky dietary predilections and coffee-consumption habits, her entry was just-the-facts minimalist: "Elena Martin is a first-year student." He'd held out a little hope, still, that she might have an ethnic background worth noting.

"So, where are we doing this? The faculty lounge?" he asked Nathaniel after he sank into the leather chair in his office and the men traded empty remarks about their respective Thanksgivings. (Paul's mother had had dinner with Marvin and one of his daughters, so he'd happily eaten microwaved pad thai on his own and rewatched, for the first time in years, *The Searchers*.)

"Sorry, what?" Nathaniel asked.

"We obviously can't fit everyone in here. Unless we're reenacting *A Night at the Opera*."

"*A Night at the Opera*?"

Nathaniel had probably never seen a Marx Brothers movie in his life.

"Never mind. Are we having the hearing right here? Is it just a few people?"

Nathaniel's expression shifted.

"We think it's not in your or the department's best interest to have this situation made more public."

"A grade dispute? Who cares?"

"I'm referring to the related situation. With, ah, your car."

"My car? What're you talking about?"

"Elena claims that you promised to get that other essay of hers published if she got into your parked car with you one night," Nathaniel said. "And she alleges that you gave her the D on the last paper because she refused."

"That's ridiculous," Paul said.

"We were able to confirm with a garage that you parked your car there that day and retrieved it at night, several hours after your last class ended."

He flushed with the indignation that covers a trace amount of culpability but quickly recovered his equipoise.

"Yes, that part's true. We were working on her essay together in the student union, as I told you—you can *confirm* with them that I bought us coffees on my credit card, as I recall—and they kicked us out when they closed. We went to a coffee shop first, but it was also closed, and I didn't know where else to go. My time in the garage was going to expire soon, and I suggested we finish working in there so I wouldn't be charged a penalty. As you know, I don't get paid very much here. And I certainly never 'promised' she'd get published. That's the ridiculous part."

"No? You didn't say"—Nathaniel consulted his desktop screen—"something to the effect of, 'I think it'll get published if you work with me'?"

"I'm sure I did—to boost her confidence, since she didn't think it would be accepted. And I said 'work with me,' not 'sleep with me,' which is what you're clearly implying. I was going out of my way to help her. Jesus, Nathaniel. I thought assisting students with their writing was what I was hired to do, not a fireable offense."

Nathaniel typed on his computer.

"How about saying that you could push the seats back in your car so you would be, quote, 'more comfortable'?"

"So she had space to use her laptop!" Paul said. "Obviously I meant *shift* them back horizontally, not *recline* them."

"And when she did get the paper accepted for publication, did you tell her she should get drunk in a bar with you?"

"Of *course* not."

"She's completely making that up? You didn't invite her to go to a bar with you?"

He remembered what he'd said to her.

"I told her she should go out and celebrate," Paul said. "And I guess I must've told her about the time I published my first essay in my college lit mag, I went out with friends and my writing professor, and maybe I jokingly mentioned that we drank a lot that night. But to take that as a suggestion that she and I—"

"Did you also say something to the effect that you were"—Nathaniel nervously smiled as he read from the screen—"'obsessed with muscular and toned butts'?"

"Obsessed with *muscular and toned butts*? What the hell?"

"You didn't say it?"

"Does *that* sound like something *I* would say?"

"She claims you were discussing the use of the conjunction 'but,' then you repeated the word multiple times and said something like, 'Not that I'm obsessed with butts.' And then you described the ideal butt as being 'muscular' and 'toned.'"

"If I did, it was obviously a joke," Paul said. "And I apparently said I *wasn't* obsessed with—wait, now I remember the muscular thing. I was saying a sentence that starts with 'but'—b-u-t—should be a muscular sentence. Or have a muscular tone, whatever. Then I suppose I made another joke. A pun. Sorry for having a sense of fucking humor."

He was protesting too much, playing defense, reciting the slanderous accusations while failing to poke holes in them by way of dubious rhetorical devices. He should have asked for a lawyer from the start—not that he could afford one.

Nathaniel typed more, each keystroke further incriminating him.

"C'mon, man. I *know* you find this as absurd as I do," Paul said.

"Are you disputing any of the observable facts?" Nathaniel asked, ignoring the subtextual appeal to their shared gender. "I have to notate that if you are. Did you definitively not say anything similar to what she attributes to you?"

"No, I—well, yes, I technically *said* those things, or versions of them, but she misinterpreted them all. I mean, I understand how she could have taken them that way. And if my words caused her to feel—" He was both confessing and making a conditional apology, the most evasive, least placating show of remorse. "Doesn't my intent count for something? Is it just 'he said, she heard'?"

"Paul. A male lecturer suggests to a first-year girl that if she works with him she'll get something published, and talks about being obsessed with—or not obsessed with—muscular, toned butts, then invites her to edit it in his car, where he says they can push back the seats, inside a garage at night. Just think for a second about the optics."

Optics: an ugly word that had sprung up in recent years and was now used by stupid people trying to appear smart, yet another chunk of the once poetically homespun language mauled by corporate strategy sessions, the American vernacular so disfigured that a man whose vocabulary barely extended beyond *tremendous* and *horrible* and *very, very strong* could become the country's most audible speaker.

"I'm an adjunct instructor now," he said. "Not a lecturer. Remember?"

Nathaniel pursed his lips. At least he, and presumably Elena, hadn't brought up the cleavage glimpse, a less defensible transgression. It was only his words that had gotten him into trouble.

"Just give me the verdict," Paul said.

"The administration has terminated your contract. As the cause for firing was an allegation of misconduct, we can't rehire you. You're entitled to appeal or, if you really want to, file a lawsuit, but my advice to you—as a friend, not your chair—is that you'll almost certainly lose, it'll draw public attention to your case, and you'll be wasting a lot of time and money and rendering yourself untouchable for future employment." Nathaniel had on a face suitable for expressing condolences at a funeral. "I'm very sorry, Paul. I believe everything you've said about your intentions, for what it's worth, and I fought the good fight, but there was too much working against you. I got them to agree to pay you for the final weeks of the semester, and I'll be happy to write you a strong letter of recommendation. Though I'd have to acknowledge this situation."

Paul doubted he'd put up any fight for him, good or not. Nathaniel was just another moral mouse fearful of putting himself in the crosshairs. A lot of help that scarlet letter of recommendation would be, too—if anyone were even hiring.

He planned to leave without saying a word. Nathaniel didn't deserve the chance to apologize further and expiate his guilt. Let him sit in his lukewarm, pusillanimous puddle of good optics.

"Is she Latina?" Paul asked at the door.

"What?"

"Elena. Is she Latina? Latinx, Hispanic, whatever the right term is now?"

"I don't know, nor do I see how that's relevant," Nathaniel said. "And if you're trying to impute a racial motive to her complaint, that's a very dangerous road to go down, and I think it's best addressed through lawyers."

"No, I wasn't imputing—forget it," he said, leaving without satisfaction of any kind.

73

On Saturday he was cleared to refill his Adderall prescription. He needed it to get back in the freelance game, rustle up some pitches, reacquaint himself with old editors, introduce himself to new ones; with a book on the way he finally had a shot at the splashier national outlets.

After this final paycheck from the college, he wasn't sure where his next was coming from. Until he found another job, he'd drive full time, and with the medication assisting him, he was going to try for a big night.

But first he had to go to his mother's birthday dinner. He drove her to a seafood place in Riverdale with beige faux leather banquettes and large-font menus catering to its senior citizen patrons taking advantage of the early bird special—a dining population Paul felt more at home with, anyway, especially in their preference for quiet atmospheres. It was their first time dining out together since he'd moved in; he'd tried to avoid the self-pitying experience of being a bachelor at a restaurant with his elderly mother-cum-roommate.

Now a third wheel—and an unemployed bachelor, too, though he wasn't sharing that information with her.

"I heard the cruise was a great time," Paul gamely said when Marvin arrived.

"It was," Marvin said. "Except for the family next to us for the first week. They had little kids, but they were Japanese, so I figured they'd be quiet and obedient. Guess what happened?"

"They weren't," said Paul.

"They were loud."

"They weren't so bad at first," his mother said. "At first they—"

"Loud as hell," Marvin blustered. "Roughhousing and crying around the clock. I complained to the management, but they didn't do anything about it."

"I guess you'll have to change the title of your memoir to *One Complaint*," Paul said. "Or *A Supposedly Fun Thing I'll Probably Do Again*."

Marvin angled his ear toward him. "Whuh?"

"So it sounds like they were normal children. Just goes to show that you can't make judgments about people based on their ethnicity."

"Usually you can." Marvin held up a finger of ostensible wisdom. "Forty-seven years as a doctor treating all kinds, you can tell a few things about them just from their name and age. Jews and Asians are the healthiest, except not the older Chinese men, because they smoke, and some Jews eat too much. The women and younger Chinese are good. Old Italians and Greeks, forget it—overeat, drink like fish, never exercise. Young Italians are either very fit or very fat. Same with Hispanics. The Blacks—"

"Should we order a bottle of wine or do people want their own glasses?" Paul quickly asked.

He hardly spoke the rest of dinner. Marvin, an indefatigable monologist, didn't notice.

"Would you like another glass of wine, sir?" the weary-looking waitress asked him.

"Yes," Marvin said. "But you should say, 'Would you like *a* glass of wine,' not 'another glass of wine.' My father taught me that."

She smiled with strained pleasantness.

"Thank you, I'll remember that," she said.

When the bill came, Marvin grabbed it in a showy gesture, slapped an American Express into the card holder, and immediately gave it back to the waitress. When he filled out the tip upon her return, Paul saw he'd given 15 percent.

"I'm happy to get the tip," he offered.

"Already paid it," Marvin said.

"Well, I'm happy to supplement it with cash. It's nice for the waitress, since they don't get taxed."

"We're fine. I gave fifteen percent."

"I think the going rate these days is twenty."

"Twenty is for excellent service. The appetizers took fifteen minutes, and I had to remind her we'd asked for more bread. You give people extra for doing nothing, they get used to it, creates a vicious cycle."

"Or maybe they feel better about other people being kind to them for doing a difficult job and try harder next time," Paul said.

Marvin's rheumy blue eyes stared him down.

"When you're the one who pays the bill, you get to choose the tip," he said.

Paul couldn't tell if Marvin meant this as a truism—that the check payer, in general, decides on the tip—or if it were an ad hominem taunt, that when Paul made enough money to treat the table, he'd be in control of the gratuity.

"And from what your mother tells me," Marvin added, dispelling any doubts, "that won't be anytime soon."

A tap of rage opened in Paul's chest, flooding outward. Was this how he came off to his students, to Elena? Couldn't they see that he was on their side, allied against the Marvins of the world—or did they just see them as a grotesque monolith, a lame herd of out-to-pasture men railing against their imminent redundancy, aging despots clinging to power?

Marvin drove his mother back to his house. Once they were out of sight, Paul returned to the restaurant and handed the waitress a twenty, apologizing for a miscalculation in the tip. In the restroom he unscrewed the new bottle of Adderall with the feral hunger of a bear breaking into a camper's food and swallowed forty milligrams.

74

After his time off Adderall, the high dosage sloshed through his system like a gallon of coffee as he sped into Manhattan. Normally a defensive driver, he treated the ride like a video game, weaving and passing on the Henry Hudson Parkway, accelerating through lights just as they turned red.

He was in the flow state of driving, cutting time between fares to the absolute minimum. He downed another pill at eleven; he could stay up till the wee hours and make a killing; who needed demeaning adjunct wages? At midnight he picked up two men outside a bar in Tribeca, their destination another on the Lower East Side. They jostled into the car, both in Santa Claus outfits. Hordes of young men and women in Manhattan were also in Christmas costume that night, for that stupid annual custom Paul had managed to avoid during his years in South Slope.

"Driver, we've grown bored of this den of vice," one said in a pompous, put-on English accent. "Chauffeur us to the women of ill repute, posthaste."

Paul nodded diplomatically as he started off. He was used by now to finance bros and their peacocking assertions of dominance camouflaged as jocularity. The key was not to give them any material to work with.

"Go east, young man," the other guy said.

"*Middle-aged* man," corrected his friend.

"Tragic, isn't it? That the automobile driver, symbol of American self-reliance and freedom, has been effectively emasculated through this geolocational service as he scurries from pickup to pickup."

"Neutered, as he scrounges for tips."

"Castrated, as he takes his directions from a phone app."

These men, perhaps a decade and change younger than he, were in the last generation to have grown up as brutes, inculcated with the values of "toxic masculinity." In a few years their kind would be at the precipice of extinction, at least in New York City, and good riddance.

"But the nice thing about this, as opposed to a cab, is you actually have a chance at getting a white guy as your driver."

"Right. As opposed to a dude whose name on the ID card is a fucking paragraph."

"And who doesn't know where the fuck he's going."

"Because he just snuck into the country under a fence."

"And he sucks at driving."

"Because he's used to driving two miles an hour through marketplaces full of goats and shit."

They were saying these things not just out of their native racism, not just because they were granted permission by their president, but also as a power play, a test: would Paul chime in, would he dissent, or would he merely sit there, quiet and timorous, afraid to provoke a confrontation or say anything that might tarnish his rating.

Their remarks grew more rancid as they drove, touching upon women, homosexuals, transgender people. It wasn't possible they were this ghastly, even while drunk or on coke; they had to be ratcheting it up for their captive audience.

At a stoplight three blocks from their drop-off, one of them, observing a lineup outside a bar, said, "Check out the one in the green skirt."

"She's twelve years old," his friend sang.

"My point exactly," the first sang back in the same melody.

They tittered like schoolboys.

He hadn't said anything that time the couple had had sex in his backseat, and they'd still given him a bad tip.

The light turned green, but Paul didn't hit the gas. The car behind honked.

"Dude, it's green."

"Out," Paul said.

"What?"

"Get out of my car."

"We're not there yet."

"Yeah, *Dad*, we're not there yet."

"I don't care," Paul said. "I don't want to listen to another one of your vile comments."

"Ooh, *vile comments*," one of the men said. "Keep fucking driving. We paid for the whole ride."

Paul put the car in park. "I'll refund your money. You can walk the rest of the way."

His back was to them and he felt exposed. It was a terrible sensation, the anticipation of being struck while defenseless.

The driver behind him leaned on the horn.

He waited, tense and braced, more jammed cars joining the chorus. This was unlike all the other verbal confrontations he'd had. There was a potential for violence, and his anger and anxiety bubbled mostly in his body, not his mind.

He'd never been in a physical altercation in his life. If they made a move, he'd grab the ice scraper, untouched this winter, from the floor on the passenger side. It wasn't much of a weapon, and he was outnumbered, but he could jab with it, and they were intoxicated by something.

They didn't hit him, though. They didn't even speak until, just before they slammed the door, one tossed in, "Get a real job, fucking loser."

As he drove up the FDR Drive to head home, the prick's parting words lingered. Maybe it was that the elision of "you" had felt like an erasure of his personhood.

No, that was euphemizing it: even at forty-six, it still hurt to be insulted, however generically. Words matter.

At Thirty-fifth Street, instead of continuing north, he swerved off the FDR and onto the Long Island Expressway.

75

It wasn't hard to find the address on his phone, and the drive took just over half an hour without traffic, through progressively exclusive waterfront hamlets, until he reached a bucolic two-lane road that funneled into a stiletto of land. No movement anywhere, no cars out; in the summer you'd likely hear crickets and peepers. Hedges barricaded all the houses. Occasionally a fraction of tennis court or swimming pool peeked through a gap.

Paul's car crawled past the home, which was completely hidden, likely set back hundreds of feet from the road. A security gate with a darkened booth blocked a driveway. Tall wooden fences, their coiled tops silvered in the moonlight, further discouraged intruders.

If only his viewers could see where Colin Mackey lived, the costly lengths he went to for segregation and protection from the barbarians—though they probably deluded themselves into the fantasy that they, too, could someday attain such wealth and would also have to defend their ten-million-dollar homes like medieval lords stocking a moat with alligators.

He executed a three-point turn and scoped out the property from the reverse direction, in the closer lane. As he inched toward the security gate, a figure stepped out of the booth, the white cone of a flashlight preceding its advance. Paul's instinct was to flee, but that would only arouse suspicion, maybe occasion a call to the authorities. He stopped and rolled down his window.

"Can I help you?" said the man, his face obscured in the beam of light trained on Paul's face.

"I'm a little lost," Paul said. "Trying to find my way back to the LIE and my phone's not getting service."

The man gave him directions. Paul thanked him and took off before he could get his license plate.

He'd sometimes wondered why the super-rich were fine with causing societal collapse; they had to know that the chaos would eventually boomerang around to them, too. They must figure their money meant they'd always be able to insulate themselves from cataclysm, with curlicues of barbed wire and security personnel and surveillance systems for their remote homes. They never had to experience the primitive fear Paul had with his passengers earlier, completely vulnerable to attack while their backs were turned.

76

He was awarded a zero-star rating and no tip from the obscene duo, and, as punishment from the ride-sharing company for "verbal abuse of a passenger," one month's suspension. He could dispute it, but the injustice inflicted upon him by the college would be replicated even more heartlessly here, under amoral profiteers who viewed him as anonymous disposable labor. If he'd had proof, if he'd had the presence of mind to record their comments on his phone, he would have had a chance. That was all anyone believed anymore—and even then, not always, not when the latest technology could fool anyone, not when the administration had convinced the citizenry to discredit their own lying eyes and ears.

Forget them all. He was a writer, a lone wolf, no conforming institutionalist or timid company man. He wasn't made to operate in their exploitative systems. His wits, and *The Luddite Manifesto*, would save him.

77

Paul eased up on the Adderall and slept late for a few days, cruised around Van Cortlandt Park on longer jogs spliced with intervals of sprinting, augmented his push-ups and pull-ups, watched DVDs, reread some of the books from college that had gotten him into writing. Self-care, it was now called. An already cosseted, solipsistic nation convinced that the remedy to its woes was further pampering.

On Saturday afternoon he saw Mabel. She wore, for the first time in his presence, the cashmere sweater he'd bought her. She asked to see a new animated movie, so he took her to the Nitehawk Theater off Prospect Park, then, at her request, a café that served overpriced organic food.

"What'd you think of the movie?" he asked as they were served a grilled chicken sandwich for him and a farro salad for her.

"I thought it was really good," she said. "Thanks for taking me. What did you think?"

Her Emily Post routine was conspicuous, as if Jane had coached or bribed her to be nice to him. She'd probably forced her to wear the sweater, too. Paul almost wished she were sullen; at least he'd know he was seeing the real her. As she forked a ladylike bite of farro into her mouth, he could envision her a few years ahead, a teenager with her own life that she didn't share at all, thoughts and feelings she jealously guarded from him like a diary with a lock. He'd turn into one of those divorced men who dropped in on birthdays and holidays and graduations, a living ghost in his daughter's life, the dad she barely saw and rarely talked about, until one day she'd be an adult who wanted nothing to do with him and sourced all her psychological defects to her absent father.

He should confront the issue head-on. Acknowledge his failings without letting her off the hook for her own behavior. Ask questions and let her speak her mind and listen. Above all, emphasize that he loved her, would always love her, and though things weren't great now between them, she was what mattered most to him, and he'd do everything he could to repair their relationship. It would be an uncomfortable conversation for them both, but he'd screw up his courage and get through it. That's what a good father did.

"I thought it was good, too," he said, cleared his throat, and took a bite of his sandwich.

78

He had emailed his book editor a few times, hinting that he had some free time for edits without mentioning the reason for it, and each time Charles had apologized floridly (more than one use of "alas") for not getting to it yet.

Paul was preparing to leave for a date with Lauren when his ringing phone displayed the name of Charles Haskell. He picked up excitedly; it had been a while since he'd had a business call in which real work was conducted, and the drought had left him feeling increasingly unnecessary, a person without whom the world of commerce could rotate quite merrily.

"Do you have some time to talk?" Charles asked, his cautious pitch reminiscent of Nathaniel's when he'd called to say his position had been downsized.

The book was not what Charles thought he'd be getting from the proposal or Paul's original opening chapters. It was a jeremiad, a freewheeling tirade, the arguments scattershot, and not in a way that fruitfully resonated with the theme of distractibility. He had expected a carefully reasoned and restrained book for fellow academics, something evenhanded. This, frankly, was not that.

Paul hadn't met Charles in person, and they'd spoken only a couple of times over the phone, but his editor's picture on the university press site—bow-tied with thick owlish glasses, like a computer programmer from the 1980s—and email prose style suggested the disposition of a man who'd never gone a day without shaving. He'd wanted Cole Porter and Schubert, and Paul had given him the Clash and the Sex Pistols. But

Paul wasn't daunted by laborious edits, and if a stylistic overhaul was what it took to get *The Luddite Manifesto* published, he would do it.

"Well, I wrote this draft pretty quickly, so I expected it might be a little rough. My apologies for the extent of the roughness. I'm happy to make edits, of course. Do you want to take a pass at it, or should I just start revising with this in mind?"

"My email to your school address bounced back yesterday," Charles said in a curious tone. Paul hadn't checked his inbox since his firing. Already erased from institutional memory with his body barely cold.

"Yeah, I've left it, now the semester's over. I'm focusing full time on writing these days. I'll send you my personal email."

"Then I called you, but your phone was disconnected."

"You had my landline. I moved over the summer and I just have my cell now. I had to upgrade to a smartphone, actually." Paul chortled. "I suppose I should revise the prologue."

Charles didn't laugh. "Your agent had an out-of-office email, so I called your department to track you down. And I was told you no longer work there. When I asked why, they said it was an internal matter. I asked to speak to your department chair, and after I explained who I was, he said he was obligated to tell me."

"It's not true," Paul said.

"The student's lying?"

"She's not *lying*, per se. She has a vendetta against me, motivated by a bad grade on a paper, and she twisted my words out of context."

"Your chair said you're not disputing it."

"Because of the legal costs. And it would just drag my name through the mud, and even if I didn't do anything—I mean, I *didn't* do anything—but even then, once the rumor's out there—"

"When I raised the issue in a staff meeting, some of the younger women expressed their fears over working with you."

"Their *fears*? Are you kidding? I'm never even going to meet them in person! What do they think I'm gonna do?"

"I have to remind you," Charles said in a calm voice, as if trying to subdue a toddler throwing a tantrum, "that we have a morality clause here, which you agreed to in your contract, that stipulates that we can revoke a book's publication if the author does something that might diminish our reputation. You can keep the portion of the advance we've already paid you, but we think you'll be best served by publishing the book elsewhere."

A sickly sensation seeped through him akin to when Julian Wolf's book had taken off, the feeling of squandered and irrecoverable opportunity.

"I know I don't know you all that well, so maybe this isn't my place to say"—Charles paused—"but I was a little concerned by . . . the tenor of your writing. Is everything . . . fine for you right now?"

"Absolutely," Paul said. "Everything fine for you?"

"For me? Yes, but I wanted to make sure—"

"Then everything's fine for everyone. The whole world is fine. Hunky-dory. Let's not upset anyone or do anything to diminish their reputations."

He pressed the red icon to end the call, the recompense of prematurely and loudly hanging up eliminated on a cell phone. He felt even more wronged for initially apologizing to *him* for the state of his manuscript—after essentially being told it was unreadable.

But maybe Charles's issues with his writing had just been cover for the morality clause. He should have expressed more remorse about the incident with Elena, said it was a misunderstanding that he felt terrible about, to both Charles and Nathaniel. And to Elena, if necessary. He'd been too pugnacious, too lawyerly. If the slew of controversies like this in recent years had shown anything, it was that defending yourself never went over well.

Nor did apologizing, though, in the end. Nothing would have satisfied them short of renouncing his manifold privileges with theatrics of kowtowing and self-flagellation, the hara-kiri of autocancellation. Of *amenability*. At least if you stood up for yourself, you could maintain your pride.

And fusty Charles was wrong about the manuscript. He'd find another publisher, one with more subversive taste, not to mention courage. He'd get his voice out there, somehow.

79

At dinner, Lauren told him a long story about how Colin's chair had gotten stuck at the wrong incline just before airtime Thursday, and she'd had to personally hunt for a suitable backup, finding one with only a minute to go.

He waited for an opening. It had been a few weeks since he'd last inquired about his chances of being booked on the show, plenty of time for them to reach a decision.

"I don't suppose Emily has said anything about whether they want to have me as a guest?" he asked.

"She did," Lauren said without looking up from the dessert wine menu. "They didn't think it'd be a good fit. Sorry to be the bearer of bad news."

He tried to appear impervious. "I thought you said she liked my book."

"She read another thing you wrote, too. Something about global warming. She didn't think Colin would like it."

"Global warming?" Paul couldn't remember addressing the topic directly, and nothing in his sweep of his online writing had touched on it.

"In some magazine I hadn't heard of—I forget the name? She showed me the copy. It had a picture of a mountain on the cover. I didn't read the article."

It was an environmental journal he'd written a short essay for, when Mabel was a toddler, about having a child in the midst of impending natural apocalypse. The journal had a minuscule circulation, had paid him probably a hundred dollars plus a few contributor copies, and was now defunct, with no website of its archives.

"They found a copy?" he asked, stunned that they'd managed to track one down. Then, afraid it sounded like he'd had his cover blown, he said, "I wrote that a long time ago, and I've really changed my thinking on it, if that's what they're afraid of."

"She was also confused that when she looked into your book, it had a different title with the publisher. *The Luddite Manifesto*, I think she said."

"We thought about giving it an ironic title at first, but we're sticking with *The Technophile's Manifesto*. Not enough people know what Luddites are, anyway."

"And she said it's being published by some small college. They usually only book authors with the New York publishers."

"It's a highly respected academic press," Paul said. "They publish much more serious work than the corporate houses."

Lauren didn't say anything.

"You can't lobby for me at all? You're the senior producer. Don't they listen to what you say?"

"Sometimes." She smiled slyly. "But things are about to change next week."

"Why?"

"I didn't want to tell you and jinx it until I get the official offer on Monday"—the smile broadened—"but I'm finally going to be an executive producer."

If she were executive producer, then she could override the booker's rejection—it might just take longer.

"That's amazing!" He waited a beat so he didn't look too single-minded. "So your title changes next week?"

"No, I'll give my two weeks' notice once I accept it, which runs through Christmas vacation, then I'll start in the New Year."

"Two weeks' notice . . . for a promotion?"

"A promotion?" She was also confused. "Oh, you thought the job's at *Mackey*." The position, she informed him, was for a daytime talk show at another network.

That was it, then: months of this pricey charade, all to be rejected and with no shot in the future.

He couldn't break up with her immediately; he didn't want to have to defend himself against truthful accusations of using her for access to Mackey. He'd do it over the phone later that week. Cowardly, but less painful for them both.

He was unable to come up with a plausible excuse to go back to Riverdale at that hour. Or perhaps the desire to role-play professor and student and sleep with the enemy one more time was too strong. The moment he stepped through Lauren's door, though, surrounded by her high-end furniture, about to drink a cocktail he didn't want, his libido softened. Maybe the booker's rejection was for the best. If he spoke his mind on the air, he'd just be dismissed as a leftist kook, mocked on social media, reduced to a risible meme. He'd been kidding himself to think it would accomplish anything; his appeals to his mother had only made her position more hidebound. He'd simply wanted a moment of glory to distinguish himself from the Russes and Larissas with their courteous protests.

He was trying to figure out a preamble about not being in a good place for a relationship when Lauren's mother called.

"Mom?" she asked. "What's wrong?"

Paul gave her some space as Lauren teared up over evidently bad news. When she hung up and restated the details—her father's prostate cancer had recurred, they'd caught it early enough that they had reason to hope for the best, but he would have to undergo chemotherapy again—he held and consoled her as she mopped her face on his shirt, reminding her that her dad had beaten this once before and that his own father had overcome the same common diagnosis, feeling a natural empathy for a person in pain yet simultaneously wondering how she could justify her boss's pitiless stance on health care, and most of all kicking himself for not being cutthroat enough to go through with the breakup at the restaurant.

80

He was running in Van Cortlandt Park on a trail fringed by leafless oaks when Jane called.

"I'm jogging," he said between cloudy gasps of wintry air. "Anything pressing?"

"Uh," Jane said, "no, I guess not."

"What is it? You're still taking her to Steve's mother's for Christmas, right?"

"Yes. Never mind. We can do this another time."

"Jane, what's going on?"

She took in an audible breath but didn't speak. He stopped running.

"I'm sure you've noticed some changes in Mabel the last few months," she said.

"Some."

"It's all very normal for a young girl. I went through a similar thing when I was a teenager." Jane forced a laugh. "So I guess she's a little precocious."

"Oh, God," Paul said. "Does she have an eating disorder? She's been mostly eating salads, but I haven't noticed any—"

"It's not that. Mabel—"

Jane started crying. Paul hadn't heard her break down in a while. When they were together and she wept, no matter how acrimonious things had been up until that point, it always activated his caretaking instinct.

"What is it?" he asked softly.

"She doesn't want to stay with you anymore," Jane managed through a sob. "I tried arguing with her, but she won't budge, and I don't want to force her to do something against her will. I think it'll make things worse in the long run. I'm sorry. I'm so, so sorry, Paul."

Bare branches slivered the gray December sky. A crow perched overhead cackled. Paul opened his mouth but no words came. There was nothing to say. His daughter didn't want to see him.

He'd been rejected in affairs of the heart before, and though he'd never been the invulnerable type, he had always thought of himself as possessing a hide toughened by years of freelancing and striking out his fair share. But this cut deeper than any unforeseen breakup, any spurned essay. His father's brusque words that night at the kitchen table, doubting his ability to support a family, clattered around his head. He'd long ago given up on that qualification of fatherhood, ceding fiduciary duties to Steve, but he'd thought of himself as highly capable on the interpersonal front. Now his daughter was telling him he was no longer needed there, either. He was irrelevant, a paternal skeuomorph, with useless design features of his past self: a wallet with no money, an apartment she wouldn't visit, a lap she didn't want to be held in.

"I'm sure it'll just be while you're at your mother's," Jane said, sniffling. "Once you move back to Brooklyn, she'll come around. And you'll still see her in Park Slope on weekends, she just won't sleep over. It's just a phase we have to get through."

"Did she say why?" Paul asked, though part of him didn't want to know.

"I . . . don't know."

"Come on, Jane. At least give me that."

"She said that . . . that things seem sad with you now."

"She thinks I'm depressed?"

"No, not depressed. That your—that . . ."

"Please, just say it."

"She said your life seems sad," Jane said. "And it makes her sad to be around it."

Had it been an immature charge—that his mother's apartment and Riverdale were boring, that she didn't like his old movies, that he took her to "gross" museums—it wouldn't have bothered him that much. But to be pitied by your young child was terrible; to be shunned by her because of that pity was even worse.

"This isn't an easy question to ask," he said, the idea crashing with sudden force, "but are you sure Steve hasn't done anything?"

"You're suggesting *he* put the idea in her head?"

"No. Are you sure that Steve hasn't done anything . . . untoward with Mabel, and that's why she's going through this phase?"

"Are you fucking kidding me, Paul? You think Steve has done something *untoward* with her?"

"I'm just asking, if maybe that could explain—"

"Steve is a *fantastic* stepfather. He works with her on her homework every night, he reads *Harry Potter* to her at bedtime, he takes her to all her birthday parties and playdates when he's around. Whereas I hear you just let her watch TV at your place. *You*, of all people."

"Okay. I was just making sure we were covering all our—"

"And here I was feeling sorry for you. Jesus Christ, Paul. You're a real piece of work."

"I'm sorry," he said.

He staggered home after the call, his muscles sapped. It hadn't been the right moment, but even if it had, he would've been afraid to ask about Mabel's allowing Steve to read to her. Paul had refused to entertain *Harry Potter*, deeming the series unworthy based entirely on its gargantuan readership without ever having scanned a page. He pictured Steve's reading it aloud in her room, which he'd seen just a few times. It was spacious, with a wrought-iron bed, dolls and stuffed animals neatly arranged, the walls painted a warm pink, the windows opening onto their garden. A nice room for a girl to grow up in, in a nice brownstone on a nice street in Brooklyn. Steve was, in Jane's phrase, good at life.

What had he amounted to, after four and a half decades? No job, no prospects. A few essays that no one had cared about when they'd appeared, most of them now nearly impossible to locate (except, it seemed, for bloodhound-like employees at totalitarian news networks). He'd passed up Julian Wolf's offer years ago to be his research assistant because the job wasn't stable, because he'd wanted to be near his sick father, but those weren't the real reasons. It was because he knew, in his marrow, that he was a good writer—but not *good enough*. Even if he hadn't failed at that task, he wouldn't have made much of the opportunity afterward, would have spent his days alternately treading water and grasping the side of the pool. He was his father's son, unwilling to test the mettle of his talents for fear of confirming their modesty. He didn't have the killer instinct, as Mackey had said of the president, a greater determinant of the careerist's success than skill. He wasn't the type to go for the jugular.

And after his work? He'd lost touch with nearly all his friends, alienated the remainder. No real partner, and if he went back on the dating scene, good luck finding takers for an unemployed, morality-clause-violating writer who lived with his mother in Riverdale. An ex-wife who viewed him as feckless, a daughter who found him too tragic to be around. She might come around in a few years—but maybe none of this would be around in a few years. He'd always told himself he was working to improve the world, to leave a better one behind for Mabel. Yet he'd been deceiving himself there, too. He'd led a small existence by any measurement, even those taken within his cloistered literary microcosm. He'd justified his inaction outside of writing as the regimented behavior of a dispassionate intellectual, regarding the scene from a distance, coolly pontificating without biasing himself by leaping into the mayhem. But in the end he was no better than Russ, Nathaniel, Charles, all the white-collar professionals unwilling to take a real stand for what was right out of fear of losing what they had. If he died tomorrow, his legacy would be nothing but mixed memories from a handful of people. He hadn't even given Mabel his last name. And when she went, all traces of his time on earth would vanish.

He wasn't good at life.

He passed wordlessly by his mother in her armchair in the living room. He hadn't yet contacted his agent about the nullification of his book contract, nor had she reached out to him. She was probably finished with the project, too. He could try selling it himself to another small publisher, but even with her help he'd barely found a home for the more "evenhanded" proposal. Others would take issue with the same things Charles had, or discover his firing from the college and express their own discomfort about working with an unreconstructed ogre such as himself. Meek cogs cowed by their sanctimonious left flank, terrified of the monstrous right, waving a white flag of "civility" to the passionate intensities of the worst.

In his room he posted the entirety of *The Luddite Manifesto* to a RealNews article about social media data harvesting, in a marathon thread of four-thousand-character chunks. His publisher could fire him, but he wouldn't be silenced. The people who were receptive to his ideas could still read him. The thread would go viral; it would attract the attention of another publisher; he'd make Charles regret his myopic decision.

Minutes after he finished posting the final piece of the thread, his phone trembled.

RealNews does not permit the publication of comments intended to sell a commercial product or promote a personal brand, read the notification. Your account will be suspended for fourteen days. Any additional infractions will result in deactivation.

He lay on his bed. The crack in the ceiling looked wider, almost wide enough to stick a finger into, a major river on a map—or, more accurately, a fault line.

He had nothing to lose.

81

Why would you want to eat dinner in my *office*?" Lauren asked Sunday morning in bed.

She sounded suspicious of the admittedly cockamamie plan, perhaps thinking he was still angling for a last-minute spot on the show.

"I don't know. I just woke up with this idea to bring you a nice dinner there," Paul said. "Something better than the catered food. I guess I wanted your co-workers to see."

"Why?"

"You've had a rough time lately, with your father and everything, and I thought you deserve a romantic gesture in front of them, before you leave the job. But maybe it's stupid. We don't have to do it."

Her smile remained half-closed, like that of a shy teenager with braces, as she nuzzled her head against his neck in affirmation—her first expression of real tenderness he could recall, the softening possibly a byproduct of her father's fragile health. With anyone else he might have felt a wave of guilt. But certain aims required one to discard conventional rules of decorum. And besides, as she'd said, Lauren could take care of herself.

82

Paul handed the screw-top bottle of wine to the same security guard as last time and carried a bag of takeout Japanese food through the metal detector. He wore different pants from the ones that had set it off last time, and he passed through without incident or inspection.

Kelsey met him at the elevator and again escorted him to Lauren's desk. Paul set up their dinner as the night-shift employees swam about and closed captioning dropped in clusters of abysmal language over Colin Mackey's face on the wall-mounted screens.

"I got extra sushi for you, too," Paul told Kelsey.

"You didn't have to do that," she said.

"I insist." He poured a plastic cup of Cabernet and served her a California roll. "And a little wine, too."

Lauren joined him shortly after the show ended.

"Aw," she said, eyeing the spread and stashing her office ID card in a zippered pocket inside her bag.

"He even got sushi for me," Kelsey announced from her desk.

They ate and talked about their days. Lauren complained quietly about a human resources meeting that had devoured her entire afternoon.

"Were there any technical problems during the show? Things not working right?" he asked once she was on her second cup of wine.

"No. Why?"

"There was that chair issue recently. I thought maybe these things happened all the time."

"Not really."

"Huh," he said. "You know, I've never actually been on a TV set. Or news studio, whatever you call it. I guess I don't know what they're really like. Or even *look* like."

"It's not very exciting. Especially not our studio. It's pretty bare-bones, not like what you see in movies."

Her voice had taken on the flat tone that prevailed whenever she was bored by the conversation.

"Because there's no audience?"

"That, and Colin likes an intimate space without any clutter. He's pretty old-school."

"Sounds interesting," Paul said.

Her chopsticks swirled a piece of sashimi in a cup of soy sauce.

"Could I maybe see it sometime?" he asked.

"It's a closed studio. Visitors aren't permitted."

"Not during a show, of course."

"There are still no visitors allowed."

"What if no one's there? Like now?"

"There are all sorts of protocols for any outsiders, and if they knew you're a writer, they definitely wouldn't let you in."

"You couldn't get me in?"

"I don't really have much leverage around here anymore. I could show you the control room later."

"Can you see the set from there? Are there windows? Or a door I could poke my head through?"

"No, it's just on screens."

"Oh. Well, I've actually seen a control room before," he lied. "I can't peek in the entrance, just for a second?"

"Definitely not."

"Why? Are there security guards there who won't let me look in?"

"Several." Her forehead squinched. "This isn't for your book or anything, is it?"

"No," he said, acting offended. "I just wanted to see where you worked all these years, before you leave."

Lauren had mentioned before how nearly all the men she'd dated spoke nonstop about their own jobs, rarely asking after hers, and how refreshing it was that Paul was interested in her work.

"Well," she said, cocking her head thoughtfully, "there *is* a fire exit from the set, a door with a little glass window. I guess I could take you there from the other side, and you could get a glimpse of it through the window. If you really want."

"There aren't security guards there?"

"There's one guy, but he likes me. I think he'd let you in. You *really* want to do this? I'm telling you, it's nothing special."

He shrugged. "If it's a hassle, we don't have to. But if you're up for it, I'd love to see it."

She agreed to show him, and when they finished their meal Lauren retrieved her ID card from her bag. She led him out of the office, past the elevators, swiped the card over the reader on the opposite side, and opened the glass door to the studio wing. They entered an identical-looking office, populated by similar-looking drones in their cubicles. Paul wended through the aisles after her.

"Like a rat in a maze, right?" he said.

"Mm," she said.

They reached a nondescript door manned by a security guard chewing a Snickers.

"Lovely Lauren," he said.

"Candy Bar Kevin," she said. "Gotta watch the refined sugar. Worst thing for you."

"It's chocolate. All natural."

She laughed her hawkish laugh as Kevin grinned. Lauren could make small talk, knew how to leave people feeling good about their interactions with her, social skills that, despite having no bearing on their aptitude for their actual jobs, catapulted certain employees in office cultures up the managerial ladder while others with more talent but less easy smiles languished in the cellar.

"Hey, you mind if I let my boyfriend in here? He wants a sort of behind-the-scenes tour."

Kevin smiled at the word *boyfriend*, said he'd make a special exception for her, and opened the door. A hallway lined with closed doors forked twenty feet away. Lauren made a right then turned at other forks: right, left, left.

"Sorry if the boyfriend thing surprised you," she said on the walk. "If I said you were some random guy, he might not have let you in."

"It's fine," Paul said. "I mean, it was nice. So what else is back here?"

"Entrances to other studios and control rooms, storage rooms, freight elevators. I told you, it's boring."

"Is this how Colin exits the building? I imagine he doesn't take the regular elevator."

"No, there's a private exit and elevator for talent. Then they whisk him off in a car to the helipad. Tough life he's got."

They finally reached a metal door with a small gray device that looked different from the ID card reader. Lauren pressed a button and leaned in close.

"My voice is my password," she spoke into it.

The door clicked and she opened it. One more short, unlit hallway connected to another door with a narrow glass panel. Lauren motioned for Paul to look through it.

Near the end of the room, some thirty feet away, was the desk at which Colin Mackey sat for his show, currently unoccupied. The view was from its side, and three cameras at different angles and what looked like a teleprompter were stationed before it. It was a stripped-down set, as she'd said; there was nothing on the floor between the door and the desk, not even any loose cables. The slender window limited him from seeing much else in the room, including whether anyone was there.

"I don't see any monitors, except for the big screen behind the desk," he said. "I thought news sets had them all over the place, showing the thing they're taping."

"You don't really need them unless there's a studio audience," Lauren explained.

"What about if he's interviewing someone remotely? Doesn't he need to see them?"

"There's a small monitor the crew uses that they turn around for the interviews. But Colin thinks it ruins people's focus to have too many screens around. Even him—he says he freezes up when he sees himself onscreen. It's actually a pain in the ass for us."

Paul couldn't help but respect him for this sensible, non-narcissistic restriction. He adjusted his view through the panel but still couldn't see much other than the desk.

"I can't just poke my head inside?" He reached for the knob. "If they can't see me?"

"No," she said, staying his hand. "We're really not supposed to be here. In fact, we should go. I don't want to get Kevin in trouble."

He took a last look and followed her out, past the voice recognition door, then through the hallways—left, left, right, right this time.

83

Paul found a spot for his car right in front of Steve's brownstone on Saturday afternoon. It was too cold and blustery to go to the park, so he proposed to Mabel their old standby activity of checking out books from the library. They walked to the Sixth Avenue branch, where they'd whiled away so many weekend days together, Mabel poring through the aisles of nature books as Paul blissfully read cross-legged on the floor.

This time, when Paul led her to her favorite section, she just stood there.

"I don't really need anything," she said.

"Yeah, but that's the fun of going to the library. You never know what you'll find."

"Steve took me to the bookstore last weekend. I've got enough books for a while."

"Oh." He wondered why she'd agreed to come to the library in the first place. "Well, should we just get an early dinner? Maybe at the diner?"

She agreed without enthusiasm. At the South Slope diner she ordered the kale Caesar.

"How about pancakes?" Paul asked.

She said something he couldn't hear over the music. He asked her to repeat it.

"Steve made us French toast this morning."

After all these years, Paul still didn't know how to make French toast.

"Well, I'll get them, and you can have some of mine," he said, though he didn't want pancakes for dinner.

When the food came, Mabel picked at her salad and declined a bite of his meal.

"Mabel," he said. "I hope you know that it's important to stand up for what you believe in. Even if others don't understand why you're doing it, or disagree with it, if you know in your heart that it's the right thing to do, you have to do it."

She listened as she swallowed a morsel of kale.

"A lot of people right now, in government and in regular life, aren't really defending what they know is right. There's a famous quote that goes something like, 'The only thing necessary for the triumph of evil is for good people to do nothing.' You understand that idea?"

She nodded, scratched a rosy blotch of eczema on her neck, and drank some water. His speech hadn't left the mark he'd hoped it would.

"Sure you don't want any pancakes?"

"I'm sure," she said.

He walked her home after their dinner. It was already dark out. They didn't speak until they reached the gate to Jane's brownstone.

"Hey." He clamped his hand over hers on the latch of the gate. "I love you. You know that, right?"

"Yeah," she said, squirming her hand free and unlatching the gate.

He'd blamed the president, TV shows, phones and iPads, failed birthday parties, anyone and everything for why his daughter didn't want to be around him anymore. But maybe it was simply his fault. He'd shown up for his appointed rounds but was too straitjacketed by his own thoughts and values—"checked out," as she'd said that time in the car—to pay real attention to his daughter and give her what she wanted as opposed to what he thought she needed. Good parents should guide their children, not dictate to them—his father and mother had inadvertently taught him this lesson—yet he couldn't follow his own advice. His intuition in the hospital after her birth had been right. He wasn't cut out to be a father.

"Hey, there, kiddo," Steve said when he opened the door. "Hi, Paul. You guys have fun?"

"Uh-huh," Mabel said as she wriggled out of her jacket. Steve hung it on a hook, securing it with the little loop in the back.

"Your cheeks are bright red," he said. "You look like a little raspberry."

"It's freezing out."

Steve placed his hands over Mabel's cheeks and rubbed. Paul used to do that for her when they came in from the cold.

"Better?" he asked. She nodded. "Bradley's waiting to play video games with you. One hour, max."

Mabel started off.

"Can I take a picture of you?" Paul asked.

She looked confused. "You never take pictures with your phone."

"Can I, just this once?"

She posed, unsmiling, as if for a mug shot. He took a photo, his first ever on his phone.

She turned to leave, but Paul said, "Wait—give me a hug." She took a step back to him and, arms passively dangling, consented to a hug. He inhaled the lavender and baby-powder aroma of her head.

"Goodbye, Mabes," he said, and after a couple of seconds had passed, she ran upstairs.

"Sorry—I know you don't like her playing video games, but she really bonds with Bradley over them, and we're strict about cutting them off," Steve said.

Paul mumbled his permission.

"Everything go okay?" Steve asked. "You're back a little earlier than expected."

"Yeah," Paul said.

"Need me to get Jane?"

"No thanks."

"Great," Steve said. "See you next time, Paul. Happy holidays."

He swung the heavy door.

"Hold on!" Paul said, stiff-arming it. "I forgot something in the car."

He hustled over, popped his trunk, and carefully transported the object he'd stored there, protectively wrapped in towels.

"It's Mabel's terrarium," he said. "I think you should keep it here."

"You sure?" Steve asked. "Isn't it kind of your guys' thing?"

Contained in his arms was the small world they'd created over the years: new bugs, new worms, new soil, but the same pebbles that they'd first collected together in the park when Mabel was a little girl.

"It's better off with you," he told Steve, and handed over the tank.

In the car, before he took off, he texted Jane.

I'm sorry I wasn't a better husband, he wrote.

He stopped halfway down the block.

And I'm glad you found Steve, he texted again. For you and Mabel.

He blocked her number so he wouldn't see her response.

84

Paul emailed Kelsey with his plan for surprising Lauren on Thursday, her last night of work, by bringing a cake to the office for after the show.

Great idea! she wrote. The office is also throwing her a little party but I'm sure she'll appreciate you coming by. She suggested he arrive after ten, as she expected to be busy until then and Lauren wouldn't emerge before that.

Do you mind if I come around 9:30? he asked. I'll be in the neighborhood with the cake, plus I'm afraid of an issue with the metal detector stopping me from getting upstairs on time again.

10 really is a lot better for me, she replied. Thursdays are crazy and it's our last show before Christmas so there's a ton of loose ends. You can still surprise her just by showing up whenever!

I hear you, he emailed back, but I desperately want to make sure I'm there before she gets out. I'm planning to make this a *very* big surprise! (Not a word to Lauren . . .)

In that case, I'll make an exception! came her response.

He texted Lauren, asking if she wanted to get dinner Wednesday night. It's a school night, she wrote.

I know, he sent back. But I want to be there to see you off the morning of your last day.

She texted him a few thumbs-up emojis.

85

Paul called Lauren after work Monday night.

"I think this is our first phone call," she said. "To what do I owe the pleasure?"

"I just wanted to hear your voice," he said. "Have you been told you have a sexy voice before?"

"Yeah, right."

"Really. It's got this, I don't know . . . sexy, throaty quality."

"That's a nice way of saying abrasive and hoarse. A doctor once told me if I got a tonsillectomy, it would make my voice a lot smoother."

"No, never do that. It's sexy. Say it with me: my voice is sexy."

She laughed it off.

"C'mon," Paul said. "I want you to have self-confidence about this. Say it."

"My voice is sexy," she said in a jokey intonation.

"Take yourself seriously. Say it for real."

She was silent, then said, at her normal pitch, "My voice is sexy." She giggled self-consciously. "Is this a ruse to get me to do something with you right now, professor? Is *that* why you're calling for the first time?"

"No," he said with a chuckle. "I honestly just wanted to say good night and see how your dad's doing. Actually, I almost couldn't even call you. I somehow forgot my phone's whaddyacallit . . . and now I'm blanking on the word. When you have to press the numbers to get in."

"The passcode."

"Right. I clearly need to get more sleep. Wait, is it passcode or PIN? Or password?"

"It's passcode."

"I think it might be pass*word*," he said.

"*Bor*ing," she sang.

She gave him an update on her father's health, they recounted their days—Paul claimed he'd tinkered with his book—and Lauren said she had to get ready for bed.

"Before you go, I want you to say one word," he told her.

"What's that?"

"Just one word. You know what it is."

"I don't."

"One word. You know it."

"I honestly have no clue what you're talking about."

"The word is . . ."

"Yes?"

"The . . . word . . . is . . ." he repeated slowly.

"Come *on*. What's the fucking word?"

"The word," he said in a mock whisper, "is *sexy*."

She snorted.

"You come off as this straitlaced, cerebral professor," she said. "But you're a little cray-cray."

"What's 'cray-cray'?"

"Crazy. Jesus, you're *really* behind the times. Doesn't your daughter teach you the new lingo?"

"She's not really into it," he said.

86

He returned to the bakery in Riverdale from which he'd ordered Mabel's birthday cake and surveyed the selections behind the glass.

"You need a serrated knife for angel food cake, right?" he asked.

"Or a cake cutter with tines," the employee told him. "A regular knife will make a mess."

Paul ordered one for Thursday.

"You want anything on it? Fruit, frosting, sugar glaze?"

"Frosting," Paul said. "Chocolate. Lots of it. I'll pay extra."

As she rang up his request, he asked why an identical-looking cake in the display case cost a few dollars more.

"That's gluten-free. Would you prefer that instead?"

Paul thought about it.

"We use completely different baking equipment for the regular and gluten-free," she went on. "Even the ovens. Zero cross-contamination."

"I'll take one of each," he said.

87

On Wednesday night Paul ordered in takeout at Lauren's apartment. After they ate he gave her, as a present for her new job, a cashmere sweater, this one the proper size for its recipient. She silently fingered the fabric.

"You can return it and get something else if you don't like it," Paul said.

"I want to have a baby," she said.

He'd been worried about this subject's coming up nearly the entire time they'd been together, but had also thought she'd be practical about her chances of conception at forty-two.

"I'm not sure Bloomingdale's can accommodate that exchange," he said.

She didn't laugh.

"Sorry, I shouldn't joke," he said. "But aren't you—has your doctor indicated that this is something you should get started on soon?"

"I guess I never told you," she said. "I mean, I *know* I didn't tell you. It scares most guys off. I froze my eggs when I was thirty-seven. I promised myself that if I turned thirty-nine and I was single, I'd get them fertilized and try to get pregnant right away. Then, every birthday, I kept punting it a year, thinking I might meet someone and . . . Anyway, a few months ago, right around when I met you, my doctor told me I had to do it soon or she was afraid it might not work."

So this was why she'd wanted to be with him, despite their being a mismatch on every level. It wasn't only because he was a professor; it was because he'd already proven himself to be a responsible father (in her eyes, at least) and was a good candidate to have another child with her.

"I'm planning to do this in the next couple months. It's a big reason why I switched jobs, so I can work regular daytime hours," she said. "So I want to know if you're in or out."

He took his time responding, to simulate sober deliberation over a monumental request but also because he saw Lauren, for the first time, as not just an unprincipled senior producer for an abominable TV show who chased lucre at the expense of everyone else while still grumbling about her work, but also as a woman with the fundamental desire to take care of and love a child, so much so that she'd been willing to do it alone.

"I might need a few days to get completely used to the idea," he said. "But yes. I'd be honored to be the donor. Or to try it the old-fashioned way first."

Her somber countenance turned to a smirk of repressed laughter.

"Oh, honey," Lauren said. "No. No. I'm sorry. I didn't explain. I want to use an anonymous donor."

"So you . . . *don't* want me to be the father?"

She put a hand on his knee. "Nothing against you, but we just started seeing each other, and I don't want any custody issues down the line. Or alimony. I don't know your salary, but I assume I make a lot more than you do. And no offense—I think you're really smart and everything, but you're not totally what I had in . . . I'm just asking if you still want to hang around while I do this. On my own."

Though it made things easier, he still felt insulted, deemed both genetically unacceptable and a potential leech.

"Okay," he said. "I mean, yes. Definitely."

"Good." She smiled as if clinching a business deal. "I'm going to make preparations as soon as my job ends."

Paul waited an hour after Lauren fell asleep. Then he crept out to the living room and nabbed her ID card from the zippered pocket in her bag. He hid it in a compartment of his own bag and returned to bed.

She murmured at the disturbance, half-conscious and sleep-masked, and turned over to him.

"Shh." He arrested her motion and spooned her. "Go back to sleep."

88

In the morning he said he had to leave early for a book fair at Mabel's school. He returned to Riverdale and picked up the two angel food cakes. Around noon he received a call from Lauren.

"You didn't see my ID card in the apartment, did you?" she asked.

"Your driver's license?"

"My ID card for the office. I can't find it."

"No. When did you have it last?"

"Last night at work. And I always put it in my bag when I get back to my desk."

"Could it have fallen out?"

"I zip it up."

"Don't you have a backup?"

"No. Stupid security thing. You're only allowed to have one at a time."

"But they'll still let you in the building—someone can vouch for you, right?"

"Getting in the building isn't a problem. It's swiping through doors. I use it a dozen times a day."

"Oh. Well, I'm sure it'll turn up somewhere."

"Now I have to get a replacement made just for my last day of work," Lauren said. "Such a pain in the ass."

"Maybe you should hold off on reporting it today, in case you find it at home?"

"Why would I do that?"

"They might cancel the old card. They did that with my card at school once."

"Why would I care if they canceled the one I lost if I already had a replacement and if it's my last day?" she asked. Paul didn't have an answer. "You know, for a professor, sometimes you don't think things through."

"Shit, I have to go, the teacher's calling me over," he said. "Talk to you later. Sorry you lost your card."

He hung up, his heart a bee flailing against the glass of a closed window.

89

When his mother was in the bathroom, Paul stole into her room and opened her top dresser drawer, where she unnecessarily hid her modest cache of inexpensive jewelry. He gingerly lifted a stack of beige undergarments to uncover a black velvet box. Inside was her wedding ring, bought near half a century ago: plain gold, no diamonds.

He uploaded *The Luddite Manifesto* to his website.

This is my final comment, he added to the top. The rest is silence.

90

The first snowflakes of the year spangled the sky, with a forecast of four to eight inches by morning, the kind of storm that deniers loved pointing to as evidence that global warming wasn't real.

After dinner he heard his mother start her palate cleanser of state TV. He didn't look at her as he passed through the living room.

"Going out," he muttered.

"You look very nice in your sports coat and slacks," she said. "But don't you think you should wear a pair of loafers instead of tennis shoes?"

"No," he said, still not looking at her.

When he opened the door and double-checked the contents of his plastic bag, though, he inadvertently caught sight of her, in her armchair with its pilling green velvet, alone before the flickering television.

He thought, briefly, of an alternate existence—not the one he frequently conceived of having had himself with a more educated and worldly mother, but of her own roads untaken, her privations, the unjust circumscription of her life.

"I'm sorry, Mom," he said, and he stepped out before she could reply.

91

Paul's sneakers stamped from the express bus over a carpet of snow through Midtown's neon holiday cheer. At the headquarters, Merry Christmas signage was omnipresent. He listed Kelsey as his contact at the front desk before stepping through the metal detector, which beeped as predicted.

He set down his plastic bag as the same buzz-cut guard from before wanded him.

"It's just the clasp in my pants," Paul said. "Remember me? We've done this before."

"What's in the bag?" the guard asked.

"Two cakes and some paper plates and plastic forks," Paul said. "I'm running late to a party upstairs."

The guard asked to inspect it. One box had REGULAR scribbled on the top, and the other was marked GLUTEN-FREE. Scotch-taped to the bottom of the box with the regular angel food cake was a nylon knife sheath. The guard withdrew the eight-inch serrated knife belonging to Paul's mother.

"No knives in the building," he said.

"You can't cut the cake without a serrated knife," Paul said. "I'll keep it in the case when I'm not using it."

"Steel knives aren't permitted anywhere on the premises without an advance request. You have to use plastic."

"Have you ever tried to cut angel food cake with a plastic knife? It'll destroy it."

"Can't help you. Should've thought of that when you got the cake."

Paul told him he'd be back. He returned to the front desk and asked them to call Kelsey down, saying there was a problem. In a few minutes she met him at the metal detector.

"She's an employee," Paul said. "Now can I come through?"

"You have to issue a written request for anything banned by the building the day before," the guard said. "Knives, box cutters, gasoline, bleach—"

"Can't you make an exception, just this once?" Kelsey asked.

The guard looked resolutely indifferent.

"Sir," Paul said to the guard, "the woman this is for upstairs is having a hard time. It's her last day on the job after twelve years. Her dad was just diagnosed with cancer. I wanted to do something nice for her. This is her favorite kind of cake. Please don't make me run out to get a supermarket cake."

"Just cut the slices here," the guard suggested.

"Great idea!" Kelsey said, clearly itching to get back upstairs.

Paul sliced the regular cake. When he was halfway through he stopped.

"Damn it," he said. "I should've cut the other one first. Now the knife has gluten on it. I've got to wash it with hot water and soap."

"Wipe it with a napkin." The guard offered a clean napkin from his consumed bag of takeout food.

"Do you know what would happen if someone with severe celiac disease ate from this, if all I did was wipe it with a napkin instead of using hot water and soap?" Paul asked. "They'd have to go to the emergency room. They could die. You'd probably get sued."

"Then go to a public restroom and wash it off."

"You need dish soap, not hand soap," Paul said. "My daughter's got celiac. You don't mess around with this disease. The bakery even uses separate ovens."

The guard looked annoyed at the layers of complexity Paul kept adding. "I don't know what to tell you, man. You should've put in the request yesterday."

"You can just leave the cakes here and give her a slice after," Kelsey said to Paul. "We've got tons of other—"

"Look, she's getting out of her show in twenty minutes, and I really wanted to surprise her," Paul said to the guard. It was time for his final gambit. With a smile of corny, masculine sheepishness, he pulled the ring box out of his pocket. "I call her 'my little angel,' so I was going to hide the ring inside a slice of angel food cake."

He opened and closed the box quickly so Kelsey could see the flash of gold but not that it wasn't the diamond-encrusted engagement ring that Lauren would undoubtedly demand. She clapped a hand over her mouth.

"I can leave my wallet here with you as collateral," Paul said to the guard. "And I'll come down right after I propose to her. Please, sir. I've been planning this for a while."

The guard sized up Paul, the ring box, then the knife. He sighed performatively, a demonstration of his essentially good-hearted nature that had overcome his bureaucratic constraints. "All right, man," he said. "Good luck. Merry Christmas."

Paul thanked him and sped ahead of Kelsey to the elevator.

92

Does Lauren have any idea?" Kelsey asked, trotting to keep up with him.

"No," Paul said.

"You sure this is the time to do it? With her dad and changing jobs and all?"

"Yeah, I think so."

"It's been pretty fast. Only around two months, right?"

"We're older than you," he told her. "We have to move a little faster."

Any romantic zeal she'd had at the sight of the ring had reconfigured into a pragmatic skepticism. It occurred to Paul that Kelsey might know that a proposal from him would be unwelcome; maybe she'd felt Lauren out on the subject after their email exchange about the "surprise." She could text her a warning, which could ultimately lead to Kelsey's telling him to head home, that this wasn't the time to spring a major life decision on Lauren.

"Now I'm having second thoughts." He pressed the elevator button. "You really think I should hold off?"

"It's hard to say. I might. Just because of her dad and everything. But it's your call."

"You're right," he said after some ostentatious mulling. "It's a little too fast. I'll just come upstairs with the cake as a going-away thing."

"I think that's a good decision," she said.

They waited for the elevator, stalled on the seventh floor.

"Is angel food cake really her favorite?" Kelsey asked. "I thought she doesn't even eat sweets. She always gets wine when everyone else is getting dessert."

"It's the one dessert she likes."

"Oh." She looked at Paul's outfit. "Love the suit-and-sneakers look, by the way. You must be one of those hip professors."

"I guess," Paul said, jamming the elevator button.

93

The office was shellacked and wreathed in Christmas decorations. A festive spirit was in the air as some employees had prematurely begun drinking in anticipation of Lauren's going-away party. In the kitchen, Paul put a hefty slice of the cake and a fork on a paper plate. He wiped clean the knife, tucked it back in its case, and dropped it into the inner pocket of his sports coat, which he buttoned.

He carried the plate out of the office and past the elevators to the door to the other wing, where he waved Lauren's ID card over the reader. The light switched from red to green.

"Merry Christmas!" two separate employees said to him as he steered through the aisles.

The same security guard was on a chair outside the door Lauren had taken him to before, looking bored.

"Kevin, right?" Paul asked as he approached. His hands bearing the cake trembled.

He squinted. "Yeah?"

"I'm Paul, Lauren's boyfriend. We met before?"

"Oh, yeah."

"I got her angel food cake with chocolate frosting for her last day here. You want a piece? It's really good."

Kevin examined the cake. "Thanks, man," he said.

Paul extended the plate but, before the transfer was complete, caused it to tumble to the carpeted floor. He cursed and kneeled to pick up the cake, which somehow had landed right side up and remained on the plate. Blocking Kevin's view, he overturned the plate onto the gray carpet and in the process daubed frosting on his knee.

"Oh, shit," said Paul. "It's all over the carpet. And my pants. Is there a men's room around here with paper towels?"

Kevin scowled at the soiling of his workplace. "Around that corner."

"I'm really sorry. I'll get to this after I clean myself up." Paul walked away and said, over his shoulder, "If you want another piece, it's in the kitchen of the other office. It's going pretty fast."

He turned the corner he'd been directed to, waited, and peered back around. Kevin was leaving.

Paul hurried back to the door and opened it, the shakiness in his hands compounding, his whole body now vibrating with a rubbery giddiness, muscles and joints buzzing like a diclofenac hit.

He made a right in the hallway, walked fast, another right, a left, the Adderall he ingested earlier giving him military-grade strides but also making his heart and gut somersault, a final left until he reached the door with the device. On his phone, he summoned the recording that he'd stitched together with a sound-editing app on his computer.

"My voice is—my—pass—word," played Lauren's staticky rasp in the halting cadence and uneven pitch of rearranged words filtered through two separate audio outputs.

The door clicked.

94

Paul trod lightly in the dark toward the glass-paneled door, as though someone might hear him through its soundproofed barrier.

Thirty feet beyond its slim glass aperture, in ramrod profile at his desk, talking live to three cameras, was Colin Mackey.

The room, generally illuminated and with a backlit glow from the screen behind him, darkened except for the white spotlight on the host.

The “Final Comment” segment.

Paul shed his sports coat and slipped the knife from its case. This was the moment he’d prepared for, envisioned a hundred different ways, but his jumpy excitement from before was gone; he felt only uncertain and lightheaded. His mother was watching. Jane would be bombarded by calls within minutes. In the faculty lounge the next day, Russ would talk about their Coop spat with the self-important grandiosity of those circumstantially adjacent to historic events.

A sacrifice was meaningful only if it incurred a real cost.

He placed a call. It went straight to voice mail, as expected at this hour.

He had assumed other people and institutions would protect them, that the Hegelian dialectic meant we were always synthesizing toward progress. Only the thesis now was too powerful, too malignant, too much in the image of one terrible man, and no antithesis commensurate to the task had stepped up to counter it.

These were not concepts or words she would understand.

“Mabel, it’s Dad,” he said.

He should have sent a letter in the mail, given himself time to think things through, to phrase it in the medium in which he felt most at home.

"People are going to ask you what I was thinking, and you're going to be wondering it, too," he continued. "And what I'm thinking now, what I've been thinking for a while, is: If I don't fix it, who will?"

Too abstract, cryptic. She would also be making a sacrifice, and unwillingly. It would haunt her the rest of her life. He couldn't do this to her. He'd retrace his steps, tell Kevin he'd taken a wrong turn, and, tomorrow, figure out how to start over. This was America; with hard work and talent, you could always make something of yourself, always get another chance.

No, the first part was never true, the second certainly now a lie.

And in the next room, Colin Mackey was setting fire to what was left of the country.

"I just want to protect you, even if that doesn't ever make sense to you," he said. "I love you."

His words were still inadequate. He looked at the picture he'd taken on his phone. Despite the glum preadolescent set of her face and stiff body language, he could still see, in her brown eyes, the little girl whose unbridled laughter had once given him the deepest happiness he'd ever known.

"You might want to delete this message, but I hope you'll hold on to it, and maybe you'll listen to it again when you're older and it'll make more sense to you," he said. "And I know you don't like the name now, but I want you to remember how I used to call you my little dumpling."

Before he choked up, he shut off his phone, tightened his grip on the knife's handle as his strength revived, turned the knob, and burst through the door.

95

Against the blackness of the set, no one noticed the sprinting figure at first. When he was halfway to the desk, someone raised a noise of alarm, which spread to others in an escalating rumble. Mackey looked around, like a panicked politician at a lectern as a protester rushed the stage, but didn't see the intruder bearing down.

And then Paul was hunched over behind his chair, one arm around the man's broad shoulders and proud chest, his free hand holding the glinting knife to Mackey's throat.

Woodsy cologne. The fine sandpaper of his inchoate stubble against Paul's thumb. Moist heat from the back of his suit. The spotlight drilling down on them like a laser.

The set was in havoc, the crew hollering. The full array of lights came back on, blinding Paul.

"Stand up! Don't move or I'll cut your throat!" he yelled. He had thought that presenting himself as crazed at the start would be advantageous, though it turned out he didn't need to perform; his voice had not only instinctively gotten louder, but also assumed a harried, paranoid tenor.

"Do you want me to stand up, or do you want me to not move?" Mackey asked calmly.

"Stand up slowly, no sudden movements," Paul said.

"I'm just going to roll the chair back a few inches so I can get up," Mackey said.

He did this as Paul held him with the blade at his throat, careful not to break the skin.

Once Mackey was upright, Paul led him a few feet to the side and kicked the chair away. He remained behind him; in addition to that being the best position to hold the knife, he needed Mackey's body as a shield. It wouldn't be that hard for the former wrestler to break free from Paul's grip should there be a struggle. The only deterrent was the jagged steel against his Adam's apple.

"Dim the lights so I can see," Paul said.

Nothing happened.

"Do it or I'll kill him," he said.

"Dim the lights," said Mackey.

The lights waned until Paul ordered them to stop at a point where he could see the room while still retaining some cover of darkness.

His pupils adjusted. A dozen or so people, all men, a few wearing blazers or fleeces, the rest in blue-collar gear manning equipment. He didn't immediately see Mackey's bodyguard.

"Tell your bodyguard to leave now or I'll kill you," he said.

After a few seconds, Mackey said, "Go ahead, Rick."

Movement from a blazered man in a corner of the room. He must have been carrying a gun, but it wasn't visible; maybe he'd been waiting for the right opportunity and hadn't wanted to show his cards yet. He slowly made his way toward a red door at the rear, glancing backward. Someone unlocked it for him.

"Everyone else out except this cameraman in the middle," Paul said. "No one else comes in."

No one budged.

"Now!" he barked.

"Go on," Mackey told them. "Jim, you okay staying?"

"Yeah," said the middle cameraman.

The others followed in a jumbled herd, clearly eager to evacuate but trying not to advertise their cowardice.

The only people left were Paul, Mackey, and the cameraman.

He'd pulled it off.

"Paul." Lauren's disembodied voice carried over a speaker. "What the *fuck* are you doing?"

They weren't still on the air if she was cursing.

"You know this guy?" Mackey asked.

"Shut up," Paul said to Mackey. "Lauren, you too." To the cameraman he said, "Lock the door and come back. If you leave, I'll kill him."

As the man complied, Paul scanned left and right for other points of ingress. There weren't any doors other than the red one in the rear and the fire exit through which he'd come.

He looked up.

"What's up there?" he asked Mackey.

In the unlit upper level, not visible through the fire door window, were two short rows of seats behind a low-slung barrier.

"A balcony," Mackey said.

"How do people get in?"

"No one's normally there. It's just for when the execs want to sit in on a show."

"How do people get in?" Paul repeated.

"There's a door back there."

"Tell them to lock it. And put lights up there."

"Do what he says," Mackey said.

Paul waited for the lights to find the new location. Once they did, they illuminated only the first row. The back row, which presumably led to the door, remained dark.

"Get both rows," Paul said.

"That's as far as the lights can reach," Lauren said over the speaker. "They don't tilt any further back in that direction."

It was an out-of-the-way location; Paul believed her.

"If I hear anything up there, any sounds at all, I'll kill him. Okay? And it'll be your fault."

He would easily see the red door opening and could keep an intermittent eye on the fire exit. The balcony was the Achilles' heel. Someone might manage to sneak in there, hide in the shadows, crawl to the barrier, and get off a shot when Paul wasn't looking. If he were stationary, a sharpshooter could likely pick him off, even protected as he was by Mackey's wide torso. He'd have to look up periodically, like checking the rearview mirror while driving. And they both needed to be in constant motion to prevent an attempt.

"Walk with me," he told Mackey. "Small side steps. Slow. Start off to the right. If you try to break free, any sudden movements at all, I'll cut you." To the cameraman he said, "Follow us with the camera."

After coordinating their movements, Paul and Mackey shuffled together in lockstep.

"Paul," Lauren said, "I don't know what you want out of this, but—"

"Stop talking," he said. "Stop talking and listen to me. I know you've cut the feed."

The monitor near the cameraman was facing away from them. It was small, as Lauren had said, and would be hard to keep a close eye on when they were at the opposite end of the room.

"Put us up on the screen behind us," Paul said.

He didn't turn, but the quality of light coming from behind them didn't change.

"Do it," he said.

"Patch us in, Lauren," Mackey said.

The light behind them flickered off and on. Paul rotated his head—it pinched his neck, but he looked only for a second—and caught the sight of their two sidestepping figures, the desk and chair at the edge of the frame.

"Walk in the other direction," he told Mackey when they neared the wall. He reversed course, and Mackey moved with him. "Put us back on the air now. When we get to the other side of the room, I'm going to tell you to turn to another news show and put it on the screen. If they aren't talking about this, then I'll know you're not broadcasting it, and he dies."

Once they slowly traversed the room, Paul ordered them to turn to another cable news channel with the volume on.

An anchor's voice broke through the silence: "—unidentified man with a knife appears to be holding Colin Mackey hostage live on the air—"

"Turn it back to us," Paul said.

The set was quiet again. He felt a surge of power, not only from the knife and positional advantage he held, but also from an intensity of concentration and the satisfaction of a plan's perfect unfolding. The flow state.

"If I tell you to go back to the other channel again and they say we're not on the air anymore, I'll kill him," he said. "You hear me? Tell them to keep us on."

"Keep us live," Mackey said in a tired voice. "Who are you?"

Paul was silent for a moment.

"I'm the author of *The Luddite Manifesto*," he said.

"*The Lead-eye Manifesto*? What's that?"

"Ludd-*ite*!" Paul shouted, louder than he had for any of his commands. "*The Luddite Manifesto*!"

"Okay, *The Luddite Manifesto*. What do you want, man? Money?"

The fire door and the red door and the balcony: nothing.

"I don't want money. I want your audience to know the truth. The truth about you."

"I don't know what you mean," Mackey said.

"I want your recordings. Of the president."

"You want us to play clips of the president? Okay. What clip?"

"No. *Your* recordings. Your phone calls with him."

"I don't have any recordings of phone calls. You're crazy."

Paul had to respect the man's defiance, his obstinacy at the brink. He could smell coffee on his breath now, a hint of cigarette smoke. Mackey's triceps strained under his suit against Paul's leaner biceps as they sidestepped. He was a big man; he might take a chance breaking free.

"I'm not crazy." Paul looked over Mackey's shoulder at the camera, addressing the future audience of one he cared about most. "I'm not crazy. You have the recordings. Lauren, confirm it."

There was a pause, then Lauren said, "I don't know."

"Lauren," Paul said, "I'll kill him. Say what he told you."

"Colin, you said—you once said you recorded him," Lauren said. "Then you said you were kidding. So I don't know."

"It was a joke," Mackey said. "I'd never record the president."

Paul tickled the blade across his throat as a warning. The pressure was light, not enough to draw blood.

"I know for a fact that you recorded him," Paul bluffed.

If Mackey was telling the truth, if he hadn't made any recordings, he had no good backup plan. This was the only way, going all in with a bum hand.

"I'll give you five seconds to admit it," he said. "If you don't, I'll kill you. Five . . . four . . ."

He could sense Mackey thinking about the president, undoubtedly watching live, and deciding which threat was graver: the judgment of the most powerful and vindictive man in the world or the serrated knife on his soft throat.

Paul pushed harder, feeling the resistance of the peach pit under Mackey's skin.

"Three . . . two . . ."

"Don't!" Mackey said. "I may have recorded him once or twice—I don't know."

"Once or twice? Or every time? Five . . . four . . ."

"Every time!" he said.

The stalwart vocal cords that he'd used to intimidate and dissemble for decades were shaky, attenuated. For the first time in his public life, Colin Mackey sounded frightened.

"Please, man," he pleaded. "Don't do anything crazy. I've got kids."

"I'm not doing anything crazy," Paul said. "Not doing something would be crazy. Play the recordings. Take out your phone."

"They're not on my phone," Mackey said. "I swear to God."

"Where are they?"

"At home. On a flash drive. It's not connected to the internet. I wouldn't keep them anywhere else."

He was likely telling the truth; Mackey wouldn't want the recordings to leak. They were his insurance, a deterrent of mutually assured destruction.

"Who's at your home now?"

"Just my family. And our nanny and security team."

"Who can access the recordings?"

Mackey hesitated. Paul again scraped the knife. The teeth snagged on Mackey's loose skin.

"My wife. I'd have to give her instructions."

"Lauren," Paul said, "call his wife and patch it to us"—a glimmer of self-consciousness that he was using Mackey's television patois and probably mangling it—"so he can talk to her. And go to the other channel now."

Paul didn't look back, but the anchor's voice from before played.

"—of his private phone calls with the president. As you can see from our chopper through the heavy snowfall, NYPD's Emergency Service Unit, which deals with hostage situations, has arrived, as has a crowd—and I see we're now back on their screen—"

"Turn it back to us," Paul said. "If I see any police, I kill him."

He couldn't afford any lapses. No movement in the balcony. They continued limping sideways. Paul's arms were tiring from the bear hug, and his right shoulder ached from the unrelenting tension.

"Patching Charlotte through," Lauren announced.

"Colin?" a woman said frantically.

"Charlotte," Mackey said, "listen to me—"

Mackey's wife was crying.

"Babe," Colin said. "You have to stop crying. You can't be hysterical now. I'm gonna be okay. Please listen to me. I need you to go to my office. Go to the vault at the back of the closet. Okay?"

"Okay," she sniffled.

Heavy breathing and footsteps, doors opening.

"I'm here," she said.

As Mackey gave her directions to spin the lock, Paul checked the vulnerable spots in the room. Still no action.

"It opened," she said.

"Good girl." The chauvinist's binary of hysterical woman and good girl. "Now take out—"

"Paul," a man's voice cut in over the speaker. "I'm not a cop, Paul. I just want to talk. My name is Richard—"

"Stop talking," Paul said.

He looked up but again saw nothing. If a hostage negotiator was already in the control room, then so were the police, scoping out a way to infiltrate the balcony without alerting him.

"If I hear anything from the balcony, I'll kill him right away," he said.

Mackey's wife wailed.

"Babe, it's okay," Mackey said. "No one's going there. Right, Lauren?"

"No one's going there, Paul," said Lauren.

"I just want to see what we can do for you, Paul," the negotiator said, repeating his name like Nathaniel about to tell him he'd been demoted. "I want to talk with you and find a way to make everyone happy here."

Making everyone happy meant compromise. Civility. Amenability. That was how they'd let people like Mackey and the president rise to power—playing by the rules when the other side refused to, appeasing them to forestall even worse behavior, assuming their leader would eventually commit a sin so irrefutable, so unpardonable, that even their hollowed-out morality would object.

Enough, they'd said—after episodes of presidential criminality, egregious lies, mass shootings, affronts to common decency—*enough*, *enough*, *enough*, shouted so many times that the word had lost any meaning.

"No," Paul said. "If they play the recordings, I'll let him go. If you keep talking, I'll kill him."

The negotiator didn't speak.

"Do what he says," Mackey said.

"Keep talking to her," Paul said to Mackey. "Hurry up."

"Babe, you see a flash drive in there?"

"Yes," said Charlotte.

"Bring it to the computer and plug it in."

"What's the computer password?" she asked.

"It's Kathleen's middle name." To Paul he said, "That's my daughter. She's nine. And I've got a seven-year-old boy. Patrick. You have any—"

"Shut up," Paul said. "Don't talk unless I ask you something or you're giving your wife instructions. You listen to me, you don't speak. Okay?"

"Okay," said Mackey.

It was working; it was going to happen. His supporters might excuse the president and Mackey for not believing in all their public positions. They had, after all, tolerated every other misdeed and crime of their leader, found ways to justify or minimize the cognitive dissonance of supporting a philanderer, a tax cheat, even a traitor. If the other rumored embarrassments ever surfaced on a recording—bizarre sexual peccadilloes, racial slurs—they still wouldn't accomplish anything; he'd already dodged repercussions from a thousand other shames and breaches of the presidential morality clause, and had proven time and again that no denigrating words about others were off-limits; if anything, they were celebrated.

But his admirers wouldn't forgive the two men for labeling them idiots or morons, the fire hose of the president's verbal scorn that they loved so dearly finally turned on them. No one could stand being duped, finding out that the person they'd put all their trust in thought of them as fools ripe for exploitation, that he considered them beneath him, just as everyone else with power did—which was their primary reason for latching on to him in the first place, their messiah who vowed to return them to glory, to elevate their lowly status while knocking everyone else down the totem pole. The rational world had been telling them this for years, but those were the selfsame elites who belittled them.

They listened only to the president and minions like Mackey. This was the magic bullet everyone had been waiting for, the con man executioner at last hanged by his own rhetorical noose. Words matter, Mackey had said in this very studio. Words can change the world.

"Change the channel," Paul said.

The other network came on, the volume substantially higher than before. Paul glanced back at it through the complaint of his neck, the pain now linking up with the familiar tenderness in his right shoulder.

"—identified only as the author of *The Luddite Manifesto* is holding Colin Mackey hostage live on the air. We've found a personal website that has text with that title, though we're not naming the man until we confirm that he is indeed the author. Mackey's wife is currently attempting to access supposed recordings of phone calls between Mackey and the president in order to play them on the air, for purposes we don't yet know. My apologies if I'm a bit discombobulated. On top of this being a very tense situation, I'm now seeing myself directly on the screen in Mackey's studio, as proof that they're airing this—"

"Richard—the man from before—would like to talk to you in person," Lauren said over the din. "He doesn't have a gun. He's going to open the front door and put his hands on his head—"

"Stop!" Paul screamed. "No one comes in!"

"—he's just going to stand at the door, he's not going to come in—"

Paul curled the knife around Mackey's neck and nicked its side, avoiding the carotid artery. Mackey cursed.

"I cut his neck," Paul said. "If that door opens, I'll do the throat."

"Colin," Mackey's wife broke in, "what's happening?"

"I'm fine," he said. "Don't open the door. Babe, put the drive in the computer when it's ready. Lauren, I mean it, don't open it."

There were a few seconds of silence.

"The door isn't opening," Lauren said.

The other network had been blaring the whole time, though Paul had tuned it out.

"Turn the screen back to us," he said.

It was quiet again.

"They said I was only identified as the author of *The Luddite Manifesto*. That means you stopped filming when the negotiator said my name," Paul said. "Don't do that again."

His shoulder burned. Don't think about it, the pain goes away when you ignore it. The piney scent of Mackey's cologne was strong at close range. He'd stared too long at the screen last time; he couldn't let down his guard, had to stay sharp. The Sharper Image. That ridiculous thing for drinks plus a phone charger. Stop thinking, just do. Like Al the handyman. Keep moving, look up, keep moving, look up.

"Don't come in now, baby," Mackey's wife said. "Mommy's on the phone."

"Is that Kathleen?" Mackey asked. "Put her on the phone."

"No!" Paul said. A horrible feeling sliced through him as he imagined Mabel watching him speak to a young girl on the phone while he held a knife to her father's throat. "If she gets on the phone, I'll kill you. Tell your wife to get rid of her."

Mackey gave the order. His wife's conversation with their daughter was inaudible.

"Naima took her away," she said. "But the computer won't let me get into the drive. It's asking for a code."

"It's two-factor authentication. The only way to get the code is on my phone," Mackey said. "Can I take it out?"

"Use one hand," Paul said. "Take it out very slowly."

Mackey's left hand sank into his pants pocket and came out with his phone. "I have to turn it on," he said.

They waited for it to power up as Paul eyed the balcony. Mackey punched in his passcode, swiped several screens to the right, and opened an app. He directed his wife to enter the number that came up.

"Play the recordings," Paul said.

"There should be a bunch of folders," Mackey said. "Go to the one called 'golf.' "

"There're a lot of files with numbers," Charlotte reported.

"Those are the recordings," Mackey said to Paul. "Now what?"

They needed to play multiple recordings, to prove it wasn't a single doctored audio file.

"Play them into the phone," Paul said. "Start with the most recent and go back, one by one."

"That'll take hours," Mackey said.

"I don't care. Keep us on the air the whole time. If they stop, I kill you."

Mackey would certainly value his life over the recordings, but the network might not. Airing them would not only constitute an unforgivable betrayal of the president but also expose them, via Mackey, as a two-faced New York media outlet that demeaned their own viewers. He needed the host alive as leverage until the recordings had finished playing; Charlotte wouldn't obey him if he murdered her husband, and the network would instantly take him off the air, whereas if they did so now it would be tantamount to ordering their employee's assassination. And if he killed Mackey—which he didn't have in him, anyway—it would undercut his own moral standing while giving the host martyrdom.

Better for the TV star to emerge from this alive but disgraced, his audience seeing who he really was: a hypocrite and disloyal creep who recorded his most powerful associate for kompromat. As for Paul, he could barter with the negotiator, but all that would await him outside of this studio was a life sentence and being tarred as a coward who'd surrendered to the authorities, and Mackey and the president would turn that sentiment against him to recuperate their reputations.

He would stick to the plan.

"Find the one with the biggest number and play it," Mackey said. "Hold the phone close."

They waited.

"Mr. President?" Mackey said, muffled through the speakers, the volume much quieter than the other network had been.

"Colin," said the president in his unmistakable voice, its public growl softened in private, more nostril than lung.

"Make it louder," Paul shouted.

The volume turned up as the men chitchatted about their golf games.

"Louder," he repeated.

He only had to keep his strength, keep moving, keep vigilant.

Paul and the TV personality continued their strange tango across the room as Mackey and the president batted around apolitical pleasantries on the recording.

"I don't want to take up too much of your time, Mr. President," Mackey's voice said. "But I thought we might discuss the tariffs before we cover them on the show tomorrow."

"What do you plan to say?" the president asked.

Mackey outlined, with a surprisingly astute grasp of the subject, the political and economic ramifications of imposing tariffs, though he didn't mention which country or imports they were on. Paul had a hard time following the thread while remaining observant and in motion. Step, fire door, step, red door, step, balcony.

"Well," the president said with a battle-fatigued exhalation, "what do the idiots want?"

There it was, expressed by his childlike, one-track mind with its reptilian instinct for survival: the disparagement that would reveal what these men thought of their followers.

"Stop playing the recording," Paul said. "Now go back to the other channel."

"—just stopped and are watching us again, to confirm that it's being aired," said the other host. "Just before they cut away, the president asked, quote, 'What do the idiots want?' We do not yet know who the quote-unquote 'idiots' are, but it wouldn't surprise me if that's his way of referring to the Washington establishment he makes no secret of disdaining."

"Turn that off," Paul said, letting the erroneous hypothesis stand. He couldn't stage-manage this and act as though he knew in advance what the recordings contained, or else the network's viewers would think he'd manipulated them; they had to process the facts for themselves for once. Only by his not speaking would the audience hear what they needed to hear.

"Put us back on the screen and keep playing the tape," he said.

The host was muted, and the phone conversation resumed, with more pointed political strategy from Mackey.

His shoulder was in pain; he wasn't sure how long he could hold it in place, let alone restrain Mackey if he struggled. The other network hadn't needed to be so loud the last time they'd played it. A trick to bring in more customers. He'd used *tape* for a recording that had no material tape. Kelsey's data analytics for social media must be going crazy. Would Hannah's father be the one to write about him in the *Times*? Would he know his daughter was friends with Paul's?

Mabel. If not for this, she'd be sledding in Prospect Park tomorrow, one childhood pastime she had yet to outgrow, she adored the snow, though there would be fewer and fewer snow days for her in the future, perhaps none at all for her own children, offspring he'd never know.

His mind was wandering. Focus: step, fire door, step, red door, step, balcony.

"How we do get them on board?" the president asked.

"I'll discuss messaging with a few people here," Mackey said. "We'll round up all the troops. Morning shows, too."

"I've got a big speech in Iowa in two weeks," the president said. "You think they'll be into it by then?"

"Once we've given it the full-court press, absolutely."

"My voters," said the president, "must be the stupidest fucking people in the world."

"Thank God for the idiots," Mackey said, and both men laughed.

He'd said it, unequivocally. They'd even embellished the sentiment with mockery, two coastal elites cackling at the peasants, played live on a network his followers believed more than their own eyes and ears.

It hurt too much to turn his neck, so he rotated both their bodies to confirm that they were still on the screen, that the evidence had been entered into the public record. They were. He and Mackey were in the center of the studio, right behind the desk. He hadn't noticed before, in his split-second glances, the infinite regression in the image that obtained when they were in that spot: the desk and their figures and, behind them, the screen that displayed the same tableau, only smaller, and so on, replicating in an endlessly narrowing tunnel of rectangles, any motion from them jolting their digital forms in unison like tethered marionettes, until the diminishing iterations disappeared into the vanishing point, a single pixel encompassing the two men, an effect somewhat reminiscent of the televisions of old, which, after powering off, had enough residual voltage in the electron gun to produce a white horizontal line that contracted into a dot before extinguishing its last bit of light, a period pronouncing its own death sentence. Surprising no one had brought that back to new TVs to cater to his demographic, a nostalgic skeuomorph of their simpler childhoods of VHF dials and rabbit ears antennae.

Then the sickening fear that this was futile, he'd just lie and say the recordings were fake news, his cult would take his word like they always did, or, worse, they'd embrace the abuse like Stockholm syndrome hostages, with #ProudIdiot posts and matching campaign merchandise, a new hat for the rallies, nothing could deprogram them, it was a hopelessly damaged nation made of a hopelessly damaged people, and by next week they would move on to another scandal and forget all about him, a mere dot on a screen.

No; that was cynicism speaking. He'd done it. Tens of millions before their own screens had been witnesses, billions more in the future. They were going to read *The Luddite Manifesto*, over forty thousand views a minute. His actions would silence the most noxious voice in the media and topple the worst tyrant America had ever known. He had taken the biggest swing of his life and connected. With nothing but his wits and a blade of serrated steel he'd held off collapse, fixed the broken country all by himself. Democracy's handyman.

The studio suddenly went black, the overhead lights and screen snuffed out simultaneously. But Paul, rather than panicking at the tomb-like darkness, felt his heart beating peacefully, as if on the gliding cusp of a fairy-tale slumber on a mossy forest floor. The world still had beauty, still had good sandwiches, nice parks, cool breezes under angel food clouds in autumn's fading bronze light. Still had Mabel. My little dumpling. She'd be proud of her father. Her daddy. The great man. Not tomorrow, but someday—

ACKNOWLEDGMENTS

I would like to thank the following people:

My constant agent, Jim Rutman, and Will Watkins and Drew Foster for film and TV.

My two editors—Liese Mayer for her initial feedback, and Daniel Loedel for gracefully taking the baton; Emily Fishman; Elizabeth Ellis; Olivia Oriaku; Barbara Darko; Emily DeHuff; Missy Lacock; and everyone else at Bloomsbury.

My early readers—Alena Graedon, Robert Kuhn, Aryn Kyle, Diana Spechler, John Warner, and Piper Weiss. Paul Starke patiently answered many questions for me about television production; all errors are mine or intentional.

A phrase Paul uses in reference to video games, "dice up various foodstuffs," is a variation on a quotation from Andrew Epstein in an article I published in the *New York Times* on March 25, 2012. The substance and spirit of numerous exchanges with Lev Moscow and Nathaniel Popper found their way into this book.

Frances Greathead, Molly Greathead, and Christy Pennoyer for, among other things, hours of childcare without which this would have taken much longer to write.

Kate—again, with this and more important matters, and for the place to hang my own bags.

Angus—I wrote most of this as you napped by my side, usually wedged against me while I typed. I suspect that I will someday look back upon those days as the happiest of my writing life.

And Phoebe—born at the start of the darkest of years, a joyful light.

A NOTE ON THE AUTHOR

TEDDY WAYNE is the author of *Apartment*, *Loner*, *The Love Song of Jonny Valentine*, and *Kapitoil*. He is the winner of a Whiting Writers' Award and an NEA Creative Writing Fellowship, as well as a finalist for the Young Lions Fiction Award, the PEN/Bingham Prize, and the Dayton Literary Peace Prize. A former columnist for the *New York Times* and *McSweeney's* and a frequent contributor to the *New Yorker*, he has taught at Columbia University and Washington University in St. Louis. He lives in Brooklyn with his wife, the writer Kate Greathead, and their children.